"I'm sure you think I had a motive, and that's why I'm still considered a suspect."

Harry stayed quiet. Let her talk, get it out.

"I have no motive. In fact, I have only the motive for him to be alive. I didn't kill Axel."

Sara stared out the window. "I'd have given anything to at least have met him. Even with all the bad things I've heard about him, he was still my dad. Now he's gone. I'll never have the chance to determine for myself what kind of man he was."

"Perhaps you found out what type of man he was and decided you were better off without him permanently."

She scowled and shook her head. "It's not in my nature. Do you really think I'm capable of killing another human being? No matter how vile that person is?"

His chest tightened. "I don't know you, Sara. I've only met you. You can tell me everything about your past, but I rely on evidence, motive and facts. The fact is, we found the coffee mug on Colton's counter with your fingerprints on it."

* * *

Colton 911: Chicago—Love and danger come alive in the Windy City...

* * *

If you're on Twitter, tell us what you think of Harlequin Romantic Suspense! #harlequinromsuspense

Dear Reader,

Have you ever wanted something so badly, you would do anything to have it?

That's how Sara Sandoval feels about meeting Axel Colton, her birth father. She had a successful career in St. Louis and sacrificed everything to move to Chicago after discovering her father still lived. Sara dreams of meeting her father, but her dream turns into a nightmare when Axel is murdered and suddenly she becomes the prime suspect.

Though Harry Cartwright is a jaded and skilled police detective investigating Axel's death, he can't help having feelings for the lovely, vulnerable and spirited Sara. After suffering unimaginable loss, he vowed to never fall in love again, but Sara is breaking his resolve. When her life becomes endangered, he will do everything in his power to protect her while finding out who killed her father.

I thoroughly enjoyed writing Sara and Harry's story and bringing you the completion of this exciting series, Colton 911: Chicago. I hope you enjoy reading this book as much as I loved writing it.

Happy reading!

Bonnie Vanak

COLTON 911: UNDER SUSPICION

Bonnie Vanak

HARLEQUIN

ROMANTIC
SUSPENSE

Special thanks and acknowledgment are given to Bonnie Vanak for her contribution to the Colton 911: Chicago miniseries.

Recycling programs
for this product may
not exist in your area.

ISBN-13: 978-1-335-75953-5

Colton 911: Under Suspicion

Copyright © 2021 by Harlequin Books S.A.

This edition published by arrangement with Harlequin Books S.A.

For questions and comments about the quality of this book, please contact us at CustomerService@Harlequin.com.

Harlequin Enterprises ULC
22 Adelaide St. West, 40th Floor
Toronto, Ontario M5H 4E3, Canada
www.Harlequin.com

Printed in U.S.A.

New York Times and *USA TODAY* bestselling author **Bonnie Vanak** is passionate about romance novels and telling stories. A former newspaper reporter, she worked as a journalist for a large international charity for several years, traveling to countries such as Haiti to report on poor living conditions. Bonnie lives in Florida with her husband, Frank, and is a member of Romance Writers of America. She loves to hear from readers. She can be reached through her website, bonnievanak.com.

Books by Bonnie Vanak

Harlequin Romantic Suspense

Colton 911: Chicago

Colton 911: Under Suspicion

Rescue from Darkness

The Coltons of Red Ridge

His Forgotten Colton Fiancée

SOS Agency

Navy SEAL Seduction
Shielded by the Cowboy SEAL
Navy SEAL Protector

Visit the Author Profile page at Harlequin.com for more titles.

For the real Harry in my life, my heroic dad, Harold Fischer. Love you, Dad. Miss you.

Chapter 1

On some days, life was worth living again. This wasn't one of them.

Lifting the sheet covering the victim, Detective Harry Cartwright squatted down by the body, the eyes staring skyward at nothing. A neat round hole punctured the victim's forehead and a small-caliber firearm rested near his outstretched right hand. Christmas lights adorned the red-brick mansion and several reindeer decorations grazed near a red sleigh filled with brightly wrapped boxes.

"How can anyone hate Santa Claus?" he mused, his gaze scanning the red suit, the immaculate white ruff ringing the cuffs.

He dropped the cloth over the body. Out of habit he touched the gold medal he always carried in his trouser pocket. The last thing he expected before coffee was a dead Santa Claus. Naperville was a peaceful suburb of Chicago, a place where Santas were more than likely to bounce kids on their knees for photo ops than end up with slugs in their foreheads. But Jimmy had driven him out here, a stop on the way to where another vic—Axel Colton—had died.

Though it wasn't his case, Harry could no more resist a quick look at a crime scene than a dog could resist a meaty bone.

Jimmy Curry, lead investigator with Major Crimes in Naperville, thrust a steaming paper cup at Harry. He gulped the coffee gratefully, glad for the warmth scalding his throat. A veteran of the force, Jimmy had been his old partner in Naperville before Harry moved to Chicago.

"Who called it in?" Harry asked.

Jimmy jerked a thumb at a patrol cop standing nearby. "Junior here. First week on the force."

The cop, who looked all of eighteen years old, flipped through a notebook. "Vic's name is Devin L. Duell. Ex-con, in for breaking and entering, paroled last month. Neighborhood security guard shot him. She was making rounds and saw him trying to break in around oh six hundred. He turned, lunged at her and she fired. Single shot to the head. Homeowners are Mr. and Mrs. Henry Ladd, away for the week at a convention."

"Where's the security guard?" Jimmy asked.

The uniformed cop gestured to a woman standing nearby. "Maureen Markam. Robber meets security guard armed and ready."

Harry glanced around at the snow dusting the elegant sweep of driveway, the immaculate lawn, the house locked up tight.

"You think this was a burglary?" he drawled to the patrol cop.

"Miss Markam said there's been break-ins over the last few weeks. Some guy in a Santa suit. Meets the description."

"Security cameras?" Harry pointed to the house behind them.

"Blacked out with spray paint. Just like the ones at Axel Colton's house." The newbie's eyes brightened. "Hey, you think this has to do with the Axel Colton murder?"

Harry resisted the temptation to roll his eyes. He pointed to a red sack a crime scene investigator photographed. "What's in the bag?"

The newbie frowned. "A soccer ball and a kid's toy truck. I still think this is a robbery gone wrong."

Jimmy sighed. "Harry, why don't you give the kid an education?"

"Why not?" Harry squatted by the body, lifted the sheet again. "Look here, kid. This is execution style." He pointed to the bullet wound. "See the gunpowder residue? Close range, against the forehead."

He dropped the sheet again, dusted off his hands. "You know the drill, Jimmy. Have your team check reports of local burglaries to see if the vic's description matches. Interview all the neighbors. Check all incoming emails, letters, phone calls and visits to our Santa in prison before he was paroled."

He narrowed his gaze at the security guard talking to another detective. "Something in Miss Markam's story doesn't match. See if she had a relationship with Santa."

As Jimmy shooed off the newbie cop, Harry saw a familiar face among the gathering throng of bystanders outside the crime scene tape.

His day went from mildly bad to excruciating.

"Harry Cartwright!"

Dominic Anthony Russo the Third. Shock of white hair neatly swept back, his coat impeccable. Snow melted soon as it touched the man's shoulders. Funny about Dominic making anything melt. Harry always thought the man was as icy as Chicago in winter. Even when Marie and John were alive.

Never one to obey rules, the old man ducked under the tape, ignoring the protests of the uniforms guarding the scene. Harry walked toward him before Dominic trampled all over the crime scene. He touched the medal again. It was a family heirloom, had belonged to his wife.

"Dominic." Short and clipped greeting, hoping the old man wouldn't cause a scene this time.

"Harry. I can't say it's a pleasure to see you back here." Russo flexed his fingers as if he longed to punch him.

Again.

"I'm here on official business and this is a crime scene." Harry pointed to the sheet-covered body, one black boot sticking out from beneath it.

"Right. Cop business." Russo shook his head. "Low pay, chasing criminals. You screwed up, Harry."

Here we go again. Harry remained silent. Russo couldn't say anything worse than what Harry had said to himself over the past two and a half years.

"You could have had all this, Harry." Russo swept a hand up and down the tree-lined street and the multimillion-dollar mansions. "You should have stayed in Naperville and taken that job with my firm. Head of my security. And then Marie and John would still be alive."

Russo fisted his hands in Harry's jacket, bunching his tie. "You killed them as much as that crook who was after you did."

Harry shrugged off the man's grip. He smoothed down and straightened his tie. "I'm not a rent-a-cop. And I told you, I'll live with their deaths on my conscience as long as I breathe. But I'm not your lapdog, Dominic. I don't answer to you. In fact…"

He narrowed his gaze at the older man. "Where were you this morning around 6:00 a.m.?"

His ex-father-in-law sputtered. "How dare you…"

"This is an official homicide investigation." He crooked a finger at Jimmy, who hurried over. "I asked a question. Where were you?"

"I was home with my wife! I'll call my lawyer…"

"Call your lawyer, but that makes you look even more suspicious," Jimmy drawled.

"Jimmy and the major case squad may have more questions for you. Don't leave town." Harry walked off to a string of curses from Russo that would make a sailor proud.

Harry felt a wave of relief as a uniform pulled Russo back behind the tape. Not his case. Not his problem. Not his town anymore.

He stared at his reflection in the window of a police cruiser and straightened his tie. Tiny, scowling Tasmanian devils peppered the black fabric. Marie had given him that tie for his birthday. She thought it was whimsical and fun, something he needed in his life. And then a few weeks later, a car crash ended her life and John's and anything whimsical and fun died with his family.

Jimmy joined him, shutting his notebook. Jimmy, bless him, knew the strained relationship with his ex-in-laws.

"Intense."

"Yep. He can be." Harry rubbed the nape of his tensed neck. He withdrew the medal, staring at it.

Marie's great-grandmother brought it over from Italy, passing it down to Dominic, who gave it to his only daughter. Treasured family heirloom and his wife had given it to Harry on their wedding day.

"St. Jude is the patron saint of hopeless causes, darling," Marie had told him with an impish smile. "Our marriage is a lost cause, according to Dad, so you might as well have it for protection."

Damn, he felt like a wrecking ball smashed into his guts the day she died. Every time he touched the medal, it reminded him of her, but along with the good memories came the bad, the guilt…

Jimmy popped a piece of chewing gum into his mouth as Harry pocketed the medal once more. "We'll handle this. What did you dig up on the Colton case?"

Axel Colton. Blunt force trauma, his head bashed in in his luxurious Naperville home recently. Out of Harry's jurisdiction, but Naperville's major crimes unit asked him to be point man on the case. With Christmas coming up, Naperville's police department had their hands filled. The murder of wealthy Axel Colton took prominence, but the department was slammed, so they called in a favor and asked Harry to be lead detective on the investigation. The sooner Colton's murder was solved, the sooner good citizens could sleep easy.

Didn't hurt that Harry had met the Coltons while dating Carly Colton, Ernest and Fallon Colton's daughter. Carly's father and her uncle Alfred had been murdered by a serial killer Harry had helped to collar.

Harry glanced around. Too many ears and mouths, and he knew how this neighborhood gossiped. He inclined his head at Jimmy's car. "If you're done here, let's roll."

Jimmy nodded, left the investigation to two other detectives and soon they were driving away. Harry felt another wave of relief, as if he'd escaped the yawning jaws of a steel trap.

His old partner guided the car down a tree-lined street. "Why do you want to visit the crime scene again? Got any leads?"

"Maybe. Whoever killed Axel Colton wasn't Santa Claus."

Jimmy slid the car into a parking space before Axel Colton's mansion. The house loomed, silent and dark in the snowfall.

Harry pulled out his phone, showed Jimmy a photo he'd come across.

Jimmy whistled. "Your latest love conquest?"

"Hardly. Her name's Sara Sandoval. Came across her photo when I was checking out Vita Yates, Axel's ex-wife. Met her at Yates' Yards, the nursery where she works, when I was chasing a lead on Nash Colton, when we thought he might have killed Axel."

"Quite a looker."

"Yeah, reminds me of Carly Colton." Harry pocketed his phone. "I used to date Carly."

"Lucky you. You questioning this Sara? What connection does she have to Axel?"

"I plan to talk to her." Harry rubbed his beard, his jaw tight. "I did a little digging. Found something at the crime scene as well."

He laughed.

His former partner glanced at him. "What's so funny?"

"The Coltons." Harry snorted. "Everywhere you turn, there they are."

But in this case, his dating Carly, and attending a couple of family dinners with her, proved beneficial to the case.

Because after meeting her at Yates' Yards, he realized Sara Sandoval wasn't just a pretty face who reminded him of Carly Colton. But unlike with Carly, he'd felt instantly smitten, the chemistry between them like an electric shock.

Harry knew he had to forget the attraction he'd felt upon seeing her. The family resemblance was plain. Sara was related somehow to Axel Colton.

He'd made it a rule to never get involved with suspects. Especially during a homicide investigation.

What did you do when all your hopes and dreams shattered like brittle glass?

You picked up the pieces and started all over again. Survived. She knew how to survive. Hadn't she done exactly that since the day her mother told her the truth about her real father?

Sara Sandoval took in a deep breath of the chilled Chicago air. Paste on a bright smile, push forward. But first…

The Yates were kind enough to give her time off after Sara requested it for personal reasons. She insisted on working from home. Go home and rest, they'd said.

Vita and Rick, her employers at the nursery, thought she simply had a stomach bug. They didn't know her connection to the dreadful news about Axel Colton's death.

No one did. Easy enough to hide in plain sight from everyone with her last name. Her marketing expertise had gained her a job while she'd watched the Coltons from a distance.

She'd gone home but had not rested for the past few days. She'd worked on the accounts she'd scored for the nursery and between working, tried to reconcile herself to what happened.

Shivering, Sara used her key to open the lobby door to her apartment building and shouldered her way inside before the door banged shut. She took the stairs to the third floor, the bags filled with groceries feeling like lead weights. But the elevator was finicky again, and she didn't want to get trapped.

At Apartment 302 she knocked loudly. Widow Pendleton was slightly deaf.

The door opened to reveal an elderly woman, a yellow

knit shawl draped around her shoulders, her rheumy blue eyes peering behind spectacles. The woman brightened upon seeing Sara.

"Sara my dear! Come in!"

Sighing, Sara went into the kitchen and set one bag down on the cracked linoleum table. "Mrs. Pendleton, I told you, you need to use the peephole before answering the door and find out who is there."

"No one comes much to visit these days, dear. Except you." Her face crumbled. "My Amy never visits, not since we had a falling-out last year."

The widow reached into a cookie jar and withdrew some worn dollar bills. "How much do I owe you, dear?"

"Keep it. It wasn't much." Sara thought of her slim budget and winced, but it seemed more important for the widow to have food than she did.

Vita will probably ply me with chicken soup when I go back to work at Yates' nursery tomorrow. Her kindhearted employer was like a second mom to Sara.

"Now, Sara…you're always doing everything for me. Please, take the money."

Pride was a tough thing to swallow. Sara knew about that, and sensed the elderly woman disliked handouts. "I'll tell you what. Make me one of those delicious apple pies you enjoy baking and we'll call it even."

Mrs. Pendleton frowned. "You can't have apple pie for dinner."

"Says who? The apple pie police?" At the woman's chuckle, Sara added, "I love to eat homemade apple pie."

The woman beamed. "I'll get started on the pie right away."

After they said their goodbyes, Sara walked down the hallway to her own apartment. When she was inside, she set the bag down, shrugged out of her winter coat and then put away the few purchases.

Though it was almost noon, she had no appetite. Instead, she made coffee and paced the kitchen. Before it finished dripping, she poured herself a cup.

Sara picked up her mug of coffee and brought it over to the postage-stamp-sized table. On the table a scrapbook lay open.

She hadn't looked at this album in a long time. So very long, until this morning.

The mug was warm beneath her fingers. She read the inscription, her throat tight.

WORLD'S GREATEST DAUGHTER!

She'd taken the cup home from Yates' Yards and planned to return it. The Yateses had an assortment of customized coffee mugs in the employee break room. Sara had gone through the entire collection. Her favorite proclaimed WORLD'S GREATEST DAD. She always selected that cup when it was clean and she wanted coffee from the break room. But she hadn't seen it for days now, so she'd settled for WORLD'S GREATEST DAUGHTER!

The irony of the sentiment wasn't lost on her.

Sara cut out the photo of Axel Colton from a recent newspaper article on his death. Snip, snip, the scissors moving methodically as if she were cutting wrapping paper for a gift and not a photo from a news article about a murder.

Four quick strokes of the glue stick across the back. She placed the photo on the empty page.

Something splashed onto the newspaper cutting. Sara swiped a hand across her face. No tears. *Don't let anyone ever see you cry.*

Axel Colton was dead, along with her dreams of ever knowing her real father.

Since February, she'd been observing the Coltons. A few

times she'd seen her birth father from a distance. Every time she saw him, she tried to work up the courage to approach him, tell him the truth about her origins.

Each time she'd failed.

Now she had nothing but regrets, and a photo album filled with clippings.

With an angry swipe, she sent the album sailing off the table. It landed on the cheap linoleum and lay open, like a wound.

Hands shaking, she sipped her coffee and stared out the window at the streets of Chicago below her. Snow had fallen, then stopped. It would be another cold winter.

Was this move here, and the changes she'd made, all for nothing?

You have cousins. You have other family. Confess to them who you really are and there's a chance they'll accept you. It's not too late.

Her throat squeezed tight as she realized her mother might not like the idea of Sara cozying up to the Coltons. She'd been less than enthusiastic when Sara told her she was moving to Chicago to finally meet her birth father.

Now Axel was dead. Her mother had been mysteriously out of reach since Jackson, Myles Colton's son, had been kidnapped last month. The little boy had been safely found, the thirty-million-dollar ransom paid with fake bills and the man who picked up the ransom money found dead.

Vanishing like this after Axel's death didn't bode well for Regina. If anyone had reason to kill Axel Colton, it was her mother.

Sara called Regina and left another voice mail.

"Mom, call me. It's urgent. Please call me as soon as you get this message!"

Sara hung up and began to pace the tiny kitchen, side-stepping the album. She couldn't bear to look at it anymore.

She needed to come clean with the Yateses and tell them who she was, and hope for the best. They'd hired her for her expertise in marketing the nursery. Maybe they wouldn't fire her for her origins.

Sara glanced at the clock hanging on the wall above the window. Almost noon. She couldn't simply stay here any longer. She had to get out, clear her head.

As she headed for the winter coat hanging on a peg in the hallway, the downstairs buzzer rang. Sara frowned.

Surely Mrs. Pendleton couldn't have baked a pie that quickly. Few people knew she lived here. She hadn't made many friends since moving in, simply because she'd been too busy with work...and stalking her birth father.

I'm a father stalker.

Not anymore.

Sara pressed a button by the door. "Yes, who is it?"

"Detective Harry Cartwright, Chicago Police Department. I need to talk with you."

Her heart did a happy dance for a minute. The detective who'd been at Yates' Yards when he informed Vita about Axel's death. Sara had fainted and had woken up to see his handsome face furrowed with concern.

After buzzing him through, Sara smoothed down her cranberry sweater and opened the door the length of the chain lock when he knocked.

He put a badge up for her inspection.

"Sara Sandoval? I have a few questions. May I come inside?"

Sara unhitched the chain and opened the door, letting him inside. The rush of pleasure faded as a cold chill rushed down her spine. The detective wasn't here to pay a social visit.

"What's this about?"

"Axel Colton. I'm investigating his murder."

Sara bit her lower lip so hard she tasted blood. Sooner or later, she knew it would come to this.

The sharp-eyed detective seemed like the type who would never stop until he got the answers he wanted from her.

Chapter 2

Harry had been chilled before, now he was hot. Surely it wasn't the surge of pure male interest that slammed into him as he entered Sara's apartment.

No, it was the heat coming from her radiator, bathing him in warmth as he walked into her apartment hallway. Though it was December and not the icy cold of a true Chicago winter yet, she had the thermostat turned way up.

And Sara Sandoval wore a sweater. A cranberry-red sweater that clung to her curves like glue. He gave a brief, appreciative look. Polished and professional, even while relaxing at home. But she looked anything but relaxed.

At first glance, he recognized the slight resemblance to Carly Colton. But it was like comparing a skyscraper to the pyramids of Giza. Sara was nearly as tall as he was, and had a classic beauty with her honey-tinted skin, black hair and high cheekbones.

She looked like a model, not a potential murder suspect.

Vivid green eyes that could snap with passion, now narrowed in suspicion. Hair bound in a braid, as if she needed it off her face. For a single moment, he wondered what she looked like with all that silky hair free of restraint. Maybe fanned out across a pillow as she lay in bed, relaxed, her arms lifting upward to pull him down atop her...

Don't go there.

Harry turned off the very male part of him and focused on the surroundings as she led him into a small living room. Sara hugged herself, finally looking at him.

"What can I help you with, Detective?"

He almost told her to call him Harry. Keep it friendly, personal. Keep her off guard, unbalanced. Get her to talk. Then turn up the heat, so to speak, and get the information he wanted.

For some odd reason, he disliked playing good cop, bad cop with her. She seemed frail and vulnerable. But he'd met homicidal people who acted the same.

Honesty was the best approach.

"I have some questions for you. May we sit?"

Silently she gestured to a sofa that looked like a Goodwill donation. Harry sat, watching her perch on the edge of an equally frayed armchair.

"How are you feeling? You gave everyone a scare when you fainted at Yates' Yards."

She shrugged. "I'm better now. I didn't eat much that day, so I guess the lack of food made me faint."

Or perhaps news someone close to you had died. That can also cause a fainting spell.

"How long have you worked for the Yateses?"

She blinked, as if the ordinary question caught her off guard. "Eight months."

No more information. His guard went up. Most people

were eager to talk about themselves, offer information before he even asked. She was closemouthed, quiet.

"And you do what for them?"

"Marketing."

Any more clipped answers and he'd have nothing more than when he'd walked into the apartment. Harry did a cursory scan of the surroundings.

"What kind of marketing can a nursery need, especially in winter?"

She blinked again, but this time his question didn't shut her down.

"Plenty of marketing. That's when business naturally slows down, so nurseries need that extra push. I'm working on a large account, the Richardson-Davis wedding. They requested a theme wedding for Christmas and we're supplying all the flowers to their florist."

"Let me guess, holly and Christmas trees," he said dryly.

Sara smiled, a genuine smile that added a sparkle to her eyes. "Far from it. Vita and Rick have been courting this account for a while, but had no idea how to cater to the couple's requests. They wanted something different, big, larger than life that would be the talk of the social set. If they liked Vita and Rick's ideas, the Yates nursery would land all the flowers for the wedding and the engagement party and the florist will use our stock before going elsewhere for large orders. I suggested a tropical wedding. Hawaiian. Birds of paradise, ferns, leis, everything. I made the contact and suggested the theme, and the couple loved it."

Now he had her warmed up like a Cubs pitcher before a big game. Sara became animated, her hands moving in the air as she described the floral arrangements for the wedding of the season.

Then she looked at him, her skin darkening, and her

mouth opening. "Oh, you didn't come here to learn about planning a Hawaiian wedding."

Charmed, he grinned. "No. Sounds fascinating, though."

He flipped open his notebook. "Have you ever met Axel Colton?"

The switch from flowers to the vic made her pretty mouth wobble. "Um, no. Never."

She fisted her hands on her lap. Now they were getting somewhere.

"Am I under investigation?" she blurted out.

Harry gave her a level look. "I'm looking at all angles and possibilities for everything and anyone connected to the victim."

He began firing off questions at her, the hard stuff, asking where she was the night of the murder, was she familiar with the vic, all standard things. Sara had no alibi. She was home alone the night Colton was killed.

Flushed now, her hands so tight they appeared bloodless, she finally unclenched her fists. "It's warm in here. I need a glass of water. Would you like one?"

Shaking his head, he watched her stand, race into the kitchen as if eager to escape him. *Sorry, not going to happen.*

Harry followed her into the kitchen and watched her fish a glass out of the dishwasher.

He glanced down, saw the album lying open. *This is interesting.*

Axel Colton's face from a magazine clipping stared back at him. Harry picked up the album.

"You dropped this."

Sara's green eyes widened. Her pulse beat faster as she carefully set down the glass on the counter as if afraid of dropping it. If he'd wanted any indication his suspicions were on target, he had it now.

He watched her bring the album to an empty drawer in the kitchen, shove it inside and slam the drawer shut.

"Miss Sandoval…"

"Sara."

"Sara, I must ask. What are you doing with a photo album of the victim?"

Caught.

Sara swiped a bead of sweat away from her perspiring forehead. She'd never been adept at lying or even evading the truth, up until the day she'd decided to move to Chicago to get to know her birth father better.

If she'd felt icy cold this morning and wondered how she could endure a tough Chicago winter, she was on fire now. Maybe being in the hot seat under the scrutiny of this detective was a way to save on heating bills. Sara almost laughed, caught herself and gathered her lost composure.

She indicated a chair at the table. "Please sit."

He sat, arms on the table, his eagle-eyed gaze centered on her as she took the opposite seat.

"You're related to Axel Colton."

The detective's statement felt like a gut punch to her stomach. "Oh? I am?"

He gestured to her face. "There's a family resemblance."

Sara touched her mouth. "There is?"

His mouth twitched, as if he struggled to hide a smile. Maybe he knew what she was doing. Surely someone as savvy as Harry Cartwright knew when one was evading direct questions through asking questions of her own.

"You came here to Chicago, perhaps to meet him. Not so much for a marketing job." He flipped through his notebook. "You were the assistant director of multimedia for Caymen Reynolds, one of the largest marketing firms in the

Midwest. One doesn't give that kind of high-powered position up to take a job advertising ferns for a local nursery."

Sara felt her stomach roil. "Maybe I wanted a big change of scenery."

"In Chicago?" He arched a dark brown eyebrow. "A big change of scenery is moving to Miami. You haven't been living here long, and it looks like you're unsure about settling in."

"What makes you think that?"

His mouth twitched upward in a brief smile. "I've never seen such a clean junk drawer. There's no signs of a real home, nothing on the walls. Only a few books and knick-knacks on the bookcase. There's also plenty of boxes still unpacked in the living room."

Despite her trepidation, she had to admire his skills. "Yes. I moved here not long ago from St. Louis. You're quite good at detecting, Detective."

Gone was the small smile, replaced with intensity. He leaned across the table.

"Yeah. That's my job. So tell me the truth. What are you doing with Axel Colton's photos in that album?"

Sara folded and unfolded her hands. "It's not a photo album, not really."

Photos were in a photo album. She had no real photos of Axel. No happy family gatherings, no father-daughter dances at school, no photos of Axel and her mother together. Just the one photo Regina had back in her house of Axel, tucked away in a drawer.

If Sara hadn't found that photo, maybe she never would have known. Never would be in this mess.

"Semantics. May I see it, please?" He pointed to the drawer.

Biting her lip, she went to the drawer, jerked out the

album and all but threw it on the table before him. "Here. I should burn it now that he's dead."

Detective Cartwright didn't flinch. Instead he began flipping through the album, his expression neutral. Finally he closed it.

"Magazine and newspaper clippings. No photos. Why were you stalking Colton? Because he's related to you?"

"I don't have any photos of him because he never knew I existed." She folded and unfolded her hands again, this time in her lap. It was hot in here. "He, he's, um, my birth father."

"Ah."

That was it? A one-syllable word? No inflection, nothing to hint what he thought or if he accused her of being more than a curious daughter. She'd never been grilled by the police before. Never had reason to, either.

Not until Axel was murdered.

Life wasn't fair. All she'd wanted was a chance to meet the man she'd dreamed about her entire life. Even though her mother warned that Axel and the Coltons in general were nasty people one did not want to know, Sara had to find out for herself.

Sara looked down at her hands again. Offer as little information as possible, yet she was already a suspect and she didn't want him asking others personal information to find out about her origins. Not before she had a chance to level with Vita and Rick. They'd been so kind to her, treating her like a daughter.

"My mother was his mistress, but they severed ties years ago, before I was born. My mother, Regina, blamed Axel for my brother's death. After my brother died, she left Axel, changed her name from Perez to her mother's maiden name, Sandoval, and moved to St. Louis to begin a new life before my birth."

"Why did you really move here?" Cartwright's voice seemed almost gentle.

Pride made her sit up, look him square in the eye. "To meet him. I never knew Axel Colton was alive until I found a photo of him in my mother's drawer. She told me years ago he was killed in a boating accident, along with the brother I never knew. It was only when my mother finally confessed the truth that I set out to find him. Axel was alive. My brother drowned in a swimming pool because Axel was too busy to watch him."

It had seemed like a crazy quest, to quit her plum job and leave behind her friends to start over in Chicago. *Call me Don Quixote, tilting at the windmill of Coltons.*

But she'd never questioned herself on the decision. Maybe some people would have taken time to think about their actions. But some people might also never grab the chance to realize a dream.

She had, and knew nothing would stop her from pursuing it.

"You got the job at the Yateses' nursery to spy on the Coltons?"

Sara's temper began to rise. "Not spy. Observe. Figure out how I could get close enough to meet my father."

"Why not just ring his doorbell?" Cartwright's gaze sharpened.

To someone as skilled and experienced, and perhaps normal, as this detective, it seemed like an easy decision. Ring the doorbell, introduce yourself. He and the others had no idea how long she'd pined to have a father and a family, and how she feared discovering the father whom she'd idolized in death would never live up to the expectations she'd built around him.

It was like dreaming of meeting a celebrity, only to have

the celebrity slam the door shut in one's face. If Axel had done that, Sara didn't know what she would have done.

"Miss Sandoval? Answer my question, please."

"Sara."

"Sara, why didn't you simply ring his doorbell or call your father? He wasn't a private person."

He waited. Silence.

"Sara?" He leaned forward. "Are you all right?"

"Fine. I'm having a Forest Park moment," she murmured.

Now he seemed caught off guard. "Forrest…Gump moment?"

She laughed, a loud, sharp laugh that contrasted to the ugliness she'd mentioned. "Forest Park. It's the largest park in St. Louis, where I'm from, but you already know that, Detective, since you did a thorough background check on me. I used to walk there to gather my thoughts."

"Don't think," he shot back. "Tell me the truth. No need to think about what the truth is. You and I both know it. You were in Colton's house. Don't lie to me."

If he'd reached out and slapped her, she couldn't have felt more shocked… "What…no! Never. I never set foot inside his house. I never even met him!"

"Then why was a coffee mug with your fingerprints found in his kitchen?"

Confused, she shook her head. "What coffee mug?"

He scrolled through his phone, showed a photo. Sara's heart sank.

WORLD'S GREATEST DAD.

"Don't deny using this cup." He tucked his cell phone back into his trouser pocket. "We ran the prints. Yours and Colton's were the only ones we lifted off the mug."

More confusion. She shook her head. "I mean, no, yes, I used it! It belongs to the Yateses, they have it in their break room at the nursery where I work. But I was never in Axel Colton's house! How did you get my fingerprints?"

Calm. Cool. Confident. The detective was in charge and he didn't need to assert any authority. It practically oozed from him. "You're in the system. Your mother fingerprinted you as a child in case you were ever abducted."

Slow rage began to build. "My mother did that to protect me and now the police are using it against me?"

"We use whatever resources are available to us to do our job, Miss Sandoval. Why were you in Colton's house?"

"I wasn't! I never even came close. I couldn't…"

"The truth."

Her temper finally snapped. "Fine! You want the truth? You want to know why I didn't simply ring his doorbell or call him up like an old friend? Confront him and say, 'Hi, Dad. It's me, the illegitimate daughter you never realized existed, I'd like to get to know you.' Why didn't I do that? Because I was afraid, all right? I was afraid he'd shut the door in my face!"

The dam burst and she spilled everything pent up inside since discovering her father had been murdered. "I was afraid he'd throw me out, or accuse me of wanting his money, and then what would I do? I'd dreamed about meeting him, dreamed about having this stupid life where he actually cared about me. I couldn't face that kind of hard rejection. I had to mentally prepare myself for it and then when I finally did work up the nerve to ask Vita and Rick to introduce me, he's dead. Gone forever. I'll never have that chance. I don't know how that coffee mug got in his house, but it wasn't me who put it there. Someone else did."

Sara slumped against the hard vinyl chair, burying her face into her hands. This was all wrong. The detective was doing his job. He wasn't a therapist or a friend. He didn't care about her lost hopes and dreams.

A hand settled gently on her shoulder. Sara uncovered her face to see him holding out a wet paper towel. She murmured thanks, scrubbed the tears from her cheeks and then carefully placed the towel into the trash bin. Threw it away, like her lost chances in life. But by the time she turned back to the detective, she felt more in control.

"Thank you." She expelled a breath. "I apologize. You're just doing your job."

His blue-green gaze seemed less harsh, but he still gripped the pen in his hand. "I am sorry for the loss of your father."

The simple condolence, so commonplace with the Coltons who could claim a legitimate family connection to Axel, eased the tightness in her chest. Part of her stress, she realized, was that no one knew she secretly mourned him. No one knew she had the right to mourn such a sharp loss.

"You're the first person to say that." Now she looked him straight in the face, not caring if her emotions showed like snow on blacktop. "Not even my mother would care."

If her mother even knew Axel was dead. But again, Sara didn't know, because Regina had been out of touch for days.

"Did your mother say anything about Axel's death?"

"No, I don't know." She gave another bitter laugh. "That's another problem. I haven't talked to her since the night little Jackson was kidnapped. I had called to let her know Myles's son had been taken and the kidnapper wanted thirty million as a ransom. It was so upsetting, I had to talk to someone who understood. Mom has a soft spot for children in trouble."

He ceased scribbling on the little notepad. His gaze sharpened again. Gone was the compassionate man, replaced by the suspicious detective.

"You haven't called your mother to tell her your father is dead?"

"I've called. Left messages. She hasn't answered. She could be gone on a company business trip…left her personal cell phone at home."

"Most people always have their phones with them on business trips." He glanced at her. "I have to contact her."

Sara rattled off her mother's cell phone number. He shut his notebook. "Thanks. Did you contact her employer?"

"Yes, but the office has been shut down for renovations the past two weeks. Roof leak. Everyone is working remotely from home and I don't have the home number of my mother's boss."

"Huh."

His tone indicated he didn't believe her. How could this detective know that she and Regina had fought about Sara's moving and her mother had pleaded with her to let the past go?

Don't go see your father, Sara, please, he's not a good man…

"Is my mother a suspect?" she blurted out.

His gaze turned level. "I'm afraid I can't say. Official police business."

Sara frowned. "My mother is not the type to end someone's life. She's a kind, caring soul."

Doubt on his face said it all. *Right. Why should I believe you?*

He nodded at her. "Don't leave town, under any circumstances. I need to be in touch with you at all times. I will have more questions."

She showed him out the door and when he left, she sagged against it, her knees weak.

Official police business. She liked this detective, against her better judgment. He had flashes of real compassion, and his rugged body and penetrating blue-green gaze could make a woman feel safe but wanting to get past that hard exterior. Secrets filled those amazing eyes. For a moment when she mentioned her dead brother, they had filled with his own personal pain before his expression turned guarded once more.

Harry Cartwright was investigating her father's death and now Regina turned into a suspect. If anyone had reason to kill Axel Colton for the misdeeds of his past, it was her mother, who blamed him for Wyatt's drowning.

A mother never forgot a child who died.

Worry built inside her again. Where was her mother and why wasn't she answering her phone?

Chapter 3

Long ago, Sara learned to set aside personal problems to focus on work. It served her well as she flipped open her laptop to work on coordinating the floral arrangements for the Richardson-Davis wedding. In two weeks, everything had to be delivered to the florist's exact standards.

With this account and the prestige of the wedding, Yates' Yards was certain to land other prime business.

She worked quietly, trying not to let Detective Cartwright's visit distract her. Oddly enough it wasn't the fact he considered her a suspect in her father's murder. It was the man himself she couldn't quite erase from her mind.

In another time and place, she'd fall hard and fast for Harry Cartwright. It wasn't so much his good looks. It was his manner, the flashes of compassion and kindness she'd seen, even when he grilled her.

Sara sighed and pushed back from the kitchen table. She stood, did a series of stretches and was shocked to see the kitchen clock read nearly 5:00 p.m. Grabbing her cell phone, she dialed Vita Yates.

"I'm so sorry," she blurted out when Vita answered. "I'll be in tomorrow. I've been working on the spreadsheets for the Richardson-Davis wedding. How are all the arrangements?"

"Don't worry, Sara. Everything's under control here. Are you feeling better?"

Vita's warm, caring tone made Sara suddenly vulnerable, wanting to dissolve into tears. Faced with a tough cop like Harry Cartwright and she could hold her own, but the moment someone as sweet as Vita showed concern, she melted like snow in Florida.

She gripped her cell phone so hard her knuckles whitened.

"I'm so much better, thanks." *And under investigation for the murder of your ex-husband.* "I'll be back tomorrow at eight, ready to work."

"Thanks, dear. You're such an asset to us. Make sure to rest plenty tonight. Thanks to you, we have many more clients to plan events for. Oh, by the way, our Instagram account has dozens of new followers thanks to your ideas!"

Sara wished her a good night and hung up, feeling like a rat for lying. Honesty was best. How many times had her own mother lied to her over the years about her father and brother?

Tomorrow morning, she would come clean with Vita and Rick about her identity. If they threw her out on her butt into the cold street, well, she wouldn't blame them.

She'd be jobless, though. Not as if she'd been through worse.

She checked the nursery's Instagram account on her phone, pleased to see all the likes and comments on the latest post. Sara had suggested to Vita and Rick to take a few selfies as they worked in the greenhouses and caption them with little stories about themselves to drive home the point that Yates' was a family-owned and -operated nursery that specialized in personal touches. Not only had they done so, but Lila, Vita's daughter, had snapped one of herself in a stylish green sweater, peeking out from an arrangement of poinsettias in the humid greenhouse. The cheerful Christmas blossoms accented Lila's wide grin, resulting in the most traffic.

Pocketing her phone, Sara stared out of the window at the windswept street. Harry Cartwright came to mind again. *Don't leave town.* She was stuck here. Not that she wanted to leave. She wanted answers as much as he did. When she found out who killed her father, maybe she'd finally have closure.

Outside, a man and a young girl of perhaps five scurried down the street. The girl had a pink winter jacket, unzipped. She slipped and nearly fell on the sidewalk, but the man caught her. Laughing, he swept her up into his arms and they continued on their way.

Her mouth wobbled as she stared after them. Memories struck like icy knives. Ten years old, father-daughter dance. Her teacher telling her with a sympathetic look only fathers and daughters were permitted. Perhaps she had an uncle who could escort her?

Remembering the white-hot embarrassment of the entire class staring at her as she'd shaken her head and mumbled she had no male relatives.

Someone had tittered.

Someone else gave her a new nickname—All Alone Sara.

Billy Barton, who had a mother and father and endless family, even made up a song about her, "Sara, Sara, all alone. No daddy to hug her when he gets home!"

She scrubbed her face with her chilled hands. At least the nicknames and singing had stopped after she'd slugged Billy Barton on the playground two weeks after the dance. She'd gotten three days detention as a result of Billy's black eye. Oddly enough he stopped teasing her and began tagging after her, giving her gifts of a Twinkie from his lunchbox or pencils with the end chewed off.

If only it was so easy to erase the hurt her own mother caused with the lies she'd told Sara "to protect her."

Her cell phone jingled softly. Maybe her mom finally decided to check in. She grabbed it, recognized the number and answered.

"Ernie, hey, how are you? What's up?"

Her former boss blew out a breath. "Finally! I had to ask my secretary to look up your number. You changed phones."

A pinch of guilt. When she'd moved to Chicago, she'd cut most of her ties in order to focus on her new life and goal of finding her father. "Yeah. I was tired of you calling me and begging me to come back and rescue you."

He laughed. "Changing your phone wouldn't ever work with me, Sara. I'm a bloodhound."

"No, your secretary is." She found herself smiling. "What's going on?"

"I'm in Chicago for a few days. Want to have dinner?"

"Hey, what are you doing in town?"

"I'm here for a client meeting. It's not until tomorrow, though. Flew in tonight."

"Who's the client?"

"Stafford & Son Electronics."

She made a whistling sound. "Impressive. All of their Midwest division?"

"That and the East Coast as well. I know you were working on nabbing that account, they expressed interest and you left us."

True to Ernie's good-natured personality, he didn't sound bitter about her abandoning ship. Ernie didn't care, as long as the client eventually landed with their company.

"They're a good client, but make sure you address the father and the son when meeting with them. The father is old-world, demands respect, and the son is always pushing social media advertising on the father."

How hard she'd worked on that account, slogging until late at night to brainstorm ideas they'd find acceptable. Now they were signing, finally, and she'd lose out on the healthy bonus. But money wasn't as important as it once was.

"Hey, have dinner with me and give me some pointers. I could use your advice, Sara."

She hesitated a minute.

Ernie Livingstone was a vice president in the firm, a gregarious man happily married with two adorable daughters. She'd always felt comfortable chatting with him. Ernie had begged her not to leave, and promised the door would remain open if she wished to return.

He knew something bothered her and prompted her departure, but didn't pry.

Suddenly the prospect of being alone in her apartment all night seemed as appetizing as swimming in Lake Michigan in winter. Dinner was too long and intimate with Ernie, who could wheedle and cajole her into returning to the firm, but a drink couldn't hurt. And maybe Ernie could even check on her mom when he returned to town.

Sara hated admitting to herself she was beginning to worry more than usual. All the scenarios playing out in her head ended up with Regina feeling guilty over Axel's death, guilty over not telling Sara the truth, maybe even guilty because she'd been the one to kill him.

She couldn't bear to think about the latter.

Sara pulled herself together. "How about a drink instead? Where are you staying?"

"The Four Seasons."

Sara laughed. "On a company expense account, of course."

"What else? You think I could afford the bill otherwise? I have two kids to put through college."

She laughed again, feeling the day's tension slide away. "Ernie, you've been using that excuse since the day they were born."

"Can't start saving soon enough. Do you know how much it costs to send one kid through Harvard? What time?"

She glanced at the clock. "It'll take me a while to catch the train and get there. How about seven?"

"Train! Girl, you need to move downtown, be where the action is!"

Rolling her eyes, she shook her head. "I'm not a veep in a billion-dollar marketing firm, Ernie. I'll meet you in the lobby."

As she hung up, she ruefully thought of her old life. Instead of a cheap one-bedroom in Evanston outside Chicago, she could have afforded a small but elegant apartment downtown on her old salary. Maybe even with a prime view of Lake Michigan.

So much she'd sacrificed simply to meet Axel Colton and call him Dad face-to-face.

What was more important? A large salary and the fast-track career path to making partner? Or trying to establish a relationship with the man you've dreamed about since you were little?

She glanced around at the secondhand furniture and cramped space. "Here's your sign, and your answer."

For meeting Ernie, she chose elegant black silk pants, an emerald green cashmere sweater and cute designer ankle boots with sturdy heels. At least her wardrobe screamed style, if her surroundings did not.

She unbraided her hair, brushed it out and stared at her reflection. Definitely a haircut was in order, but there hadn't been time. Maybe now she could find a good stylist.

The air was crisp and cold, but it had stopped snowing. Sara walked to the train station, thinking about her life back in St. Louis. She'd commuted into the city with her car, had her own parking space. Now, like thousands of other commuters, she hoofed it to the L to save on gas and parking downtown.

But there was something to be said for the time it took to reach Chicago's downtown. It gave her plenty of time to reflect.

When she finally reached the Four Seasons, she was more than ready for warmth and a drink with Ernie. She eagerly anticipated catching up with her former boss, and getting news about her coworkers and her former staff. Penny, her assistant, had cried the day Sara announced her resignation plans to move to Chicago.

The elegant lobby made her sigh in appreciation. With its majestic view of Lake Michigan and downtown Chicago, and the welcoming atmosphere, the hotel boasted a contemporary charm that catered to both businesspeople and tourists. Small wonder Ernie chose to host a client meeting here. Impressions were important, especially in their business.

Not her business anymore. No, her business was dirt and potted lilies, not multimillion-dollar clients and a healthy expense account to wine and dine them.

Ernie waited for her in a chair in the lobby. Always a stocky man who had his suits tailor-made to fit his height and girth, he seemed to have gained a few pounds. More gray feathered his hair, though he was only in his early forties. For a moment she wondered if the same would happen to her if she had stayed in her lucrative but high-pressured career path at the firm.

He waved, and when she approached with a big smile, whistled.

"Looking good, Sandoval. Real good. Have I told you lately how beautiful you are? Man I miss you!"

The praise made her squirm. Sara turned so his intended kiss on the lips landed on her cheek. She wrinkled her nose at the distinct smell of bourbon.

"Starting without me, Ernie?"

His smile dropped. "I'm celebrating. What's wrong with a little celebration?"

Sara was glad she committed only to a drink, not dinner. She patted his arm, as one would reassure a sullen child. "You have the right to celebrate. It's a big account. Let's have that drink and you can tell me about it."

A few people were in the lounge, scattered at the booths and tables. Only a few were at the horseshoe-shaped bar. Lamps on each table added a quiet, intimate effect. Maybe too intimate. Ernie ushered her toward a corner booth and took her coat, draping it on the opposite seat. She slid into the booth with her purse and he joined her on the same seat, putting distance between them at least.

Until she realized he was staring at the bar like a pointer dog at a rabbit.

"I'll get our drinks. White wine for you? Chardonnay, right?"

She waved at the seat. "Let the server do it, Ernie. No rush, no need to order from the bar."

And something about the way you're acting makes me

*feel better about a server handing me a drink instead of
you having it.*

Ernie was happily married, and always respected her,
but Sara had learned to trust her instincts when socializing.

He pouted again, but settled back against the leather
banquette. Sara scanned their surroundings. A few couples
sitting at the bar leaned close, and a man in a black suit
at the far end of the bar studied the television sandwiched
between lighted glass shelves filled with liquor bottles. He
was too far away to see clearly, but he had a good view of
everyone who entered the bar.

Probably waiting for his date.

A waiter scurried over, took their drink orders. Sara decided against alcohol. She needed to retain her wits, and
cut her ties short. She ordered seltzer with a twist of lime.
Ernie a double bourbon.

When the waiter left, her former employer shook his
head. "I invited you for a drink, Sara. When did you stop
drinking wine?"

"I have an early day tomorrow." True enough.

"Right. Working for that nursery. What do they have
you doing, digging in the dirt?"

She clamped a lid on her temper. "They're a large business in Chicago."

"Chicago doesn't need you as much as we do. You really
should return to us, Sara. You're sorely missed."

She felt a pinch of guilt and smiled. "It's good to be
needed."

Ernie grinned. "You sure are pretty, Sara. I almost forgot how pretty. Since you left, we don't have any account
managers whose good looks are an asset with clients."

Her smile dropped. "I always thought my brain and my
business acumen were my biggest asset with clients."

He waved a hand. "Of course, of course. You were the

best. You're stylish, and what you're wearing proves it. Can't have a frumpy account manager meeting with high-end prospects."

Tension knotted her stomach. All the years she'd worked with Ernie, had she missed this underside of him? Had she been so invested in the opportunities the firm offered she ignored this?

Respect was important, especially for her. Appreciation went far, and credit as well. For the first time, Sara wondered if Ernie gave all three at the office. Rumors had stirred about how he swiped accounts from younger account managers eager to climb the ladder.

Was she one of them? Did it matter now?

No. But working for Vita and Rick, who truly appreciated her skills and not the designer labels on her clothing, made her see Ernie in a new light.

Setting aside those concerns, Sara started asking questions about the office and the account.

"You should have seen me. I hooked and reeled him in. You did an okay job gaining his interest, Sara, but he needed a professional touch, a man's sales pitch."

As he talked, bragging about how he'd coaxed the client into signing with the firm, her eyes glazed over. Had Ernie always been this pompous and overbearing? Perhaps she'd excused or never noticed his behavior in her eagerness to advance at the office.

When the waiter set their drinks down, Ernie grabbed his. "Here's to the new account!"

She raised her glass, watching him down half the contents of his drink. Sara sipped hers, wondering how she could slip away. Her lonely apartment was starting to look more and more appealing.

"Sara, hey!"

She glanced up, saw Nash Colton and Valerie Yates, Rick

Yates's niece. Sara did a double take. Nash held Valerie's hand in a proprietary way, signaling his intent. It made her glad. She liked Valerie, who had been kind to her each time she saw her and gone through pure hell when Nash was suspected of Axel's murder. Security cameras at Nash's house showed the heavy candlestick in his car's trunk had been planted there by a stranger.

Now Nash was cleared. *And I'm under suspicion.*

"Nice to see you again." She made introductions. "My former boss, Ernie, is in town. This is Valerie Yates and Nash Colton. They're related to my current employer."

"But not to each other." Valerie gave a little laugh. "Only through marriage. Uncle Rick is Nash's step-uncle."

Ernie didn't get up or offer to shake hands, only nodded. "Oh right, the nursery people."

Sara's smile tightened. "We're catching up on my former company."

"Interesting coincidence," Nash murmured. "All four of us being here at the same time."

"Four?" Sara asked.

"You, us and Harry Cartwright. He's over there." Valerie gestured to the solo man at the bar.

Craning her neck, she realized the detective wasn't wearing a suit, but a silk tuxedo. Dinner dress. Intrigued, she watched him. Even from a distance, he cut a nice figure, the jacket stretched across broad shoulders, his hair and short beard well groomed.

Sara's heart raced. "Yes, interesting coincidence. I hope he didn't bother you, Nash. I mean, you're not a suspect in Axel's murder anymore."

Nash's jaw tightened and his gaze hardened. "No, I'm not but I want to find who did kill him, as much as the rest of my family does."

Why was Harry Cartwright here? Stalking any Coltons who happened to stop by?

Or worse, was the detective tailing her because he thought she was guilty of killing her own father?

Chapter 4

She'd hoped for an entertaining evening away from her small, stuffy apartment. Not this kind of potential drama. Sara fisted her hands in her lap.

"Sara? Are you okay? You look lost." Valerie sounded amused. "You should go over and say hello to Detective Cartwright."

No thank you. We already had an interesting conversation.

Ernie leaned forward, took another slug from his glass. "Sara didn't come here to pick up men. She's with me."

An uncomfortable silence descended. Sara's stomach tightened. How she wished she could throw her seltzer in Ernie's face, but creating a scene, especially in front of the detective, made her pause. She didn't want to draw any unnecessary attention to herself.

"This is a nice place," she said lamely, ignoring Ernie. "Do you both come here for a drink often?"

Goodness, she sounded like an idiot.

Nash's gaze softened while Valerie rested her head against him.

"No. Nash wanted to celebrate being cleared of Axel's murder, so we booked a room."

Too dark to see Valerie's flush, but Sara suspected it was there all the same. She smiled. "Good reason to celebrate. You both deserve it. Romance, roses and candlelight."

Valerie's expression blanked. Sara wanted to bang her head against the table. She'd forgotten about the heavy candlestick planted in Nash's trunk by whoever wanted to frame him for Axel's murder.

"No candles. Or candlesticks," Nash said dryly. "But we'll manage the romance without them. We have theater tickets, so we'd best get going. See you, Sara."

Nash took Valerie's elbow and ignored Ernie.

She waved goodbye.

Feeling the unexpected weight of someone looking at her, she glanced at the bar to see Harry Cartwright studying her. She flushed, resisted the temptation to touch her hair or smooth her sweater. He nodded at her and turned back to his drink.

For a wild moment, she wished she was sitting at the bar with him, instead of sequestered with her former boss.

"Hey, Sara. Let's go somewhere more private to talk about the account."

She glanced over, saw his glass had emptied. Then she felt a sudden quick pressure on her leg.

He was touching her. Sara squirmed away, but he slid closer. Fumes invaded her breathing space as he leaned close. She turned away, feeling trapped.

"C'mon, Sara, let's have some fun. You were always so serious at work. I've got a room upstairs."

In your dreams. Sara felt an urgent need to leave, now,

before this escalated. Ernie had never been this obnoxious. Then again, she'd never been alone on a business trip with him and seen him drink like this.

"I can't go anywhere until you slide out of the booth, Ernie."

He beamed, threw two twenties on the table and then slid out of the booth, holding out his hand. Grabbing her purse, she left the booth and ignored his hand, snatching up her coat instead.

"I have to leave. Good luck with the account, Ernie."

Harry turned in his seat, watched her. He tilted his head, as if trying to figure her out.

Nothing to see here, Detective. Only a woman trying to dump a drunk former employer who grabbed her thigh.

Ernie's mouth turned down. "You owe me, Sara. You owe me for all I did for you."

His fingers laced around her arm, preventing her from leaving.

"Let go of me." She kept her voice low. The desire to avoid a scene was rapidly fading, replaced with the urge to kick him in the shins.

Or someplace else.

"So damn pretty," he muttered and yanked her close. "Just one little kiss, Sara."

Just as she was about to wrench free, a deep voice interrupted them.

"The lady asked you to leave her alone. I suggest you listen to her."

Sara looked up into the expressionless face of Detective Harry Cartwright. No, not expressionless. Fury simmered in his blue-green eyes, though he seemed calm. Collected.

Ernie sneered. "None of your business, buddy. Take a hike."

"It became my business when you started to assault her. Step away from the lady now."

So polished and cool. Sara's heart skipped a beat.

"Stop hassling me. This is business between myself and my girlfriend. Beat it now before I rearrange your face with my fists. I'll have you on the ground long before the cops arrive." Ernie's sneer widened.

"That would be impossible, seeing that I am the police."

Harry lifted the corner of his dinner jacket, showing a badge and the glint of his sidearm. Ernie paled and dropped Sara's arm.

Seizing the moment, Sara stepped out of range of Ernie's grasp. "You're intoxicated, Ernie. Go upstairs and sleep it off if you want to close that account." She lifted her chin. "Or do you wish me to call Bill Myers and tell him you'll be indisposed and he should look elsewhere for representation? No, that wouldn't be professional. But I am concerned for you, Ernie. I could call your wife and let her know you're not feeling well, judging from your behavior toward me."

Ernie's jaw dropped. He rubbed his eyes as if awakening from a bad dream. Behind her, she felt the large, imposing and oddly comforting presence of the detective, as if he were her backup.

If she needed rescuing.

She did not.

But it was sweet of him to try.

Without another word, Ernie bolted. If they had been on a dirt road, he'd have left dust in his wake.

Detective Cartwright's mouth twitched. "I see you're more effective than a gun or a badge."

Sara's fingers tightened on her purse. "Only with married men who fear their wives finding out what they do at night on business trips."

It sounded as if she'd made a habit of doing this. Sara

flushed. "I mean, I know him. He's my former boss at the firm where I worked in St. Louis. He was never this... this..."

"Obnoxious?"

Sara sighed. "Yes. When he called and wanted to meet me for a drink, I thought he really did want to talk business, this account the firm had been eyeing for a long time that I was working on, I mean it's a huge business deal and he said he wanted advice so I thought, why not meet him for a drink..."

"It's okay, Sara," he said quietly. "You don't have to explain why you were with him. I didn't mean to embarrass you. I saw you looking like you were in trouble, and wanted to help."

"You're very observant."

What a lame remark, when she really wanted to thank him. How did one thank a police detective who had you under the microscope as a possible murder suspect?

For a moment they stood in awkward silence. Sara couldn't help but stare. Gone was the ruggedly handsome and hard-nosed detective who had questioned her earlier. In his place was a charming man in an elegant silk tuxedo. She glanced downward. Even his black patent leather shoes gleamed.

His short hair was combed, his beard trimmed. He looked like a dream date or a man about to sweep a woman off her feet as he escorted her into a formal gala.

Then he nodded. "Have a good night."

Finding her voice, she touched his arm as he turned away. "Thank you, Detective Cartwright. Thank you for saying something. Many men would not."

He looked down at her hand and then at her face. "Call me Harry. If you're not ready to go home yet, would you care to join me?"

It would be lovely. But did he plan to grill her some more about Axel Colton? She had already had enough subterfuge tonight.

"To talk about the case and Axel Colton?" It was hard to keep the bitterness from her tone.

He shook his head. "No. Just to talk, let you get your composure back. You're trembling."

She glanced at her hand still on his arm. Dismay filled her as she realized her hand shook. Sara pulled it away and gave a little laugh. Of course he would notice. The man noticed everyone. Came with the job, she guessed.

"Thanks. Yes, repressed anger does that. I'm quite good at leashing my temper. I suppose it's a good thing as it wouldn't look right on my résumé to say I punched my former employer when he got fresh with me."

A smile touched his face. Really he was quite handsome, especially with the smile, which made him look more human.

Sara drew in a breath. "Thank you for asking, but I don't want to take you away from your dinner date. Or whatever plans you had."

To her surprise, sadness pulled his mouth down, thought she could see him struggle against it. He looked back at the bar and his abandoned drink. "I don't have plans, or a dinner date."

Harry stretched out his hands. No wedding ring, but there was a slight tan line on his left ring finger. "It's my wedding anniversary. I come here…every year tonight… to honor a promise I made."

Her stomach tightened. This was not going to be good.

"You're married."

"Was. She died." He didn't look at her and that alone made him seem less of a confident police detective, more like a man who'd suffered loss.

"I'm so sorry." Hard as it had been to lose a father she never knew, she couldn't imagine losing a life's partner.

"She died in a car crash a little over two years ago, along with our little boy." He shrugged, and the gesture seemed to hide a wealth of pain. "We got married here, and she loved it so much we spent every anniversary here. We would dress in formal wear and have dinner, and after our son was born and money was tighter, we settled on one drink in the lounge. She made me promise we would always meet here on this date. It meant…a lot to her."

Her fingers stopped trembling. She'd been thinking of him as a police detective perhaps tailing her to grill her for more information and he was here simply to observe a heartfelt promise.

Sara's heart ached for him. Not merely the tragedy, but the loss of all those years ago, the loss of a child.

"It's a sweet tradition," she said softly. "It shows how much you loved her."

Harry glanced away and nodded.

She squeezed his arm. "Yes, I'd love to have a drink with you. But not at the bar. Can we get a table?"

He lost the sad look and his mouth twisted upward. "Yes, a table. Not a corner booth so if you wish to leave, you won't feel trapped."

Sara smiled. "As long as we avoid talking about work, I'll be fine."

Harry escorted her over to a table closer to the door. It was private, but offered easy access out. He pulled out a chair for her. After she sat, he took the opposite seat, his eye on the entrance.

"Are you looking for someone? You had the same kind of position while at the bar, as if expecting someone to arrive."

"And you called me observant." His mouth quirked upward again. "It's habit. I seldom sit with my back to the door. Lots of my kind don't."

"Your kind?"

"Cops. Military types as well. It's self-preservation. You want to see who is coming into the room."

"You mean you want to know if a suspect is coming into the room," she said slowly.

Harry's expression turned guarded. "Something like that. Or an enemy."

Which am I?

"But we agreed not to talk about work." He signaled for the waiter, who brought his untouched bourbon over. Harry glanced at her.

"Club soda with a twist of lime," she said.

"Shall I start a tab?" the waiter asked.

"No," she and Harry said in unison.

They looked at each other. He chuckled and she smiled.

"Not that I want to drink and run, but I do have an early start tomorrow." Sara hooked her purse on one of the tabs beneath the table. "I have to check on a client."

"Ah, work again." He grinned.

Sara sighed. "Yes, it's a hard habit to break. Especially when you're accustomed to your work being your life."

"Then you need to get out more often, see the city. Or do you like staying at home at night, kicking off your shoes and watching a good television program?"

"Not always. Back home, well, where my mother lives, I was active, had lots of friends who lived around St. Louis and I seldom stayed at home. But it's different here."

For reasons she didn't want to explain to him, reasons that had to do with her dead father.

"Chicago has a lot to offer. Theater, museums, winter sports," he told her.

"I do like ice-skating."

"Have you ever skated with Santa?" He leaned over the table. "Every Christmas, there's a skating Santa downtown. The kids, and even the adults, love it."

"Is he accompanied by eight tiny reindeer?"

"They're on vacation. Too many hooves to fit skates for."

This whimsical side of him was fun, and he was quite sober, which settled her raw nerves.

Her stomach rumbled, reminding her she hadn't eaten dinner, or lunch. Sara flushed as he tilted his head.

"If you're hungry, they have a good restaurant here. Or you can order sandwiches from the bar."

So tactful. She'd planned to take an Uber to the train station tonight. She thought of her budget, inwardly winced. "I'll be fine. I'll grab something from the freezer and nuke it when I get home."

"Sounds like my dinner when I'm on the run. Bless the invention of the microwave."

She laughed, and they began conversing about favorite foods. Harry Cartwright was charming and had an engaging smile. Certainly he was rather dashing, not traditionally handsome, but rugged, with compelling eyes.

He seemed interested in her opinion and looked at her, really looked at her, unlike some of the men she'd dated in the past.

Date?

He's a detective, Sara. Not a boyfriend.

But after the tension of the past few days, it felt good to talk about something normal like food and cooking shows, which led to a heated discussion about the merits of deep-dish pizza versus regular crust. Sara liked all kinds of cooking shows. Harry liked them as well, especially the volatile ones.

"Have you ever cooked with cast iron?" He leaned back.

"Never."

Harry shook his head. "A cast-iron frying pan is amazing for cooking. Not just frying, either. I can make a terrific chicken cacciatore with my cast-iron frying pan."

In back of the lounge on a raised dais, a band set up instruments—drums, electric piano and acoustic guitar. She sat up and watched. A blues tune soon rippled through the air.

"Does the music bother you?" he asked. "Some people dislike the blues."

Sara rolled her eyes. "How can anyone not like the blues in Chicago?"

"You'd be surprised. Probably the same people who like putting ketchup on a Chicago hot dog or think thin-crust pizza is best."

Hiding a smirk because she did love ketchup on her hot dogs, she shook her head. "I love music. I play the acoustic guitar, when I'm not immersed in a big project. I used to play in a band."

Harry leaned forward, his arms resting on the table. "A garage band?"

"Afraid so. Just my friends and me. More a creative outlet than anything, though we did get one or two paying gigs at local schools."

She wondered about him. Was he all work? "How do you relax? Do you have a hobby?"

"Art." Harry flexed his fingers. "I paint. Acrylic, mostly, but sometimes sketching when I don't have the time."

They began talking about art, art history. Harry surprised her with his in-depth knowledge of the classics. He'd even exhibited a few paintings at a local gallery.

"Ever think about doing it for a living?" she asked.

Harry laughed. "Become a starving artist? No, I'm too good of a cop. Plus my job interferes with my paintings. I end up blending the two. I also do quick sketches for witnesses at the scene sometimes if they can't get to the station to work with the police sketch artist. It helps to sketch out a rough drawing while their memory is fresh."

Back to his work as a police detective again. Disappointment stabbed her. She had started to forget about his professional life.

"Did you find it hard to leave St. Louis? You spent your entire life there." Harry sipped his bourbon, his gaze sharp.

A casual question from anyone else, but this man was a police officer investigating a homicide. Sara wondered if he was turning their conversation toward more of a casual interrogation to discover her background.

"It was, but in an odd way, it was time. I do miss Mom's house and her yard. She has a huge yard. I had a vegetable garden—amazing zucchini and carrots. I loved gardening in the backyard. So it was a little tough trading all that space for a tiny apartment of my own."

Lost in thought, she remembered all the promises she'd made to herself while in college, studying hard and working her way through school. "I needed to break free of routine, see a world outside the microcosm of my hometown where everyone knows everyone else."

Sara swept a hand across the air. "Look at these people. Everyone has a story to tell, experiences to share. I always wonder what their stories are, and back home, I already knew those stories, heard them hundreds of times before. I find people in a large city like Chicago fascinating. Don't you?"

Harry leaned back, studied her. "You're different, Sara Sandoval."

She tilted her head. "Different how?"

"Most people are interested only in telling their own stories. Or hiding secrets." He tugged at the silk tie at his throat, as if it felt too tight.

What secrets did he hide? Sara wanted to know, but the question seemed far too intimate for this cozy setting.

"Oh, come on. You mean to tell me you've never people-watched and wondered where they came from, what drives them, what they're all about?"

"Usually when they're sitting down in an interrogation room, yeah." His mouth twisted into a smile beneath his beard.

Sara changed tactics. She needed to know, for her sake, and they were back to discussing work again, so why not? "Detective Cartwright…"

"Harry."

"Harry." She drew in a breath. "Why do you think someone killed my father?"

She halfway expected him to brush aside her question, or make excuses about having to leave. Instead he looked straight at her.

"Discovery of motive is half the battle in narrowing down the list of suspects."

Now was the time to pin him down. Get real answers. "I told you I don't have an alibi for the night Axel was killed. Am I considered a suspect?"

Harry studied her, his green-blue gaze piercing. "Yes."

"Why? Because I don't have an alibi?"

His gaze never left her face. "That, the coffee mug evidence and you came to Chicago on an ulterior motive, not for a change of scenery. I can't rule out that you did meet your father and got into an argument with him and acted out of anger."

"I didn't!"

"Can you prove it?"

"Can you prove I did?"

For a moment they didn't say anything. Sara sipped her

drink and gave a bitter laugh. "I suppose we should have stuck to avoiding talk about work."

"It does seem to ruin an evening out." He traced a droplet of condensation that rolled down the side of his bourbon like a raindrop. Or a tear. "Then again, after a long day investigating a homicide, it's hard to disassociate myself from the job."

"Shoptalk can ruin a night."

He considered. "Yes. Especially when conversing with an intelligent woman such as yourself. You fascinate me, Sara."

Her anger died. Such a contradiction. Harry Cartwright irked her one moment and charmed the next. Men had called her several things—mostly complimenting her looks. None had ever complimented her mind. Harry barely knew her. They'd had only three encounters and yet she felt more alive and energized with him than with her former boyfriends.

They'd been immature, interested in sports and advancing their careers, not in justice. Or in her life.

Maybe that was what attracted her to Harry. His depth. A man who honored a promise to a wife who died certainly had much depth. And heart. Even if he thought she was a murderer.

It was certainly an odd place to be in.

She thought of Ernie, who only wanted to use her. "Thank you. Some men would not be as complimentary."

"Like your former employer?" Harry's mouth turned down. "He's a piece of work. Not only because he was drunk. There's something about him I wouldn't trust."

The fleeting impression he'd had of Ernie bothered her. "You can't tell much about a person in one encounter. He really isn't like that. He was drunk."

Harry toyed with his glass. "I don't need more than one

encounter. I'm a cop. This Ernie is ambitious, but slovenly, eager to take the easy way out, arrogant bully but backs down when faced with confrontation. Dangerous, even."

Sara paused in lifting her glass to her mouth. "Dangerous?"

"Yes. Watch it with him, Sara. Not only is he a sexual predator, but he doesn't seem like one. And he does have the mannerisms of someone who will go after you if he doesn't get his way."

His warning sent a chill down her spine.

"Huh." She made her voice noncommittal. "And what is your impression of me?"

"I'm still figuring you out."

"Because I'm a murder suspect," she said slowly.

"No, because I can't figure out how anyone can live in Chicago and not like deep-dish pizza."

She laughed and he grinned. The previous tension between them evaporated. Sara liked Harry, maybe a little too much. Harry smelled faintly of aftershave, pleasant and spicy, but not overwhelming. Even interviewing her at her apartment, he'd looked polished and professional.

Her laugh died. As much as she found him charming and attractive, Sara knew there could never be anything between them. He was a cop and she was...

A suspect.

She glanced down at the gold watch her mother had given her on her sixteenth birthday and was stunned to see it was nearly eleven. Sara pushed back from the table. "I need to call it a night. I have a date with a frozen dinner waiting for me."

He grinned. "A first for me. No woman ever left me for a microwave dinner."

Sara smiled back. "Quite the opposite of a hot date."

Harry stood and tossed some money on the table. "Did you drive?"

"Train."

"May I drive you to the train station?"

She sensed he would be the protective type loath to leave a date alone to find her own transportation. "No, that's quite all right. The station isn't far and I like walking."

"Good night then."

"Good night, Harry. Thank you for the drink, and intervening for me with my former employer."

Instead of shaking her hand or nodding, he took her hand in a gentle grip and then brushed a kiss against her knuckles. The touch of his warm mouth electrified her, sent a thrill rushing through her.

So gallant.

"Thank you, Sara Sandoval, for rescuing me from what promised to be a rather lonely and melancholy evening. I'm sure we will be talking soon."

He released her hand, nodded, and then headed out of the lounge.

She'd learned two things from him tonight. Detective Harry Cartwright was a gentleman, something few men were these days. And he had her listed as a suspect in her father's murder.

Harry Cartwright had engaged her interest. Funny how time passed with him and dragged with Ernie. Once she could have talked for hours with Ernie, but that was all about work.

It was different with Harry. She really liked him, found him attractive and interesting. Too bad he thought she killed Axel Colton.

Shrugging into her coat, she headed for the lobby doors when a voice halted her.

"Sara, hey, Sara, please wait!"

Groaning, she stopped. If Ernie desired to make a scene or worse…

She turned, saw him heading for her, hurrying as if afraid she'd slip away. This time he didn't look drunk or eager to haul her upstairs to his room. He looked…

Scared.

Gathering all her patience, she stopped. "What is it, Ernie? I'm through with you. And the firm."

"I'm sorry, Sara. I truly am. I screwed up." Ernie's jaw tightened as he stared into the distance. "I got drunk and tried to take advantage of you. It won't ever happen again, I promise."

"Of course it won't, because I'm not returning to the company, Ernie. Good night."

She started for the door. Ernie beat her to it. "Wait, please, Sara."

He ran a hand through his hair, his skin sallow, his jaw tight. "I'm in a jam since you left. All those times you helped out with the accounts, I can't manage it all. I need you back."

She would have sidestepped him but for the raw honesty in his voice. She'd seen Ernie desperate only once and at that time, Sara had stepped in to smooth things over with the client.

They'd nailed the account and Ernie returned to his confident, breezy self. Uneasy, she wondered how many times she'd missed the telltale signs Ernie had leaned too heavily on her.

He seemed ready to fall to pieces now.

"What are you saying, Ernie? The truth."

Not meeting her gaze, he rubbed a hand over his face. "It was you, Sara. You were a manager, but hell, aw hell, you were more than that. You kept our department functioning. There's at least five high-end clients I've screwed up with—oh, not big items. But every day I'm losing track of details. I can't replace you."

He finally did look up. Shocked, she realized tears swam in his eyes.

"If I don't get you back to the firm, I'm in danger of losing my job. All the clients are starting to complain I'm not following up on their needs. You always made things easier, made them run smoothly. It was you all this time, Sara. Damn, I'm sorry I never acknowledged that, but without you I'm toast. My career will sink. You know how word of mouth is important in our business. I'm too old to get back into the marketplace, not with a bad rep following me. I need you back, Sara."

She stepped back. "Ernie, I can't."

"I'll do anything." Now the tears vanished, replaced by a wild look in his eyes. "I swear, I'll do anything. You have no reason to stay here anymore. Your birth father, that Axel Colton, he's dead. There's no reason you shouldn't return, go live with your mother again…"

Had he slapped her, Sara couldn't have felt more shocked. "How do you know about my birth father?"

Ernie made an impatient gesture. "I was in your office before you left, looking for the spreadsheet for the Geckel account, and came across some notes you had about Axel Colton."

Heat suffused her, pure anger that made her want to shake him. "That was private, Ernie. It was in my computer bag, not a place for anyone to look through."

"Then you should have locked it away! You told me the spreadsheet was in your office and I couldn't find it."

"You're lying." She struggled with her rising temper. "The spreadsheet was in plain view."

"Doesn't matter. Too late. I know why you really came here to Chicago and now you have nothing to keep you here. That nursery job, it can't pay much. There's no real career here for you. Not like you had with me."

"*Had* is the word, Ernie. I doubt I could work for you again."

"You have to! Don't leave me high and dry again, Sara. You may regret it." He grinned as if the smile erased the threat. "Come back to the firm. I'll double your salary, and put you on the fast track to becoming a vice president. You don't even have to work with me, just manage the accounts the way you once did."

Instinct urged her to soothe him and get away fast. "It's something to think about, Ernie. Good night."

She fled out onto the street, turned and saw with relief he headed toward the bank of elevators.

Ernie wanted her back.

No, he desperately *needed* her back.

The idea stripped away her composure, leaving her shivering from more than the December chill as she scurried toward the train station.

Ernie knew about her birth father and the real reason she left the firm. How badly did he want her back to cover for him as she'd done in the past?

Bad enough to kill Axel Colton?

Chapter 5

From the shadows near a potted plant as he fished into his wallet for the valet slip, Harry watched the exchange between Sara and her former employer. He unknotted his tie and tugged at his shirt collar. This tradition each year was one few understood. He'd loved Marie with his whole heart, and losing her and his son shattered his world. Women he'd dated, hell, none of them understood this tradition. One had been angry he couldn't escort her to the theater because he had to have a drink in honor of his dead wife.

Sara Sandoval understood. Not only understood, but appreciated it.

He couldn't figure her out. Wanted to figure her out. She intrigued him, pulled at him in a basic sexual way he understood well. He was a guy, and guys were hardwired to respond to a lovely woman. What he couldn't figure out was why the sexual chemistry felt deeper, more visceral than mere desire, a spark that could easily burst into an inferno and settle into a steady burn promising to last a long time.

Harry knew he couldn't afford to get involved with Sara. She was a suspect. But his protective streak refused to let her walk out of the hotel without watching to make sure she was all right.

He didn't like the way that Ernie talked to Sara and the wild look in his eyes. Harry had seen other men equally desperate, usually right before they confessed to a crime.

He also didn't like the fact she was walking outside into the dark night with the subtle threat lingering around her like smoke.

As Sara stepped outside the lobby, he followed. True enough she didn't linger, but walked across the street in the direction of the train station. Not so fast.

Sprinting across the street he easily caught up with her. "Sara," he called out, not wishing to scare her. She'd already been scared enough tonight.

She stepped off the sidewalk. Out of seemingly nowhere, a dark, late-model sedan accelerated…right at her.

Cursing, Harry reached out, grabbed her arms and yanked her toward him. She fell against his chest, gasping.

Sara looked up at him. She felt so good, so right in his arms. Softness and yet beneath he sensed pure steel. This was a woman who knew what she wanted and went after it.

With some reluctance, he released her. Harry couldn't resist brushing back a strand of hair from her cheek. "Are you okay?"

She gave a breathless laugh. "I am now. For a moment, I saw my life flash before my eyes."

He wondered about that. Was it a coincidence that car happened to speed up and pass just as she stepped off the sidewalk? Harry wished he had gotten the license plate. Then again, perhaps he was being paranoid.

Harry glanced down the street. "Forget the train. My car is parked in the hotel lot. I'll drive you home."

"It's more than a thirty-minute drive."

He nodded. "I know."

"But I don't want to take you away from your plans."

Harry sighed. "Sara, my plans consisted of going into the station to catch up on paperwork. Do you know how much cops hate paperwork?"

"Probably as much as I hate walking alone at night to the train station?"

He blew out a breath, frustrated with her. "Why didn't you let me drive you? Or at least walk you there?"

She bit her lower lip, drawing attention to its lush curve. "Maybe because it's best we put space between us. I am under investigation."

"No matter. You shouldn't walk by yourself this late at night." His jaw tightened as he glanced back at the hotel. "Especially with certain undesirables around."

She shivered. "You overheard."

"Everything." *And my assessment of that jerk was right. He is dangerous.* He held out his hand. "Come on. I'll drive you home."

He thought for a moment. Maybe she would open up more in a less formal setting. Food always helped.

"You hungry? Want something better than a frozen microwave dinner?"

Sara tilted her head. "Such as?"

"The best hot dogs in Chicago."

She threw him a questioning look. "At this time of night?"

"It's an all-night joint. You in?"

For a moment he thought she'd say no. Then she put a hand to her stomach. "I am really hungry."

"I'll drive, and then drive you home. It isn't far."

Harry waited for her reaction as the valet brought his car up front. His car wasn't what most people expected a cop to drive, such as a sedan, or an inconspicuous black four-door. When the valet pulled up in a cherry-red 2019 Mustang, Sara's eyes widened.

"Wow. Lovely."

Her taste in cars equaled his own. Harry tipped the valet, then escorted her to the passenger side. He ensured the door was closed before taking the driver's seat.

"Cold?" he asked.

"A little." Sara touched the leather seat. "Seat warmers. Nice. Classy car. Standard issue for all homicide detectives?"

He chuckled. "My personal vehicle. Call it a teenage wish finally fulfilled. I don't get to drive her much since my department-issued car is what I usually drive."

"You should put flashing lights on it and get to crime scenes faster."

Harry put the heater on. "Not in this state. Illinois law forbids police equipment in personal cars."

The hot dog restaurant wasn't far. Fortunately, they had inside seating. Wicked cold out.

Harry parked the car. Sara got out as he did and walked with him to the entrance. He opened the door for her, hoping she wasn't the type who would bluster or protest at this simple courtesy. Sometimes when he did this on a date, he got a ten-minute lecture.

Instead of protesting, she smiled and thanked him. Okay, good first step.

No one else was inside except a bored-looking teen wiping down the counter. They paid for their own dogs, hot tea for Sara and coffee for Harry, and took them to the counter for garnishes. His eyes widened. Couldn't believe it. Just as he started to like her, against his better judgment…

"You aren't seriously doing that?" He stared in incredulous amazement.

She blinked. "What? I like ketchup on my hot dogs."

"No." He shook his head. "No. I'll have to arrest you."

Her jaw dropped. "What?"

Harry pointed to the sign hanging above the counter. "See? You're violating all kinds of rules."

She looked up, laughed, such a cheerful and carefree sound, it made his heart turn over. "That's just a frivolous sign."

They took their dogs to a nearby booth and sat.

Harry bit into his dog and chewed, swallowed. "That sign is real. It's against the law, and good taste, to put ketchup on a hot dog within the city limits of Chicago."

Grinning, she bit into her dog. Chewed thoughtfully, and wiped her mouth with dainty motions with a paper napkin. "Since we're on the subject, what do you do with suspects who put pineapple on deep-dish pizza? Lock them in prison? Beat them with a wooden spoon?"

"Worse." Harry finished his dog in two quick bites. Wow, he was hungry after all. "Send them to Miami and force them to watch a Dolphins game."

She laughed again and sipped her tea. "Might sound like torture to some, but Florida in the winter would be worth Dolphins tickets."

"Not for me. I like the cold." He did. Even on the worst days, when the wind cut through you like a steel blade slicing through warm butter, he felt alive. Invigorated. Sometimes the weather, more than humans, reminded him of one simple rule.

Stay alive.

But he was tired of surviving. So he stuck to the job, to the facts, and ignored the past, pushed aside the idea that there could be more than what life had dished out to him.

Dished out things that tasted much worse than ketchup on a hot dog.

Harry drank more coffee, had a sudden craving for a beer. As if they were on a date and he wasn't trying to coax information from her, this pretty suspect with the wind-chime laughter. As if there could be more between them than his suspicions.

He was about to ask her about her mother's relationship with Axel when Sara turned her head to look out the window. "Such a sweet car. It's too bad you don't have much chance to drive it, except when you're off duty. Must be horrendously expensive to garage it."

He shrugged. "I leave it at a friend's house. Let him drive it in exchange for free parking."

"You're a trusting soul."

Odd remark. Trusting? He was a cop. Harry glanced at her. "Only with close friends in my personal life. Life can be damn hard without them to get you through. Even more than family."

"I don't know about that. I always thought family was more important. If I had to sacrifice friendships for family, I'd do it. That's what happens when you're brought up to think you're an only child, no relatives except your mother."

Detecting the note of bitterness in her voice, he decided to follow it. Now was his chance to dig further into her life, and a motive for killing Axel. If she did kill her father.

"I'm sure it was difficult growing up without a father, and then finding out you had one all along."

But Sara was intelligent, as he'd already noted. She didn't fall for the bait. She drank more tea before answering.

"Look, Harry, what my childhood was like and what my life is now are two separate matters. You mentioned motive is important to a homicide investigation. I'm sure you think I had a motive, and that's why I'm still considered a suspect."

Harry stayed quiet. Let her talk, get it out.

"I have no motive—in fact, I have only the motive for him to be alive. I didn't kill Axel. I know that's a lame thing to say to you, a police detective, but it's the truth."

Sara stared out the window. "I'd have given anything to at least have met him, had the chance to tell him he was my father. Even with all the bad things I've heard about him, and how my mother feared him…he was still my dad. Now he's gone. I'll never have the chance to determine for myself what kind of man he was."

"Perhaps you found out what type of man he was and decided you were better off without him permanently."

She scowled and shook her head. "It's not in my nature. You assessed Ernie and determined his personality by observing him just for one evening. Do you really think I'm a person capable of killing another human being? No matter how vile that person is?"

His chest tightened. "I don't know you, Sara. I've only met you. You can tell me everything about your past, but I rely on evidence, motive and facts. It's how I operate. The fact is, we found the coffee mug on Colton's counter with your fingerprints on it."

"And I have no motive, forget the coffee cup! You have no evidence I killed him and those are the facts." She spat out the words in a staccato rush, and then took a deep breath.

"I want to find out who killed him as much as the Coltons do. I'm family, even if not acknowledged. If you want to look at a Colton, consider this. Maybe whoever did this was simply greedy and wanted their inheritance from Axel. Had you considered that angle?"

He wondered about that. Sara had not been named in the

will. Of course not. Axel hadn't known of her existence. What she said made sense. But he had to rule out every single suspect. The family was demanding answers. Carin, Axel's mother, had complained long and loud to the media about Naperville and Chicago PD's tortoise-like progress on the case. The brass was starting to squeeze him as well. They wanted Harry to solve this and work on the backlog on his desk.

"I've considered all angles." He crushed the hot dog wrapper in his hand. "Still considering. There are thirty million angles to consider, now that Dean Colton's new will is in probate, naming your father and his brother as his heirs. Thirty million dollars is a lot of money. People have killed for less."

Sara finished her tea, took his crumpled wrapper and hers, and dumped them into the trash.

"If I did kill my father, it wouldn't have been for money, certainly not for money still tied up in the courts."

"But you have other reasons," he stated calmly. "Like I said, I have to consider all angles."

"Can we go now? I have an early day tomorrow."

In the car, she said nothing more. Harry doubted she would spill anything. She was too much on guard, too smart.

Harry switched on the heat and turned the satellite HD radio to a blues station. The soothing wail of music filled the empty space between them.

He was exhausted, and even fortified with food, he was letting his guard down around her. Sara smelled like fresh flowers and sunshine. He wondered if anyone ever told her that.

She smelled like paradise. For a wild moment he remembered that old Meatloaf song, "Paradise by the Dashboard Light," and wanted to laugh.

Sex with Sara was as unlikely as snow in Miami. But Miami, ah, the beach and the turquoise water, Sara in a little blue bikini, her sexy, slumberous gaze on his as she waded into the ocean, playfully splashing him…

He shook his head. Damn, he was tired. These fantasies, they had to stop. Yeah, she was a beautiful, intelligent woman, but he had a job to do.

"Detective Cartwright?"

He blinked. Guess they were back to formal names again. "Sorry, I was focusing on the road."

And other things.

"Like I was saying at the restaurant, you need to look at other suspects. You seem like a methodical person. Who was that man who planted the candlestick in Nash's trunk? Did he do it? It seems logical."

Logic had nothing to do with that act. "I can't discuss that."

She blew out a breath. "This is my street. Turn here."

"I know. I've been to your apartment, remember?"

He pulled up to the curb before her building, started to turn off the engine. She shook her head.

"Don't bother. I can see myself in."

Sara sounded angry. He didn't blame her. Still, his protective streak wouldn't let her simply go. He'd seen too many women who'd been victims of violence.

Harry pulled out his cell phone. "Give me your cell phone number."

He had it already, but wanted to be polite.

Sara frowned. "Why? We're not dating. I mean, you're nice, and maybe, but it just wouldn't work…"

He almost laughed. So he wasn't the only one thinking about them being more than a cop and a suspect.

"So you can text me when you're inside your apartment and I'll know you are safe."

By the dashboard light he saw her skin darken with an obvious flush. "Oh."

Harry pointed to the keys in her hand. "You've already done one thing right. Always have your keys ready before going into a building or a car. You can use a key as a weapon, strike an attacker in the eyes."

She sighed. "I know. Trust me, I'm a single woman. I know how to protect myself."

He pressed harder, hoping to find an answer he hadn't seen all night. "Use the key to open the door and then pull it open with your left hand."

Sara shook her head. "Sorry, Detective. I'm hopelessly right-handed."

He tilted his head. "Oh yeah? Some people are, but you can learn to use your left hand. I did when training for the police academy. I learned to shoot with both hands. Is your mother right-handed as well?"

Suspicion flared in her pretty green eyes. Sara wasn't stupid. "She uses both. What do you care?"

"Just asking."

He tucked away that bit of information for later. Right-handed. Not left-handed. *Check that homicide file on Axel Colton.*

When she texted her number to him, he plugged it into his contacts. "Good night, Sara. Remember. Don't leave town."

Best to leave her on that professional note. Funny how they'd both not wanted to talk business and then ended up like this.

He watched her storm off into her apartment building. She did not look back. Still, he waited until she headed for the stairs.

Less than five minutes later, he received a text. I'm inside my apartment, you can leave now.

Then another text, as if an afterthought. Good night. Thank you for driving me home and seeing I'm safe.

Harry pulled away from the curb and headed back to his precinct. Sara seemed eager to find out who had killed her birth father. Did she express that interest to clear herself?

Or did she have something else to hide…or someone to protect? Like her mother?

Instead of heading to the precinct, he drove to Axel Colton's Naperville home.

The mansion was cordoned off as a crime scene. He had a key. Harry parked on the street and let himself into the house, flipping on the lights.

The air inside seemed heavy and smelled like fingerprint powder and blood. Triangles still marked where Axel's blood had pooled on the floor. He walked over to one and squatted down.

Axel had been killed by a vicious blow to his head with a heavy object. Blood on a marble candlestick planted in Nash Colton's trunk matched Axel's. No fingerprints. It had been wiped clean.

They had the murder weapon.

They did not have motive.

Security cameras on Nash's home showed a man planting the murder weapon in Nash's trunk. They'd identified the man as Dennis Angelo, a petty thief. Before they could bring him in for questioning, Angelo was killed in a car crash as he headed home…to St. Louis.

Harry stood and walked around the living room. He couldn't let Sara know that she had soared to the top of the suspect list not only because of the coffee mug, but also because the man with the murder weapon was from her hometown.

Dennis Angelo had no known association with Axel or any of the other Coltons. It might be a coincidence.

He didn't believe in them. But he hoped, for Sara's sake, he'd be proven wrong.

Chapter 6

Sara decided to come clean with the Yateses. It might cost her the job, but she had to do it. She only wished she'd been able to tell the truth earlier. The next morning, she dressed in a violet sweater, black silk trousers and ankle boots, and added a purple-and-red pashmina scarf with sparkling strands woven through it. Instead of braiding her long hair, she left it loose.

One should always look stylish and presentable when being fired.

She arrived at the nursery around 7:30 a.m. and parked on the street. The Yateses lived in an upscale Chicago suburb.

At least the day was warmer than yesterday and she didn't have to worry about slipping on an icy walkway. Sara opened the iron gate and marched along the brick pathway leading to the office building. The nursery grounds were speckled with light snow. Several greenhouses scattered throughout the expansive property protected delicate plants from cold Illinois winters.

Since the business didn't open until 8:30, she wasn't surprised to see the lights off and the building locked. Probably Rick and Vita were either having coffee in their house much farther behind the nursery grounds, or more likely, checking on the plants to ensure they'd survived the cold. The landscapers had their hands full, ensuring the flowers would blossom and no insects would dare show their face on the tiny buds.

Much easier to deal with plants than people. More predictable. Plants don't have motives. Or lie.

Using her key to open one of the double doors, she made sure to lock the door behind her. Sara headed for her office and closed the door, breathing a sigh of relief. At least she'd have time to organize files before facing Vita and Rick.

If they fired her today, she wanted to make sure they had all the sales contacts she'd made at this job.

Sara placed her laptop bag and paper cup of coffee on her desk. After shrugging out of her coat and hanging it on the coatrack by the door, she powered up her computer and got to work.

She was so absorbed, she almost didn't hear the knock at the door. Sara glanced at the clock on the wall that featured a whimsical arrangement of yellow daisies. Nearly 8:30!

"Come in," she called out.

The office door opened and Lila, Vita's daughter, strolled inside. Sara brightened. "Good morning, stranger."

Lila smiled. "Hi, Sara! Good to see you again. You look better than the last time I saw you. You feeling okay now?"

Not really, but that has nothing to do with my physical health.

"I'm good. Are you having breakfast with your mom and Rick?"

Lila nodded. "They asked me and Myles to stop by this morning. Mom said they needed to talk with us. Something about Axel's death."

Sara's heart beat faster. She sipped her coffee, hoping Lila couldn't detect her surprise. "Oh. What's going on?"

"Good news. The police are narrowing down a list of possible suspects in Dad's death." Lila wandered over to the window overlooking the nursery grounds. "Mom said Detective Cartwright has a new suspect and he has more questions for her this morning."

What time did police detectives arrive at work? Harry had said last night he was going to do paperwork after he dropped her off. Did he remain at the station all night?

She had to meet with Valerie and Rick, and include Lila and Myles, before Harry could out her.

Bad enough she was Axel's illegitimate daughter. That alone would present a shock, but to find out she was suspected in his murder?

Sara felt like a spy whose cover was about to be blown, except she would be the one revealing her secret.

Lila pulled out her cell phone. "I've got an important meeting at ten at my art gallery and have to return to the city. I'll talk to you later, Sara."

Sara pushed out from her desk and stood so fast the chair almost toppled to the floor. "Wait. I need to talk with you, your brother, and Vita and Rick. It's important."

"You're not going to quit on us, I hope." Lila gave a little laugh. "Just when Mom was so excited about the possibility of new business for winter. She and Rick are even talking about expansion."

Not quit. Not willingly.

"It's better if I explain when you're all together."

"Sounds serious."

"It is."

Worry clouded Lila's pretty face. "I'll call everyone together. They're still at the house."

"I'll meet you in the conference room in ten."

Ten minutes later, refreshed by a new cup of coffee Lila had brewed earlier, Sara sat at the elegant mahogany table in the conference room used for conferring with clients. Rick had told her he'd found the table in an estate sale. He loved the hand-carved rosettes on the sides. Perfect for a nursery.

Sara traced one of the flowers now with a trembling finger. This was tougher than she'd expected. When she'd taken the job months ago, she'd been cool, confident in her abilities and absolutely neutral about her father's family.

Now she'd come to regard them as friends, even more.

Rick had last used this room to plan a funeral with a busy florist client. Someone had left a pot of lilies in the corner and the heavy fragrance filled the air.

Leaves still clinging with stubborn insistence on a majestic oak outside the conference room window fluttered in the wind. *I'm like those leaves. I refuse to accept the inevitable and move on. But at some point, I'll be forced into it.*

The conference room door opened and Vita and Rick entered, followed by Myles and a worried-looking Lila.

They sat across from her. *My firing squad.*

"Sara?" Vita's voice was gentle. "Lila said you had a matter of great importance to discuss with the family. I gather it isn't business."

The family. Once she might have regarded them as her family. "No." She drew in a deep breath. "It's got nothing to do with the business. This is personal."

As personal as it gets...

Harry hadn't been able to sleep much after he drove home from Axel's house. The department would soon release it to the family, after Carin, Axel's mother, had pestered the brass.

He couldn't stop thinking of Sara, and went over in his mind all the angles and motives she would have for killing her own father. Each one unraveled like a stray thread on a sweater.

Doubts filled him the next morning as he showered and mulled over her involvement. Was he being entirely objective?

Or had Sara enchanted him so much with her intelligence and beauty that he searched for an excuse to eliminate her as the top suspect in her father's death?

Yesterday he'd stopped by Yates' Yards and questioned Vita Yates about the coffee mug collection in the employee break room. Vita told him sometimes employees took the mugs home. Sometimes clients used them as well if they came into the nursery for meetings. They didn't keep track of them.

He'd gotten a list of all the employees, clients and visitors for the past two months. It was extensive. It included the murder victim—Axel Colton.

Colton had been there on a day when Vita and Rick were gone. In fact, he'd insisted on meeting Lila there before taking her to lunch at his house.

After he contacted Lila, Colton's daughter told Harry she couldn't remember if Axel had taken the coffee mug. He might have. She was too focused on hustling him out of the nursery before Rick or Vita returned. Rick in particular did not hold any fondness for Axel.

When he'd further questioned her on what they discussed, Lila told Harry the lunch was peculiar. Axel acted as if he wanted to discuss something of great importance, but in the end, he only asked about her business and if she was happy with her life.

If Sara told the truth and hadn't visited her father, and Axel himself hadn't used the mug, someone else must have planted the coffee mug in Colton's house. Someone who had known she used the mug, and had been watching her.

The last fact bothered him on a visceral level. If Sara had a stalker, she was unaware of it.

The station was busy today, swarming with people, but he had no time for chatter. Enough pressure squeezed him to try to solve this case.

To his surprise, Sean Stafford was at his desk. Now this was worth a stop. Sean had been on leave for more than three weeks. He and his fiancée, January Colton, had eloped shortly before she'd given birth to the couple's twins.

Busy with a file, Sean didn't look up. Harry rapped on the detective's desk. "Hey, papa."

Sean glanced up, grinned. "Harry! Good to see you."

"Welcome back. I thought you were taking an extra week of paternity leave."

"January's mom is helping out and the captain asked for everyone who can spare time to work on the Colton murder case." Sean leaned back, yawned.

Harry grinned. "And you needed to get away from the crying. Twice the crying. Welcome to the joys of parenthood and never sleeping again."

"Never?" Sean rubbed his cheek. "Ever?"

"Probably not for the next twenty years," Harry said a little too cheerfully. "How are the twins?"

Sean's expression softened. "Man, they're so little but growing so fast. Already have personalities. Leo's demanding and if he doesn't get what he wants right now, you'll hear it. Laura's a sweetheart, doesn't fuss, waits her turn."

"So Leo's like you and Laura takes after her mom." Harry mock punched Sean's arm.

Sean beamed. "Yeah. Oh, thanks so much for the two bouncy seats. Awesome gift, Harry."

"I figured they would come in handy."

"They are. You knew just what to give us. Last night the twins kept crying and January put them in the bouncy seats for the first time and they loved them. I remember you saying how John never wanted to leave his bouncy seat except when Marie fed him. Seems the same with Leo," Sean said.

His former partner went on talking about the twins. Harry kept his smile, but his guts did that little twist the way they always did when anyone or anything reminded him of his own son. It wasn't Sean's fault. The man was caught up in the glow of being a first-time father.

He clapped Sean on the back. "Congratulations again."

At his own desk, he could focus on work and forget his personal life and the bite of his painful past. Harry opened Axel Colton's file and read through it, searching for anything he could use to tighten leads on the case.

A few minutes later, Sean came over, sat on Harry's desk. "I thought I looked tired, but you look absolutely beat. What's going on?"

Harry didn't look up. "You're sitting on my desk."

"All the chairs are taken. Carin Pederson was here a while ago. Good thing you missed her."

A paragraph in the notes stood out. Harry took a yellow highlighter and circled it. The candlestick used to deliver the killing blow to Axel's skull weighed a little less than eight pounds. Its mate sat on an elegant table near the spot where Axel died.

Axel and Sara were about the same height. She was slender, her arms toned. But strong enough to lift an eight-pound marble candlestick and hit her birth father over the head?

When she claimed she had not even met him, and only wanted to face him in person?

"Thought I'd update you on what's happening. The Coltons are putting pressure on the brass about this case, Harry, turning up the heat. Carin was complaining not enough is being done to find her son's killer. She was practically screaming she wants more police on this case to bring her son's killer to justice or she's holding a press conference and accusing the Chicago PD of dragging its heels," Sean said.

Harry flipped through the autopsy report. Axel died from a blow to the right side of his head.

Sara admitted she was hopelessly right-handed.

Her mother, Regina, used both her hands.

It was nearly impossible for Sara to face Axel and hit him with her right hand on the right side of his head. Unless Sara had been walking away from Axel and turned... striking him on his right side. Didn't make sense. The vic had collapsed to the polished floor face flat. As if struck where he stood, by someone standing in front of him who was left-handed or at least ambidextrous? Axel faced his killer. Harry felt a chill rush down his spine that had nothing to do with the gush of relief he felt.

Sara couldn't have killed her father.

But her mother might have.

Was he grasping at straws to find ways to clear Sara instead of doing his job? Harry rubbed his eyes and set the highlighter down.

"Harry?" Sean waved a hand in front of him. "Did you hear anything I said?"

"What?"

"I heard you were having a drink with Sara Sandoval at the Four Seasons."

The tone in his former partner's voice made him finally look up. "So?"

"You had a drink at the Four Seasons, and not that landscaping place where she works. Sounds social. Get anything out of her?"

"No." Harry leaned back, the chair creaking in protest. He didn't like where this thread was headed. Much better to listen to Sean talk about his newborn twins.

"Huh."

"Huh what?"

But Sean didn't go there. "I went over that file again and again. The chief asked me to work with you because Carin is yapping she wants answers. Brass wants them, too, and the sooner we, or Naperville, solves this, the happier everyone will be."

"You think I'm dragging my heels?"

A heavy sigh. "No. I'm telling you the heat is growing on this, Harry."

No kidding.

"Okay, here's a recap." Harry sat up. "I have a candlestick used to kill Colton, no prints, no DNA except for Colton's blood. I have a dead suspect who planted the weapon in Nash Colton's trunk. And I have security cameras that were damaged in Colton's house so there's no evidence of anyone entering and leaving his house around the time of the murder. If Sara visited her father, we don't know."

"It wasn't premeditated. Whoever killed Colton used the candlestick that was available," Sean mused.

"Right. This was a crime of passion." Harry pointed to the file. "Someone got mad at Colton and hit him. They didn't visit his house to kill him. It happened spontaneously."

"If you're going to kill someone, a candlestick isn't a good weapon," Sean said dryly.

He nodded, glad his ex-partner followed his line of reasoning. "Knives, guns, hell, poisoning is much more reliable than trying to hit someone over the head."

"Someone had to have seen something. Did Naperville check the neighbors? That's a posh area. Security patrol."

Harry laughed, but there was no humor in it. "They did. My old friend Jimmy talked with all the neighbors and the security patrol. He's working another case now—a Santa Claus shot and killed outside a house. Looked like a burglary gone wrong, but Jimmy and I had the feeling it wasn't."

"And there's no way the two cases are connected."

"Not that we know, but Jimmy's checking all angles." Harry drummed his fingers on the desk. "We need more than forensic evidence, not that we have much of that. We need motive to seal this and get a conviction. But right now we have little to go on."

Sean shook his head. "Tough break. What do you want from me?"

Harry picked up a ragged piece of paper. "Neighbors across the street from Colton do have security cameras. They're out of the country, supposed to return today. Soon as they do, check their footage. Might get at least a glimpse of a license plate."

He shut the file. "I'm headed out to do a little more digging."

Sean held up a hand as Harry pushed back from his desk. "Harry, I'm here to help you. I have a full caseload of my own. I'm glad you're back at Homicide. You're a damn good cop. We need you here."

He held his tongue. Things had been distant for a long time between him and Sean.

"I'm glad you're getting your life back together. But remember, Sara Sandoval is a suspect. Don't get personally involved."

Harry rubbed his jaw, suddenly weary beyond belief. "Don't go there, Sean. Because I sure as hell won't."

Sean nodded. "Deal. I'll let you know what I find out about that security footage."

He nodded, and then looked over the file again. His phone buzzed. Incoming text from his sister, Linda, who lived in Rogers Park.

When are you coming over for dinner? Amelia misses you and Elliott and I do, too.

Soon, he texted back. I'll be in touch.

The weight of several pairs of eyes sat upon him as Harry left the squad room. He sure as hell was impartial in this investigation. No matter how much he was attracted to Sara Sandoval. Justice had to be served.

Besides, he really wasn't getting his life back together. Sean was wrong.

Didn't matter now. He would find out who killed Axel. No matter what.

Growing up as the child of a single, busy mother who worked long hours as an office manager, Sara had long ago learned to deal with problems head-on. Facing this family, who had treated her like one of their own, was no different.

Why then did her insides feel as if she were on a roller coaster and the track ahead was missing?

Taking a deep breath for courage, she looked at all four of them. "I asked you here because I need to tell you the truth. I'm sorry I wasn't open with you before. I wanted… to get to know the Colton side of the family…my father's side, before I announced my connection. Axel Colton was my father."

Their expressions were blank. Lila's mouth opened and Myles's gaze narrowed. But it was Rick and Vita she focused on the most.

Her employers, who had treated her with such fairness. Such kindness.

Rick blinked and made a pursing motion with his lips as if to whistle, then thought better of it and sat back. He glanced at his wife.

Oddly enough, Vita did not looked surprised. Her expression composed, she studied Sara with the same thoroughness expressed during Sara's employment interview.

"My mom is Regina Sandoval. She was Axel's mistress and changed her name after leaving Axel when my brother died. I was born after she moved to St. Louis to begin a new life. Mom never told Axel about me, and…only this year did I find out my father hadn't died in a boating accident with my brother, as my mother always said. She finally told me the truth. I came here to meet Axel…to see what the Coltons were like. I suppose some might call it spying, but for me, it was trying to work up the nerve to announce my parentage to my father, and get to know him from a distance."

She threw back her shoulders and thought about everything that had happened since getting hired. "I understand the shock you must feel. If you wish me to leave, I don't want you to lose all the accounts I lined up for your business. I have all the information on a spreadsheet in your server's cloud, as well as the information on the contacts, meetings with potential accounts, and of course the clients I already signed on."

Dignity was so important. She did have a professional reputation and standards. Any transition would be as smooth as possible for whoever assumed her marketing responsibilities. She wasn't certain where she could work next. Certainly not her former job, not with groping Ernie lurking about. Too bad she had deceived them because she genuinely liked Valerie and Rick, and their kids. Her half siblings. The work provided a challenge she hadn't felt in a long time.

Myles drummed his fingers on the table. "Wow. Great news, Sara. Welcome to the family, sis."

She dared to hope she heard him right. Sara glanced at Lila, who beamed. "Yes, welcome, Sara. This is great. You're family!"

Vita was unreadable, but Rick's expression softened. "I understand why you remained quiet, Sara. I'm glad you told us. Your skills here are exceptional."

"Does that mean Sara now has to take a cut in pay? I mean, she is family," Myles teased.

She smiled, the first real smile of relief felt since walking onto the property this morning.

Then she remembered the other part of her news and her spirits dropped.

Her hands trembling, she fisted them in her lap, hiding them from view. Sara mustered her strength.

"There's something else you need to know…something you must know while I'm here." Sara licked her lips. "Detective Cartwright, the lead detective on the case, considers me a suspect."

Silence descended, as thick and cloying as the scent of lilies in the corner. Funny how she always associated that smell with death.

Myles sat up. "Wow. That's… He thinks you killed our father?"

"*Your* own father?" Lila blurted out. "Why?"

Nodding, Sara stared out the window, unable to meet

their shocked gazes. "I have no alibi. I was home the night of the murder. He said I could have gone to confront Axel and became enraged when he denied my claim, or sent me on my way. Or laughed in my face."

For the first time, Vita's blank expression cracked. Her mouth thinned. "Yes, Axel was capable of all that. He was not always a pleasant person."

"I don't know." Sara brought her hands to the table, wondering if she had the same elegant fingers as her father. "I never did meet him. I didn't kill him. But there's no evidence I didn't."

"There must be no evidence you did, either, Sara." Lila blinked rapidly. "I mean, the police seem like they are grasping at straws these days. Grandmother Carin is putting extreme pressure on the department."

Best to tell them everything. "I'm higher on the suspect list because they found a coffee mug with my fingerprints in Axel's house. It was one that came from the employee break room."

Vita frowned. Rick and Lila looked bewildered, while Myles the lawyer looked thoughtful.

Myles spoke slowly. "That's not evidence you killed our father, Sara. It's circumstantial evidence that merely puts you in the house. That's all. Someone could have taken the mug and put it there."

She had to level with them. "The mug only had Axel's fingerprints on it, and mine."

Little frown lines deepened on Vita's face. "That's why Detective Cartwright wanted a list of all our clients who'd visited the nursery over the past two months. He's probably trying to make a connection to whoever put the mug there."

The tightness in her chest eased. "He is? That must be a long list."

"Quite long," Vita said, leaning forward. "If someone is trying to frame you, Sara, we may be able to help."

"Unfortunately, everyone uses that break room and it's hard to narrow down who might have taken the mug. We only have security cameras on the outside of our business." Rick's expression tightened. "Do you remember what day you used the mug? That might narrow it down."

She shook her head. "I did like using it. So it wasn't one time or anything like that."

Silly of her, having a little fantasy that she'd given the mug to Axel, for Father's Day, perhaps.

Doubt flickered in the gazes of Myles and Lila. Rick glanced at his wife, who nodded.

"Sara, please come with me. I'd like to have a word with you in private," Vita told her.

Lila threw her a sympathetic look, while Myles sighed. Rick left, presumably to oversee the landscapers.

This is it. She swallowed hard.

She followed Vita to the back of the building, where Rick had built a sunroom to accommodate high-end clients. In contrast to the stark, sleek conference room, this room was light and airy. Oak-paneled ceilings gave it a warmth and richness, while the floor-to-ceiling glass windows overlooked the lush grounds outside. Ferns and other plants filled in the corners, showcasing the nursery's plants. Instead of stiff leather chairs, a cream-colored sofa and a few matching chairs were arranged around a glass-topped coffee table. A smaller table and chairs sat near the door leading to the gardens.

It was a peaceful place where the Yateses encouraged staff to take their breaks and relax.

She could not relax.

"Please sit, Sara."

Vita indicated a chair by the sofa. Sara perched on the

edge, every nerve taut as piano wire. She crossed her legs at the ankle. Despite the lack of warmth in the room, sweat poured down her back, pooling in the waistband of her fine silk trousers.

Here it comes. They're going to fire me. I deserve it for not telling them the truth. Maybe I can get a job somewhere in Chicago...there's plenty of good marketing firms.

Vita sat in the chair opposite Sara and folded her hands into her lap.

"I knew Axel had a mistress."

Not the words Sara expected to hear. She watched Vita's face, the careworn lines and usually friendly gaze growing hardened. Vita stared down at her hands.

"I knew he had a mistress even before the truth of my husband's affair with your mother emerged. A wife... knows. I should have divorced Axel back then when I discovered he was sleeping with Regina, but I waited, for the sake of Lila and Myles. Then Regina's son, your brother, Wyatt, drowned. It was Axel's fault for not watching the baby."

Vita folded and unfolded her hands. "I felt for your mother, but I was more than scared for my own children. Axel was careless and responsible for Wyatt's death, the death of an innocent child. What about our children? It needed to end. Myles and Lila needed to feel safe, and protected. I didn't care what the cost or the price I'd pay for leaving him. I had to do it. It was not easy being a single mother. Eventually I met Rick and he was everything I dreamed about in a husband, and he became a good, loving and caring stepfather."

Silence draped between them. Knowing the struggles her own mother faced raising one child on her own, Sara ached for Vita.

"I'm glad you found happiness with him."

Vita lifted her head. Stunned, Sara watched the tears swimming in her employer's eyes.

"I truly was sorry for your mother's loss. I can't imagine… the horrific pain she felt at losing her child. I could forgive Regina for sleeping with my husband. But I could never forgive Axel for Wyatt's death, even if it was an accident. Axel had ruined lives, not merely mine and my children's."

Emotion clogged Sara's throat. Her grip on the armchair rests tightened, making her hands bloodless.

"When my mom told me everything, about Wyatt, I went into the bathroom and sobbed because I've always wanted a brother. A brother to hang out with, and play catch with, to tease and maybe I wouldn't feel so alone. When Mom told me Wyatt drowned and Axel was partly responsible, I felt so hollow. Empty. And yet I still wanted, I needed, to see Axel. I needed to look him in the face and tell him I was his daughter. Only then could I have closure. Only then, after he either rejected or embraced me, could I move on with my life."

She felt a hand on her shoulder. Glancing up through her blurred vision, she saw Vita holding out a box of tissues.

"I suppose we both deserve a good cry. It's why I thought privacy was best."

Sara took a tissue, wiped her nose, blew her nose and struggled to regain her lost composure. Vita wiped her own eyes.

She crumpled the tissue and crossed the room to toss it out. Sara turned suddenly.

"Vita, did Axel have a lot of enemies?"

Her employer sighed. "He wasn't one for making friends. My ex had a tendency to drive people away with his selfish streak. But an enemy who would go to such extremes? I don't know."

Sara had to know. More than anyone else, Vita knew

her father well. "What was he really like? My mother only told me he was not a good person."

Vita stared out the window. "Axel was a selfish, arrogant and irresponsible man. But he was once a good man—otherwise, I never would have married him."

Nodding, she drew in a deep breath. "I kept hoping… for something different. I'll never know now. Vita, if you want me to resign today, I will. I don't want to cause you or your family any more grief or trouble."

To her surprise, Vita joined her at the window and took one of her hands. Her employer's hand was warm and slightly calloused. No one could ever accuse this woman of fearing hard work.

"Axel became greedy and selfish over time. I sense you only wanted to know your birth father and the relatives from his side you never met."

From what her own mother had said, Sara knew Axel Colton was a hard man. Hearing it from Vita drove home the point.

"I did," she said quietly. "I've always wanted a family."

Vita nodded. "I did not know, no one did, that your mother was pregnant with you when she left. I was simply relieved she had moved away to start a new life. But now that you are here, with us…"

Vita's voice dropped to a whisper. "I hope you'll stay. I've started to grow fond of you."

Tears welled up in Sara's eyes all over again. She stepped into Vita's warm embrace. "Thank you."

Seemingly overcome with emotion herself, Vita patted her back. "No, we're the ones who need to thank you for increasing our business and making us think outside the box when it comes to filling client needs. You're very good at your job, Sara, and I would hate to lose you, especially over Axel. He's done enough damage in my life."

Sara wiped her eyes as Vita released her. "I do like it here, and I hope you'll consider me like family. Well, not the same as your own children, but…"

"I already do." Vita smiled. "Now, shall we go see about those spreadsheets you've been working on while you were at home?"

Vita believed her. The other Coltons might have their doubts, but Axel's ex-wife did not. Sara only wished the rest of the family would have Vita's faith in her.

How would all of them react when they discovered her real identity?

Chapter 7

The next morning Harry headed out to Yates' Yards to further question Vita about her ex-husband's lifestyle. Might provide a clue to who could have killed him.

Though Sara Sandoval remained a suspect, he needed to explore other connections. For all his partying lifestyle, Axel had come into contact with many people. Each one presented a thread leading to the main tapestry. His job was to trace the dozens of threads that made a complete picture.

When he reached the nursery, the cold, crisp air hinted again of snow. Harry headed into the office. He was in luck. Vita was in the front office with her assistant going over paperwork. Her manner was relaxed, her smile wide and professional.

Seeing him, he noticed a slight tension, though the smile remained. "Detective Cartwright. How may I help you?" she asked.

"I need to talk to you in private." He didn't want others overhearing Mrs. Yates's personal past with Axel.

Vita led him down the hallway to a spacious office with leather chairs pulled in front of a mahogany desk. A matching sofa sat off to one side, along with a table and other chairs, providing a more informal setting. Vita didn't invite him to sit there, but indicated one of the leather chairs before the desk as she sat behind it.

Amused, he sat. He knew the message she handed out— putting her in a position of power behind the desk. Vita Yates might be a good-hearted, sweet woman, but she was strong.

Had to be, to have married and divorced Axel.

She offered him coffee, which he refused. Harry didn't want to waste time with social niceties. He needed answers. Already this morning the department brass had grilled him on progress on the case. They wanted this one solved and off the books so they could call a press conference and look good.

It took less time than anticipated. Vita was forthcoming and honest about Axel. She'd separated from him after the affair with Regina and sought out a high-powered divorce attorney to ensure her children would receive the support they needed. Axel wasn't a bad person, only a neglectful father and husband who liked to party too much. His work ethic was questionable.

"If you're looking for Axel's enemies, anyone who might wish to hurt him, I'm afraid I can't help you. He's been so far removed from my life I wouldn't know. Have you talked with his brother?"

Harry consulted his notes. "This morning I did. It was a short conversation."

One thoroughly unpleasant. Erik Colton was rude and arrogant, testing Harry's temper to the max.

Vita touched a silver photograph of her children on her desk. "Axel was careless and irresponsible, but Erik has been unhappy for as long as I've known him. He's an angry person. Always angry. I recall a few times I invited him over for dinner. Once all he did was argue with anything we talked about. I stopped inviting him over afterward."

Interesting. Could Erik have been angry enough to fight with his brother and in a fit of temper, hit him over the head? But Erik had a solid alibi. That night he had been at his club. Several patrons had seen him there all night, drinking.

Harry tapped his pen against the notebook. "I talked with Erik briefly. He said Axel had changed."

Now it was her turn to look surprised. "Axel changed, how?"

"He wasn't clear, just said his twin had gone soft." Harry didn't tell her Erik had scoffed as he relayed this information.

There was also the matter of Dean Colton's will, which was in probate. Harry had his own theory about that will, though anything had yet to be proven. Dean Colton's wife, Anna, said her twin sons, Ernest and Alfred, had been the legitimate heirs to the estate. Carin Pederson, Dean's former lover, had produced two illegitimate twins, Erik and Axel, and both had a healthy trust fund their father had set up for them. Now another will had popped up to complicate matters.

"You heard about the earlier will Dean Colton left, Axel and Erik's father? The one where half of the corporation's assets were left to Axel and Erik?"

Vita's expression grew troubled. "Of course. But I don't believe it."

"Was Axel the kind to commit a crime to get what he wanted? Such as forge a legal document?" Harry leaned forward. "Think hard, Vita. Because if he was, then this puts a new spin on the investigation."

"No. My ex-husband was many things, Detective, but he wasn't a criminal. His brother…"

Following that thread, Harry pressed harder. "Erik might have forged the will to get the thirty million it said he and his brother were owed?"

Vita got up, walked to the window, her back to him. "I don't know. Erik isn't a pleasant person, but I hate accusing him of anything."

"You know him, Vita. You've sat at the dinner table with him. Would you say he might be capable of forging the will?"

A heavy sigh. "Yes. Erik tended to blow through his money, even more than Axel. I heard a rumor he was hard up for cash."

If Erik had forged the will, then argued with his twin after confessing the act, Erik stood to inherit the full thirty million dollars upon Axel's death if no one discovered Erik's deceit.

Twins, yet so different.

"Did Axel contact you in the past few weeks, apologizing for anything he did to you? Want to see his children more?"

She kept staring out the window. "He had been in touch with Myles and Lila. I wished no contact with him."

"Why?" He made a mental note to ask Lila, who seemed to be less angry with her father than Myles.

Vita turned to face him and touched the photo again. "Axel was part of my painful past. I learned to forgive him to move forward, but I had no wish to revisit any part of that past."

"What about your husband? Would Axel have contacted him?"

A small, knowing smile touched her lips. "Axel knew if he ever tried to contact Rick, or contact me through Rick, he'd get a much ruder response. My husband is very protective of me, Detective."

"Of course." He wondered how Vita would absorb the news he had for her. "I wanted to give you an update on Jackson's kidnapping."

She nodded.

"The FBI has questioned all known acquaintances of Donald Palicki, the man who picked up the ransom and was later found dead. No new leads. They're still searching for the suspect who shot Myles with the tranquilizer dart during the ransom exchange. The prints we lifted from the dart aren't in the system."

Vita bit her lower lip. "I'll let Myles know. This is troubling to know the other kidnapper is still out there."

Snapping his notebook shut, he nodded. "I need to talk with Sara now. Where is she?"

Her polite smile dropped. She folded her arms across her chest. "Why must you question her?"

Accustomed to hostility while he investigated family members, he decided directness was best. "She's a suspect."

"I believe you're misguided, Detective. Sara couldn't have killed my ex-husband. I can't see any good coming of you grilling her over the death of a man she longed to know, but never met."

"Leave that to me."

"I consider Sara family now."

"So you know her background."

Vita gave him a long, level look. "Yes, she told us. Sara explained everything about herself and Axel. You should know, Detective Cartwright, as protective as Rick is of me and my children, I am equally protective of my family. I will not stand for Sara getting hurt."

"Yes, ma'am." He liked her own directness. Oddly enough, he also liked Sara having someone stand up for her. "But this is an official police investigation."

"Very well. Sara's in the greenhouse."

Harry craned his neck and gazed out the window at the scattering of greenhouses on the grounds. "Ah, which one?"

Vita laughed. "Yes, that would help, wouldn't it? Come with me."

As they walked toward a door leading to the nursery outside, she glanced at him. "Sara's been a tremendous asset to Rick and myself. She brings a wealth of marketing ideas and knowledge to our business and has helped us to increase our income. I value her not only as a family member, but as an employee."

He nodded. "I won't take up much of her time."

"I would appreciate that." She opened the door and pointed to a distant glass building. "We have an event later she is helping to arrange at the new greenhouse my husband finished renovating. Follow the stone pathway outside to the left."

The cold outside was far warmer than the chilly reception he'd received from Vita Yates. He got it. Couldn't blame her. Talking about your former spouse, dredging up a painful past wasn't on his Top Ten list of fun activities, either.

The greenhouse where Sara worked wasn't large, but it was set among several trees, shading it from direct sunshine. Even to his inexperienced eye, he could tell this one had been designed for more than cultivating plants. The pitched glass roof and clear glass walls allowed in plenty of natural light, as well as allowed those inside to see the trees and ivy-draped terraces. Bare trees stretched out their limbs skyward, yet he could appreciate how pretty they'd look in spring and even more in the fall with vivid colors.

Lately, he appreciated glimpses of beauty wherever he could find them. They were an oasis for the grim moments on the job, the sweet stench of death, the slick red of bloodstains...

The darkness of a human soul.

He paused for a moment to observe Sara through the glass. This greenhouse was different. Instead of rows of potted plants and irrigation tubes, it was mostly empty but for saplings lining the walls. Potted red and green poinsettias hung from beams overhead, and green ivy draped tastefully over support beams holding up the roof.

In her bright red sweater and a dark skirt and boots, Sara moved gracefully inside, waving her hands, pausing to help arrange the white linen–draped chairs.

Sara didn't look up when he opened the glass door. She directed two workers as they arranged circular tables in the room, and placed red linen cloths over the tops.

"Yes, like that. Good. Can you go get the silverware and place settings? I'll take care of the music system. We'll wait to set up the side table Chef Rysen required," Sara told them.

As the men trotted out, she finally noticed him. Her demeanor changed, and he sensed the temperature drop as much as he had with Vita. So much for the artificial warmth inside the greenhouse.

"Detective. You're here to ask more questions?" She palmed her cell phone. "Vita called and said you were on your way. I hope you don't mind if I continue to work as we talk. I'm on a tight deadline."

Sara walked over to a small table with what looked like wireless, portable speakers and fiddled with a laptop. Instrumental Christmas music began playing over the speakers. She turned down the volume.

No element of surprise here, but he didn't want one. Instead of delving into the interrogation, he decided to focus on the unusual greenhouse. Maybe warming her up would lower her guard.

Not that he wanted to focus on that solely to coax out answers, but for some reason he couldn't fathom, Harry wanted to converse with her without the pall of a murder dangling over their heads like the sword of Damocles.

"Amazing greenhouse. I see you're not using it for plants. What are you planning?" He pointed to the speakers. "Or are you playing Christmas music to make the plants grow faster?"

Sara looked puzzled, then smiled. "That's a gardening theory I've never heard before."

She swept an arm around, gesturing at the greenhouse. "This is partly Rick's idea. He finished customizing it for winter plants, but it's not really needed now, so he wondered if we could use it for customers. I found a ladies' Purple Hat Club in need of a different venue for high tea. They wanted to host one outside, but it's far too cold. I suggested renting them the greenhouse for a small fee, as long as they handled the catering. They were thrilled and convinced one of the ladies' husbands, a popular chef, to serve the food and tea."

Harry looked around. "Sounds impressive, but a lot of work for a simple tea."

"Oh no, not one tea, but a series of them. Each week they plan to rent the greenhouse. Not only that, they're posting the event on their social media sites. Word of mouth means Yates' Yards will pull in even more business, especially when these ladies begin their spring gardening. Most belong to a garden society as well. I arranged to have Rick speak to their club next month. It's a terrific cross-promo opportunity."

Smart and efficient. Sara had definitely brought her marketing ideas to the nursery. Suddenly doubts filled him. He looked at her slender arms, her slim figure. Sara seemed too delicate to lift a heavy candlestick and bash in someone's brains.

Then again, he'd seen stranger things in Homicide.

"I need to know," he began, then frowned as he realized she stared upward. "What are you looking at?"

"Oh good, it's happening!"

He glanced at the roof. "What?"

"Look at the sky!"

Expecting to see a meteor, or hell, considering the way this investigation was going, he saw nothing but gray skies and snow.

"Yeah? I'm looking."

She pointed upward and clapped her hands. "It's snowing! I was hoping it would snow. The ladies said it would be wonderful for their holiday theme. I have the perfect music for this."

Bemused, because it was Chicago and snow was as common as, well, snow in Chicago, he shook his head. Sara went to the laptop and switched the music to a holiday waltz.

Twirling, she laughed, arms stretched upward. "This is amazing. I'm so glad Rick renovated this greenhouse."

Enthralled, he watched her dance in the space between the tables, twirling like a ballerina, her long hair flying out, her skirt billowing. Harry almost forgot the reason why he'd visited. He could stay here all afternoon and watch her celebrate the snowfall.

"So beautiful."

"Yes," he mused, unable to tear his eyes away from her. "Quite beautiful."

Sara held out both hands. "Dance with me, Harry. I've always wanted to dance in a snowfall."

He shook his head, part of him wishing to capitulate to her spell and waltz with her around the room. "I enjoy watching you," he murmured.

Dancing alone, she whirled around the tables as she smiled, almost caught up in the winter magic of fat flakes dusting the greenhouse roof. The music swelled and rippled in the still air as Sara danced, her head gazing with rapt attention upward, her body swaying in sinuous grace to the haunting melody.

Such a lovely contrast to the grim crime scene of her father's death… Sara lifted his weary spirits. How he wished he could bottle this moment and uncork it, like champagne, when the world became too dark and ugly to bear. For the first time since Marie's death, he felt a deep connection with someone, a moment that soothed his weary spirit.

Hard to believe a man as self-centered as Axel had fathered this enchanting, beautiful woman.

Axel…the reason he was here. Harry's grin dropped. He cleared his throat.

"Miss Sandoval, as I said, I have more questions for you."

She stopped dancing. He hated this part of the job that drove away the joy on her pretty face, replacing it with sheer disappointment and then wariness. He could almost hear internal walls dropping around her as self-preservation, like a castle dropping an iron gate to keep out enemies.

"Of course. I got carried away by my work."

Her polite, tight tone swept away any lingering magic between them, as if whisked outside by a stiff broom.

"No problem." Harry flipped open his notebook and forced himself to focus on the job. Always the job.

He began hammering her with questions. What she knew about her father, or if she'd ever run into him anywhere by chance?

Hard to believe the woman had spent months studying a man she wanted to meet and never once tried to arrange an accidental meeting.

Sara admitted seeing him from a distance, but never had formally met him. Harry made a notation.

Had she ever been inside his home? Sara folded her arms across her chest.

"Never."

"Are you absolutely certain your father knew nothing of your existence? Never tried to contact you or your mother?"

Sara sighed and shook her head. "Never. I told you, I was working up the nerve to meet him."

"What about any other Coltons contacting you?"

"No." She blew out a breath. "If you have anything, any other evidence that connects me to my father's murder other than a coffee mug, I want to know about it. I have the right to know. Are you going to haul me into the station? Arrest me? Should I hire a lawyer?"

"That's up to you, and no, you are not under arrest. But as I said before, do not leave town. It won't look good for you." Harry felt his chest constrict. He hoped he would never have to arrest her.

Because as much as he hated admitting it, he liked Sara Sandoval. He liked her very much.

And that made doing his job much harder, along with being impartial regarding her involvement. It was far safer to remain distant and objective.

No matter what he felt inside, or how much he did want to waltz with her beneath the falling snow. Integrity meant everything to Harry. He'd sworn to be objective and honest as a cop.

If he lowered his guard around her and cut her slack because he felt attracted to her, and Sara Sandoval turned out to be a killer, he might not only lose his job.

He felt he would lose part of his heart as well.

As much as she enjoyed working at Yates' Yards on arranging the nursery's first afternoon tea, Sara was relieved to finally make it home to her apartment. It had been a nerve-wracking day, going from the joys of dancing inside the greenhouse as Harry Cartwright watched with a soft smile on his face...

To his grim expression as he grilled her once more on her involvement in Axel's life, and possibly his death.

Her thoughts were in turmoil. She didn't want to like the hard-nosed cop who thought she could have killed her father. Answering his questions had made her feel like a criminal and she wanted him gone.

Yet she liked having him close. Never had she felt this confused about a man.

No use denying the attraction. It flared between them in a rush of pure chemistry. Her heart leapt and her lady parts nudged her, reminding her that she was getting older, hey, time to settle down and have babies.

Each time she drew near the good-looking detective, she had to sternly remind herself it was strictly business. Even when, and she knew it would be a matter of when, not if, he cleared her as a suspect, there could never be anything between them.

Work was everything with him. Harry Cartwright was the kind of guy who would always put the job first.

For once, she wanted someone to put her first. Someone

who wouldn't neglect her the way Axel had neglected her mother, and eventually, the brother who died.

Sara unlocked the outside door of the building and checked her mailbox. Nothing. She'd halfway hoped for a postcard from Regina. Her mother used to enjoy writing. She once said handwriting thank-you notes and postcards was a lost art.

Smells of roasting beef and peppers wafted through the hallway as she climbed the stairs, along with the ever-present musty odor of a well-trafficked carpet seldom cleaned. As she walked toward her apartment, exhaustion feeling like twin weights on her shoulders, the door to #302 opened. Emma Pendleton stepped out, waved at her.

"Sara!"

She almost groaned. *Please, not now.* Lonely and seldom leaving her apartment, Emma loved to chatter. But after an emotional and physically exhausting day, Sara had looked forward to a quiet evening alone without company. She had planned to order pizza and then settle back in her favorite flannel pajamas to binge-watch cooking shows. Odd how she liked them more now that Harry admitted they were also a guilty pleasure.

Too late, she heard the shuffling down the carpet. Sara mustered a smile as she turned.

"Hi, Mrs. Pendleton. I've had a really long day. Can this…"

Her voice trailed as she saw her elderly neighbor's smile wobble. Mrs. Pendleton clutched a pink envelope in one blue-veined hand.

"I'm so sorry, dear. I wanted to tell you I haven't had the strength to make the pie for you. But I should have it soon. I do apologize."

"It's quite all right. Honestly, whenever you can. No rush. If you'll excuse me, I'm quite tired and I need to rest."

"Of course, dear. I wouldn't have bothered you otherwise, but I found this and it's addressed to you."

The woman waved the envelope like a flag.

"The postman must have delivered it to me by mistake a few days ago. I set it aside to give to you and simply forgot. I'm so forgetful these days. I am so sorry."

The widow wrung her hands after handing Sara the mail. "I hope it isn't important! It isn't a bill, is it? It looked personal, but if it's a bill, I'll gladly pay the late fee, I am so sorry…"

The pink envelope looked like it contained a greeting card. It was slightly rumpled and a silver sticker sealed it shut at the flap. The postmark was smudged. Sara stared at the return address.

Her mother's address.

Breath caught in her throat. "It's okay, Mrs. Pendleton, thanks, don't worry about it, I've got to go."

Barely had she gotten into her apartment and locked the door when she flipped on the light and dropped her purse onto the floor. Sara stumbled to a chair and tore the envelope with shaking hands.

A single sheet of white paper rested inside. She removed it and began to read.

Dearest Sara,

I've tried to find a way to say this, and every time I go to pick up the phone or text you, I fail. This is so difficult for me. I wish we hadn't parted ways with anger. I love you so much, Sara.

I suppose this is why every time we've talked since you left I haven't been able to ask much about your life or your attempts to contact your father. When Wyatt died, part of me died inside. This is why I could never forgive your father and why I felt it necessary to move away and change my name, so Axel or any of the Coltons could never find me.

I did not want them to know about your existence.

I know you have your heart set on meeting him, Sara. I fear I didn't say enough because I didn't want you to hate me.

But when I found out you wanted to finally introduce yourself to Axel, I had do something. It's hard for me to talk about this.

I called Axel today for the first time since I left him. I told him about you, Sara. I begged him to treat you with gentleness.

He laughed at me. Axel told me there is no way you could be his daughter. He said cruel and intolerable things. He didn't care, the same way he had little remorse after Wyatt died.

Axel Colton will break your heart the same way he broke mine. He deserves to die for all the misery he's caused me, and how he hurt my baby.

I need to get out of town for a while so I can forget Axel and everything he has done. I'm so sorry I didn't have the courage to say this earlier. I love you.

Mom

The paper fluttered to the floor. Sara collapsed against the chair.

"Oh, dear heavens, Mom, what did you do?" she whispered. "Mom, how could you?"

Her mother hated Axel Colton and wanted him dead. She had to tell the police. It was the right thing to do.

Heart racing, her fingers trembling, Sara fumbled in her purse for her cell phone and dialed Regina's number one more time. This time, the voice mailbox was full.

She dropped the phone into her purse and then buried her face into her hands.

With one letter, Regina had cleared Sara of being a suspect.

And put herself at the top of the list as the person most likely to have murdered Axel Colton.

Chapter 8

Harry had told Sara not to leave town because he might need to question her further.

He never expected her to call him with questions of her own.

He'd kicked off his shoes, loosened his tie and cracked open a well-deserved beer as he flopped onto the sofa to watch a cooking show when his cell rang. Harry glanced at it and did a double take.

"Sara. What's up?"

A small silence. Then she spoke in a clear, strong voice. "How did you know…oh, right, caller ID." A small laugh. "Um, how are you?"

"Good." He sipped his beer, wondering if this was a social call or if she had something to confess. Hopefully the former.

Not that he planned to date her, but Harry sincerely didn't want her to be the killer. For only the second time in his life, he wanted to be proven wrong.

The first time was after Marie and their son had been in the car crash and Harry had given up all hope they might make it. He'd prayed he was wrong.

He was right. They died shortly after arriving at the hospital.

"Is there something I can do for you?" *Keep it professional. Don't blow her off if she needs to talk, maybe she's decided to level with you.*

"I need to talk with you, but not over the phone. I have to show you something. Can we meet someplace?"

He looked with longing at the television and the beer in his hand. Harry set down the bottle and switched off the television. First time he'd allowed himself to relax at home in days. "Yes."

Not at her home. Not at his. Someplace neutral. Judging from the emotion in her voice, whatever she had to tell him, it was heavy.

"Do you know Mira's Diner off the interstate in Evanston?" he asked.

"No, but I can find it. Meet me there? When?"

He calculated the drive. This time of night, traffic wouldn't be too bad. "Give me twenty minutes."

"Yes. I'll see you there."

He hung up, gave another longing look to his beer and headed for the shower to clear his head. Minutes later, he was dressed in a blue striped dress shirt, his favorite jeans, boots and a navy sports jacket.

He took his department-issued car in case he had to haul her into the station. Harry hoped not, but he was too jaded. After thirty-four years on this earth, dealing with all kinds of personalities, he learned to expect the unexpected. So he made a call to his former partner.

Mira's Diner was a greasy spoon where local cops could get a decent meal and a great cup of coffee. It was no gourmet restaurant, but it served the purpose. Best of all, he could talk with Sara in private while still having other cops' eyes upon him. Just in case.

He didn't think she would pull anything, but Harry's spidey sense warned him something was up. That instinct had saved his hide a time or two, like when a pretty and seemingly sweet cashier under investigation for an inside robbery gone wrong had asked to meet him just to talk. She'd been terrified and didn't want to go to the station.

He'd met her in the industrial area where she worked. With patrol as backup. The cashier had been quick with her handgun, but Harry was quicker. He had her in cuffs as she screamed obscenities at him, before she fired a single shot.

Harry pulled into the diner's parking lot and switched off the engine. A neon red sign blared out Mira's Diner like a lighthouse beacon. Cars crowded the parking lot, including two patrol vehicles.

Frying hamburgers, bacon and freshly brewed coffee odors hit him as soon as he walked inside, reminding Harry he hadn't eaten lunch or dinner yet. He asked the hostess for a booth near the back. He recognized two patrol officers from his station and nodded at them in passing, but did not stop to talk.

Spying Sean at the counter near the door, he shook his head. Damn, that man was fast. But it felt good to know he had eyes on him during this meeting with Sara.

When seated, he eyed the door. This booth gave him a good view of the diner, and was private enough so they could talk without eavesdroppers.

He ordered hot coffee, black, and then texted Sean. Amused, he watched his former partner pick up his phone.

Did you get the security footage from the neighbors? Harry asked.

Yeah. Nada. Camera angle only goes to the end of the driveway and shows a little of the street.

Anything on the street?

I did see one vehicle parked on the street at 7 p.m. the day Colton was killed. It left fifteen minutes later. Dark Range Rover, late model. Got lucky, it backed onto their driveway when they left. Plate's fuzzy, but our IT guy is cleaning it up.

Let me know when you have something. He pocketed his phone.

Sara walked into the diner as the waitress served Harry's coffee. For a moment he looked at her, really looked at her, telling himself he was only assessing objectively without her seeing him. Same as he'd do for any other suspect.

Yeah, right. That wasn't a little skip-beat of his heart the moment she strolled inside, her hair mussed, her cheeks darkened by the winter chill, her long legs encased in tight jeans. She brightened up the diner with her colorful dark pink coat and a pink-and-red scarf with sparkling strands.

Harry added a few spoonfuls of sugar to his coffee, stirred, and then waved to her. She hurried over. The two uniforms he'd nodded to previously gave Sara an appreciative once-over. Harry scowled.

Sara was a suspect, nothing more. Yet he felt protective of her. Maybe it was a lingering effect of seeing that bastard ex-boss of hers manhandle her. He couldn't ignore his gut feeling this was something more. An undeniable chemistry sparking between them as certain as lake-effect snow in the winter.

She slid into the booth opposite him and shrugged out

of her coat. "Thanks for meeting me. I hope I didn't interrupt anything."

"Only the best home-cooked meal I've ever seen."

Her mouth pulled downward. "Oh, I'm sorry."

"I taped it."

Her dark eyebrows knitted together. "Taped…oh!" Sara rolled her eyes as he chuckled. "On your DVR. I see. Well, I hope it's worth the wait."

Some things are.

"Did you eat dinner?"

She shook her head.

"I'm starved. Go ahead, order something. My treat."

"You always treat suspects to a last meal?"

"Only if it's not something created on the Food Network," he told her.

She smiled and picked up a menu. They gave the waitress their orders and Sara settled back.

"Do you always eat here?" she asked. "No wonder you like cooking shows."

"Sometimes. They have a great cup of coffee."

"I've always liked diners. Mom and I used to go to one every Sunday for breakfast. Fresh blueberry muffins made in cups. Mom's the one who turned me on to British comedy. We loved watching Monty Python movies. When I would scrape my knee or take a fall riding my bike—I was such a klutz as a kid—she would calm me down by telling me it was just a flesh wound, like the Black Knight, and I'd live."

Sara was babbling, but he could wait. He knew how nervous she was, taking a chance in meeting him here. Sara twisted the ends of her scarf, fiddled with her silverware as she talked about favorite foods and British television shows. Finally he asked her.

"Sara, what's wrong? Why did you need to meet?" His

mouth quirked. "As enjoyable as it is listening to you, something is weighing on you. Talk to me."

"I don't know why, but I trust you, Harry." A small laugh. "I guess I have no one else I can trust right now. I mean, I am a suspect, but I believe you truly do want justice for my father's murder."

"Yes." It had gone beyond merely doing his job. He itched to close this case, bring resolution for the family.

For Sara as well, if she wasn't the killer. It appeared less and less likely she was.

"Tell me what's wrong. What do you want to show me? New evidence?" he asked.

Sara blinked. "Uh, not exactly."

The waitress brought their food—a chicken salad for her, grilled Brie on rye for him. He dug into his food, famished, while she picked at hers.

"I have something that may incriminate someone else in Axel's murder, but I need your professional opinion. Right now all I have is a theory and a letter."

Harry stopped eating and leaned forward. Whoa. Out of everything he'd expected her to say, this certainly was not it.

She opened her purse and withdrew a pink envelope, setting it on the table. He listened as she explained about receiving the letter, and the smudged postmark.

"At first, I thought the letter genuine. It would explain why my mother's been out of touch." She brushed back a strand of hair from her face. "I, I wasn't certain if I should show you, seeing as the letter is incriminating to her."

Harry sat back, waited.

"And then I took another look at the letter. It's printed by a computer, which isn't odd, considering my mother hated to handwrite letters. With her Christmas card letters to friends, she printed them out. Only with clients would she handwrite notes because those drew more attention and were more personal. And Mom didn't sign it. She only printed her name."

She frowned. "I mean, she always liked to write letters and said it was a lost art, but why send one instead of calling me? We've always been able to talk before."

The letter did cast Regina in a new light. Picking it up with the edge of his napkin, he read. Pretty damning against her mother.

If Regina had killed her ex-lover and then sent this letter, it would explain many things.

"Why are you picking it up with your napkin? Can you get fingerprints off paper?" she asked.

"You'd be surprised what the lab can extract. Envelope seals contain DNA if the person licked it. If it is a forgery, whoever sent it would be smart and find another way to seal it. I'll have to take this in as evidence."

Sara bit her bottom lip, the move signaling distress, yet oddly sensual on her. "I understand. I was so relieved to hear from my mother, but you must know, this is not like her."

Harry dropped the letter on the table and polished off his sandwich in three quick bites. "Sara, what did your mother tell you during your last conversation with her? When was it?"

"About two or three weeks ago. I lost track. I told her I was finally going to confront Axel. She was worried about how he would react and said she didn't want me to get hurt. She was also worried about my apartment, wondering if it was in a safe neighborhood after I told her it looked like someone jimmied the kitchen door. It leads to a fire escape."

Whoa. This was news. Harry narrowed his gaze. "Someone tried to break into your home? When?"

"Right before I talked with Mom. I remember because she urged me to contact the police."

"Your mother was right. Did you?"

She sighed. "No. I noticed when I went outside to water a plant I had forgotten I'd placed out there."

A head shake and another sigh. "Here I am, working for a landscape and nursery company and I let plants die. I picked up the plant, it was dead already, and noticed the back lock. I couldn't be certain the marks were from a previous break-in or attempted break-in. I reported it to the building super, but he never responded. So I put a table and chairs by that door, just in case."

Harry pulled out his phone and made notes, reminding himself to check out the building manager as well. "Sara, did anyone see you entering or exiting your apartment the night your father was killed? A nosy neighbor?"

Sara frowned and then a wide smile touched her face. It was like watching sunrise after a long night. "My neighbor Mrs. Pendleton. She's always watching me. Sweet lady, all alone, I think she's lonely. She frequently stops me in the hallway. In fact, she's the one who gave me this letter. It was delivered to her mailbox by mistake."

"I need to talk to her."

"So, Harry…is this letter a fake? Or does my mother have something terrible to hide. Please tell me this letter doesn't incriminate her."

Pushing aside her half-eaten salad, Sara looked at him with her incredible green eyes. Pleading and wide, those eyes could lure the toughest man into a confession. He was made of stronger stuff but felt himself melting a little.

Only a little.

"What kind of car does your mother drive?" He could look it up in the DMV, but this would save time.

"A 2019 black Range Rover."

Not good. He felt bad for her but steeled himself.

"Most likely Regina did visit your father the day he was killed. We don't have conclusive evidence, but it doesn't look good for your mother, Sara."

She did not meet his gaze. "My mother didn't kill Axel. She doesn't have that kind of temper. She's a gentle soul who wouldn't hurt anyone."

"And yet you haven't heard from her and she indicated in the letter she was leaving town."

Now she did look up and anger tightened her expression, her mouth thinning. "I told you that letter is probably fake."

"I'll be the judge of that." He beckoned to the waitress, who brought over the check.

"You're infuriating at times, Harry."

Pleased she used his first name, he handed over his credit card. "I've been told that."

"By whom?"

"My mother." He grinned and finally her ice-cold look melted. Yeah, he coaxed a smile from her.

Harry asked for an empty baggie. When the waitress returned with one, he dropped the letter into it. "Preserving evidence. I'll drop this off at the lab later. Come on. We're going back to your apartment."

A becoming flush darkened her skin. "Um…why?"

Intrigued, he leaned forward. "So I can make passionate love to you all night."

What the…where did that come from? He'd thought about teasing her, but this was too much, totally unprofessional. He took a deep breath, ready to apologize for being an ass when she gave a soft smile.

"Kind of hard to do in my apartment. The bed has a broken spring. Not very romantic. And I think the heater doesn't always work. We'd end up shivering under the covers all night."

Relieved she didn't accuse him of harassing her, he nodded. "Then let's settle for me checking out your apartment's back door. I want to make sure that lock is sturdy in case that burglar returns for you."

Her smile faded. "You think someone tried to break into my place when I was there?"

Should he alarm her? Harry settled for a compromise. "I don't know, but in any city, always best to be cautious. Landlords tell you the lock is solid, but they don't like spending extra money."

Sara shrugged into her jacket. "True. This apartment was vacant and I didn't need much money for a deposit. The rent is inexpensive and I'm on a month-to-month lease. Since I wasn't certain how long I would remain in Chicago, I grabbed it."

He followed her back to Evanston. A restful and relaxing night off had been shot, but this was worth it. Harry had a gut feeling Sara's apartment might yield some answers.

When they were inside, walking down the hallway, he stopped.

"No security cameras." He scanned the hallway. Lighting wasn't bad, but he didn't like the shadows. Bad people could hide there, jump out and harm innocents like Sara.

Innocent?

Yeah, he was beginning to think she was, at least innocent of killing her own father.

"I know. I'm always aware of my surroundings. I never take the elevator except if I have heavy bags and even then, I'm careful." She frowned. "I have to be these days. There's all kinds of criminals out there."

At least she showed some city savvy in taking precautions when arriving and leaving her apartment.

Once inside her apartment, he headed for the kitchen. They pulled out the table and two chairs she had jammed against the kitchen door. Harry examined the inside lock. It was solid and up high enough to prohibit anyone trying to unlock it if they broke the window on the door. He hated these kind of entrances to the fire escape. They were pretty and allowed in natural light, but also beckoned burglars and provided an easier way to break inside if one didn't have the proper locks.

Harry opened the door and stepped out onto the fire escape. He glanced down. Terrific. Fire escape backed up to a dark alley. Perfect for burglars.

Using his cell phone flashlight, he examined the latch and the wood doorjamb. Someone had definitely taken a screwdriver to the wood, trying to break the door open. Judging from the freshly splintered wood, it was recent, too. Maybe last month.

Sara needed to know.

But why this apartment? Was the person who attempted this targeting Sara to rob her? Or worse?

He climbed down the fire escape to check the alley. It crossed to another alleyway that dead-ended to the left, but dumped out onto the street that paralleled Sara's building. Easy access. Too easy.

Good rabbit warren for anyone trying to sneak in and out of the building.

As he climbed back up the fire escape and reached Sara's landing, the tinkle of glass breaking jerked his attention to the right. A shadow on the fire escape five doors down, one floor above.

Bingo.

The kitchen door opened. Sara stepped outside, hugging herself. "Find anything?"

He lowered his voice and withdrew his weapon. "Go back inside, call 9-1-1 and tell them there's a robbery in progress at your building. Lock the door and do not come out until you hear from me."

Sara retreated, closed the door. It wasn't until he heard the quiet snick of the lock turning that he turned around.

The suspect crept down the fire escape stairs, grunting as he hauled a sack over one shoulder. Dim yellow lights from the apartment windows glinted off metal the perp held in his right hand. Gun.

Harry called for backup, possible armed robbery in progress at the address, and waited.

He climbed down the fire escape, hitting the alleyway the same time the suspect did. Sirens screeched nearby. Two patrol officers entered the alleyway.

"Police, drop your weapon," he barked out.

The perp turned, fired. Harry dropped, rolled but not fast enough as the hot burn seared his upper arm.

"10-1, 10-1, shots fired at police," a patrol officer yelled into his shoulder mike. "Officer down."

"I'm okay," he yelled back. "He's headed west toward Johnson. Go around the building."

The suspect took off running down the alleyway. Burdened by the heavy sack, the perp was fast, but Harry was faster. He ducked behind a dumpster as the perp turned and fired again. Then the perp hooked a right and sure enough, headed for the open street, right toward the patrol car blocking the entrance. As the perp raised his weapon, Harry jammed his gun into the suspect's back.

"Drop your weapon now or you'll get a bullet in your spine," he told him.

The gun clattered to the ground along with the heavy sack. Harry kicked the weapon aside as two patrol officers rushed forward to make the collar. Only then did Harry grimace.

Damn. He examined his arm. Just a graze, but it would make showering a bitch.

A patrol officer radioed for an ambulance. Harry shook his head. "I'm fine."

Then amid the flashing blue and red lights, the chatter on the patrol unit's radios, the stream of uniforms into the alley as he sagged against the redbrick building, he saw an angel emerge from the direction of Sara's apartment. An angel with dark hair bound back in a braid, wide green eyes and a worried expression.

He groaned. "I told you to stay inside and wait for me," he barked out at Sara.

"I waited until the police arrived. I saw him shoot at you, Harry!"

"I'm fine."

In the dim alleyway light, he saw her pretty eyes widen. "That's blood. You're hurt!"

"I'm fine," he snapped.

"No, you're not."

Oh, damn. More trouble. He knew that voice. Sure enough, Sean emerged from the sea of uniforms.

"You following me? You're not my mother," Harry grumbled.

"I heard the call go out. Yeah, I followed you from the diner." Sean shook his head. "You're going to the hospital, Harry."

"It's just a flesh wound." Warm blood seeped through his fingers. He winked at Sara.

"Flesh wounds get infected. Come on, stop arguing." Sean crouched down next to him.

"Tell that to the Black Knight. You know, the guy from Monty Python." He watched Sara's mouth quirk, and then her lips wobbled.

"You're no knight." Sean beckoned to the paramedics walking toward them.

"He is indeed a knight," Sara said so softly Harry wondered if he heard her right.

His ex-partner studied Sara. "Sara Sandoval. One of the suspects in the Axel Colton murder case. We've not met... yet. I'm Detective Sean Stafford."

Sara narrowed her gaze. "Yes, I am a suspect. But that's not important now. Harry's wound is."

Harry sighed, knowing Sean would lecture him about Sara and playing the hero. Right now his arm throbbed too much to care.

"Bastard ruined my jacket," Harry muttered, and then he glanced at Sara. "Sorry."

Her expression tightened. "*Bastard* is too nice of a word for him. Do you think that's the same man who tried to break into my apartment?"

"Maybe. Hey, wait, don't cut that, it's a good shirt," he protested as a paramedic brought out scissors.

"It was. Got a tear in it now. Stop complaining. I'll buy you a new one," Sean told him as he helped Harry shrug out of his jacket and shirt.

Bare-chested, he watched the paramedic treat his graze. It bled freely, but he'd had worse. Harry glanced upward at Sara, staring at him.

Her gaze centered not on his wound, but his chest. Harry wanted to laugh. Had they been alone, he'd have teased her that this was so not the way he'd wanted to get half-naked with her. But with Sean hovering over him like an anxious mama bird, he didn't dare.

Not only was his ex-partner worried, he'd warned Harry not to get involved with a suspect.

Too late. His interest, and his emotions, were already engaged. Hell, he hadn't felt this much sheer desire for a woman since Marie died. Not exactly the way he'd thought he'd feel something in his long-dead heart again. Certainly not here in a dirty alley smelling of rotting trash and spilled beer, blood trickling down his bicep.

Life sure was strange. But lately, he'd learned to accept that fact.

The paramedics finished dressing his arm. He flexed it as they handed him a blanket.

"It's cold out," the EMS guy told him. "We highly recommend you go to the hospital, but if you refuse, you have to see your doctor tomorrow. You're risking an infection."

Man, he hated feeling like a victim. He shrugged off the blanket and grabbed his shirt and jacket. "I'm fine and I'll go see my doctor tomorrow."

Forget the shirt. He tried to shrug into his jacket, but the bulky bandage prevented that. Without words, Sara picked up the blanket and gently placed it around his shoulders. Grateful for the warmth, pride preventing him from admitting he was freezing, Harry clutched it tight around him.

She turned to the paramedics. "I'll make sure he visits his doctor."

Oh, damn. Sean tilted his head. "Yeah? I was going to offer. Do you know who his doctor is?"

"I can find out. Right now he needs a hot drink and warmth." Sara looked more like a warrior than an angel right now, fierce and protective. "Officer…"

"Detective," Sean said.

"You can join us if you're worried I might poison his drink. I have plenty of hot coffee and tea for the whole department if you want. Or you can return to Mira's Diner for a refill, since you're so familiar with the place, unless you only go there when you're watching Harry meet with a suspect."

Harry closed his eyes. Sara was a hellava lot more observant than he'd given her credit for.

"Okay, okay." Sean huffed out a breath as Harry opened his eyes. "He's all yours. Harry, get yourself to the doctor tomorrow to get checked out or I'll have the chief drag you in."

"I will," he muttered.

He'd collared a dangerous thief, had gotten his sorry ass shot and now he felt like a kid caught with his hand in the cookie jar. As he and Sara headed toward her apartment, using the hallway this time, the door to Apartment 302 opened and a white-haired woman in a pink knitted shawl stepped out.

"I heard all the police sirens, Sara, oh my!" she gasped, seeing Harry.

"Everything's all right, ma'am. Please return inside. The police have this handled. Patrol officers may stop by to ask you questions."

"Oh dear. Sara, are you all right? I was so worried!"

Sara wrapped her arm around Harry's waist. Warmth seeped into his bones, and it felt damn good.

"I'm fine, Mrs. Pendleton. Please do as Detective Cartwright asks. Please stay inside."

When the door shut behind the elderly tenant, he shook his head. "She does a much better job at listening than you do."

"Hush or you'll get no sugar for that cup of coffee. In fact, forget the coffee. Hot cocoa for you, and I need a cup of chamomile tea."

"Sounds terrific," he murmured. Right now he could drink motor oil and it would taste good, wash away the ugly smell of gunpowder and blood.

Too often he'd come close to biting it. Tonight he wasn't close, but the wound served as a grim reminder he needed to be more careful, especially when chasing down a perp on foot.

No longer did he have a wife to weep over his casket or a son to ask questions no widow wished to answer. But he knew people would miss him, knew he had to get his head straight because even on days when life didn't seem worth living again, he had to push on.

So others could live their lives.

Inside her apartment he gratefully sank onto her too-soft sofa as she busied herself in the kitchen. Then she emerged, vanished into her bedroom and returned carrying a large pink fleece jacket with red hearts embroidered on the sleeves.

He raised his brows. "I hope that's for you."

"Mrs. Pendleton donated it to me. It belonged to her daughter. I didn't have the heart to tell her it was far too large. But it might fit you."

"Pink?" His nose wrinkled. "With hearts? I'll look like a deranged Cupid."

"It will keep you warm and I don't have anything else you can wear. Better than wearing a blanket."

He gave a dubious look at the jacket as he shrugged off the blanket. "I don't know. Do you have any manly sweatshirts, like a basic gray or navy that a guy could wear?"

Sara sucked in a breath and he frowned, then realized she stared once more at his bare chest. His blood surged, thick and hot. Yeah, the chemistry was there between them, sizzling like electricity arcing on a live downed wire.

Now was not the time to entertain the idea of exploring that further. He put the jacket on, zipped up and the interest faded from her gaze.

Yeah, nothing like wearing a girly jacket to douse desire. Maybe he should ask her for a pair of bunny slippers with floppy ears. Or wear flip-flops with white socks.

"What's so funny?" she asked.

Harry caught himself grinning. "Not much. Just…this." He gestured at the jacket, winced at his sore arm.

A soft smile touched her lips. "You look good in anything. Even a silly pink jacket."

He removed the medal from his trouser pocket. Hopeless cause, indeed. That was him. Maybe the medal stopped the bullet from hitting him someplace else, like his heart.

Sara held out her hand. "May I?"

He gave her the medal and she turned it over, examining it. "St. Jude. My mom has one. She never wears it, though. It's lovely. Looks like an antique."

He pocketed the medal as she returned it to him. "It is. An heirloom belonging to my wife's family. Marie, my wife, she gave it to me on our wedding day. After she died, her father asked for it back. I refused. I guess…I keep it because it reminds me of her."

Sara smiled softly. "Then don't give it back. It is yours, after all, family heirloom or not."

She switched on a table lamp next to him, so close he could smell her light perfume. Her fingers were long and elegant. She looked pale, too pale, as if witnessing his shooting had drained all the blood from her. But he sensed a solid core of strength in her that had gotten her through past tough times and served a purpose now.

Sara Sandoval wasn't someone who fell apart in a crisis. He could appreciate that, just as he appreciated the soft sway of her hips, the classic beauty of her face and the curves hidden beneath wool and denim.

Sara glanced at the kitchen. "I promised you hot cocoa. I'd better go fix it."

She headed back into the kitchen. Whoa. Harry moved his sore arm, welcomed the throbbing. It took his mind off the throbbing much lower. He could fall hard and fast for

Sara if he wasn't careful. Focusing on the job helped as a good distraction.

He called Sean for an update on the perp, left a voice mail when his friend didn't pick up. Sara brought him steaming cocoa in a mug that read Coffee Is My Boyfriend. He grinned.

"Nice sentiment."

Her face darkened in an obvious flush. "My friend gave it to me as a Christmas gift when I skipped her party because of work. She was trying to fix me up on a blind date with this guy she raved would be perfect for me."

"Oh yeah? Did you ever go out with him?" He wondered about her social life. Did she have a boyfriend? From his background checks, Sara seemed happily single and relationship free.

"No. But she did, and ended up marrying him." Sara shook her head. "When I finally met him, I don't know why she thought I'd fall in love with him. He had money and maybe she thought that made a good match. But he was far too arrogant and this sounds petty, but…"

She laughed. Intrigued, Harry leaned forward. "What?"

"Oh, it is petty, but it's a pet peeve of mine. He wore too much cologne. Bathed in it. It made my eyes water. In my line of work, I've learned to be more sensitive to people's needs. I try to wear a light scent in case people are allergic. Does mine bother you?"

"No," he said in a husky voice. "It's perfect."

Sara gave a soft smile. "Scents are so important, and they can leave a lasting impression. I remember when I first met you, after I fainted and you were leaning over me and helped me recover. I smelled this amazing scent, spicy, but not too heavy. So intriguing and yet comforting, like the smells of home."

"I'm glad you were okay. I…was worried something bad happened to you."

"It was embarrassing. I hate looking weak in front of anyone. I've never done that before, but I was light-headed from not eating, and the news, it was too much for me." Sara touched his hand. "Thank you for looking after me."

The connection between them felt stronger than ever. Harry sipped his cocoa, his gaze centered on her. Funny how hot cocoa never appealed to him, but the scent now, along with the light fragrance of her perfume, made him think of autumn nights lazing on a wide porch, the crisp scent of wood smoke and home…

His cell rang. Harry set down his cocoa and picked up.

"Hey, how's the arm?" Sean asked.

"Fine. What's going on with our perp?"

He listened to Sean's report, deeply troubled, all his earlier peace vanishing. "I'll check in with you tomorrow after I go to the doc."

Harry hung up, toying with his cell phone, lost in thought. Sara waved a hand before his face.

"Harry? What's going on?"

He set down the phone, stared into his cooling chocolate to get a grip on reality. Reality wasn't a beautiful woman who cared about him getting hurt on the job. Reality was Sara Sandoval's questionable past and her connection to Axel Colton's murder.

"The guy they caught robbing your neighbor. He's a real creep, but dumber than a bag of rocks. Loved to brag about all his heists to his ex-cell mates. Name's Eddie Angelo. Ever hear of him?" he asked her.

Sara shook her head.

"You never heard of him?" Harry picked up his cell, scrolled through messages and found the mugshot of Eddie Angelo that Sean had texted him. The guy looked like roadkill, his hair mussed up and sticking up on end, his beard long and scruffy.

He showed it to Sara, who frowned. "He doesn't look familiar."

"They ran his name through CODIS and he's got five priors of B and E in Chicago."

At her blank stare, he added, "The federal database for DNA. Guy's been convicted five times of breaking and entering. Paroled three months ago. Lives in St. Louis." Harry set down his mug carefully on the nicked coffee table.

"That makes sense, if he was here in this building now, stealing again."

Harry drummed his fingers against his thigh. "He's the brother of Dennis Angelo, the same guy who planted the murder weapon in Nash's trunk."

Sara's mug rattled as she set it on the table. "Are you saying this Dennis and Eddie…were working together? Or is it a coincidence?"

"I'm a cop. I don't believe in coincidences." He gave her a long, level look. "You sure you've never heard of either of them? Saw them in St. Louis?"

Sara shook her head. "It's a large city, Harry. Why would I have heard of them unless they were on the news?"

"You tell me, Sara. Or is there something you aren't telling me?"

"I've told you the truth so far."

The truth. Or a muted version of it? Little white lies that seemed harmless but omitted the full story?

His arm began to throb, a pulsing ache that warned he'd get little sleep unless he took a painkiller.

"Okay. Thanks for the cocoa. I need to get home."

"You barely touched it," she protested.

He offered a bare smile. "What I did drink was good. Make sure you lock up behind me."

When he was downstairs in his car, he took in a deep breath. This night had truly been revealing. He felt glad of Sean's news about the perp. It served as a slap to his face that no bullet grazing ever could.

He needed a grim reminder that this was an active homicide case and Sara was still a suspect.

Because Eddie Angelo and his equally seedy brother, Dennis, weren't any ordinary ex-felons who lived in St. Louis and committed crimes in Chicago.

They had a real and damning connection to Sara and her mother, Regina.

Sean had traced the brothers' history and discovered Eddie had done odd jobs for Regina around the yard. The same yard Sara used to garden.

She lied to him. It was pretty damn obvious.

He'd started to believe Sara Sandoval hadn't killed her father.

With this new information? Maybe not.

Chapter 9

Sara couldn't focus the next day at work. Harry had been warm and friendly one moment, enjoying her company, and the next, he turned as icy as a Chicago winter.

As soon as he discovered someone named Eddie Angelo was the man who shot him and broke into Sara's building, Harry's attitude changed. Maybe because Harry thought she knew him? But St. Louis wasn't a small town where everyone knew her name.

I guess I'm still a suspect. But why won't he level with me?

Time to do her own sleuthing. She could also play detective. Sara typed the name Harry had mentioned into Google, didn't get much. Her mother might know this person.

Sara tried calling her mother again. Nothing. She couldn't even leave a voice mail.

Her hand shaking, she set down her cell phone on her

desk. The cursor on her screen kept blinking like an accusation. Guilty. Guilty. Guilty.

Did her own mother kill Axel Colton?

Ridiculous. Regina lacked a fierce temper…

Except when it comes to protecting you.

Pushing back from her desk, she went to the window to look out at the gardens. Vita was outside with a woman who had her back turned to Sara. Two gardeners dug up a young sapling for an order while another waited with a cart. Curious, Sara returned to her computer to look up the order.

Cold dread skated down her spine as she read the name.

Carin Pederson. Axel's mother. Her own grandmother.

She'd met her at Axel's funeral, but Carin had been cold and dismissive. She'd know Sara as a lowly nursery employee. Not family.

Suddenly she didn't want Carin to know the family connection. Not yet. Sara printed out the order form and grabbed her jacket. She scurried outside. A bitter wind nipped at her cheeks, but it felt nothing to the icy numbness in her heart.

If on the remote chance her own mother had killed Axel, how could she claim any kind of relationship with Carin? A mother's love ran deep. She knew this from her own mother, and watching Vita and her loving relationship with Myles and Lila.

As she reached Vita, the woman with her turned around. Her heart raced. She wasn't ready for this. Too late to back away now, though she felt as if she'd rushed headfirst toward the jaws of a tiger.

"Hi, Vita. Here's the order, in case you need it," she said lamely, handing her employer the paper.

"You told me there would be no charge, Vita. Or are you determined to leech money out of me, despite my grief?" Carin ignored Sara.

"It's okay, Sara. The paperwork is merely for documentation," Vita said tightly.

"Oh, that's good to know. I'll mark the file."

Vita cleared her throat. "Carin, this is Sara Sandoval. I believe you met her at Axel's funeral."

The woman sniffed and nodded.

"It's a lovely tree," Sara said, smiling at Carin. "But it is a little late in the year to plant a sapling. You should make certain to water it and fertilize it at the right time."

"It's for my son's grave. Of course I'll make sure it's watered." Carin turned away from Sara and began snapping orders at the two gardeners.

Sara wanted to back away slowly, but part of her, the same human half fascinated by train wrecks, even the one in her own life, decided to remain. She'd had so little contact with Carin. Maybe there was something, a spark of compassion or friendliness, that could connect them. Carin was her paternal grandmother.

Certainly Sara didn't inherit her grandmother's height, for Carin was short, and quite thin. But perhaps her sense of style. Beneath her coat, she wore a red Chanel suit and red designer heels. Her white hair was uncovered, pulled into a tight bun.

But her green eyes were the same as Sara's.

Family.

Sara remembered all those holidays where it was just Regina and Sara. No matter how much they'd decorated the house, it was always too quiet. Her friends all had big families, sitting around a large dining table, laughing and exchanging tales.

Their neighbors the Millers always had cars crowding their driveway, overflowing onto the street. Carole Miller, who was in Sara's science class and friendly with her, had five brothers and sisters and endless cousins, uncles and aunts. All of them always celebrated Christmas at the Millers'.

One year Mrs. Miller came over and knocked on their door. Sara had held her breath, eagerly hoping Mrs. Miller would finally ask them over for dinner. Maybe even share dessert.

Mrs. Miller had asked Regina if the relatives could park their cars in their driveway. Sara had hung back behind the front door, hoping Mrs. Miller would finally issue the sacred invitation. They wouldn't eat much, but it would have been lovely to bask in the warm glow of holiday cheer with lots of people, maybe sing Christmas carols at the big Steinway piano Carole Miller played "Chopsticks" on, and Regina would bring over her homemade apple pie…

Her mother had glanced at Sara and swallowed her pride. She'd told Mrs. Miller it was just the two of them for Christmas and since Sara was an only child and Regina had baked too many pies this year, maybe they could bring one over for dessert…

Mrs. Miller thanked Regina for use of their empty driveway, murmured something about having to get back to her simmering cranberries and rushed across the street.

No invitation.

Sara didn't cry.

Regina looked at Sara, and her expression had hardened. She followed Mrs. Miller and told her that she'd changed her mind. No cars. She had to leave because they were heading out of town for a special Christmas celebration.

Regina had taken Sara to an expensive dinner at a luxurious restaurant. Before leaving, she'd blocked the driveway with rocks to prevent the Millers from parking there.

Regina had a fierce love for Sara. Sara didn't want to upset her mother and acted happy and surprised about the gourmet Christmas meal.

Later, in the privacy of her bedroom, she cried for the father and brother drowned in a boating accident, the family she never had…

Carin was her grandmother. Blood was blood. *Grandmother.* Maybe she could call her Grandmother. Regina's parents died years ago. Carin was a living, breathing connection. Maybe she could finally have that dream come true…

"What are you staring at?" Carin snapped.

Sara blinked and looked away, her stomach clenching as if the woman had slapped her. She pasted on the same polite smile used for unruly customers. She crumpled the order form in her hands and shrugged. "Nothing, Mrs. Pederson."

Her grandmother turned to Vita. "Vita, tell them to hurry, for heaven's sake. I don't have all day. I have a hair appointment this afternoon."

Doubtful she could feel any worse than Carin already made her feel, Sara started to back away.

Vita threw Sara a questioning look and mouthed, "Do you want to tell her who you really are?"

Bless Vita for asking before blurting out the truth. Sara shook her head.

A small smile touched Vita's mouth. As Carin turned away from both of them, Vita winked and twirled her finger near her temple, the sign for "crazy." Tension fled Sara's shoulders as she stopped feeling sorry for herself. Carin was not a pleasant person. Surely she was not an easy ex-mother-in-law to have in Vita's life.

The two men lifted the sapling out of the ground and placed it on the cart. One landscaper hauled it toward the driveway, Carin and Vita flanking the cart like pallbearers at a funeral.

Axel's funeral.

Suddenly she became too aware of the cold creeping

into her bones, the pretty heels that provided no protection from the light snow dusting the ground. Her ears hurt. Or maybe it was all a reaction to seeing this.

Sara went inside, headed into her office. Once there, she picked up her coffee mug with a trembling hand.

A knock sounded at her doorjamb. She peered up to see Lila's troubled expression.

"Are you all right? I saw what happened."

Sara set her mug down carefully. "Yes. It was unexpected. Thanks for asking."

Lila sat in one of the chairs before Sara's desk. "Uncle Erik was in yesterday to pressure Mom and Rick about that tree for Axel's grave. He's always in here to pick out flowers for the girlfriends he thinks no one knows about because he gets them at a discount. So cheap."

"I know." Sara had met him a few times, though Erik had never realized she was Axel's daughter.

Her half sister made a face. "I saw Carin was coming into the nursery and I hid. She may be my grandmother, but she's difficult."

Throat tight, Sara nodded.

"Well, more than difficult." Lila leaned forward, her gaze filled with sympathy. "Sara, she isn't the grandmotherly type. In fact, I don't know if she's anyone's type. She's never been a nice grandmother to me or to Myles. I'm sorry if she made you feel awkward."

Sweet Lila. Such nice words. Sara shrugged away a lifetime of rejection. "She's a client. I would rather Carin not know my relationship with Axel. I don't think she'd take well to it."

"No, she probably would not. She's too absorbed in her own grief. I mean, Axel wasn't a terrific father to us, but Axel was her son. It's different for her."

Such honesty felt refreshing. Sara toyed with her now-cold mug of coffee. "Lila, I don't know if you or anyone else believe me, but I didn't kill Axel. I only wanted to introduce myself and get to know him."

Lila closed her eyes. "I believe you."

"You…do?"

Her half sister's eyes flew open. "Yes. I know we don't know each other that well, but I like to think I'm a good judge of character and your character doesn't seem to have it in you to commit such an act of violence. Even if Axel provoked you."

The lack of censure from Lila suddenly meant more than if Carin had expressed joy at Sara being a long-lost granddaughter.

Lila stared out the window, and Sara sensed she wanted to say something but found it hard.

"Lila, what's wrong?"

Her half sister sighed. "I'm sorry you never knew Axel. He was your father, too, but you need to know something, Sara. It was never easy around him. I don't want you getting dreamy-eyed, thinking he was this amazing dad. He wasn't."

Sara leaned back. "What was he like as a dad growing up?"

"Self-centered. Not really mean, but he was more absent than around. He was there for birthdays. Sometimes. He wasn't the kind of dad you could talk with or ask advice. Myles and I were lucky when Mom met Rick. Rick became everything Axel wasn't."

A heavy sigh from Lila. "I guess that's why I didn't feel angry or upset when I found out you were our sister. Maybe not even surprised. Axel hurt Mom a lot when he had an affair with your mother. But in a way, he was already separated from her. At least, that's how it felt for me. I learned to get along without him. As for Carin, she's not grandma material. If she even caught us calling her grandmother, she'd get angry and walk away."

"Sounds like her Chanel panties were too much in a wad," Sara said dryly.

Lila laughed. "Yes, that is a good description of Carin. Don't ever feel bad about being on the wrong side of the sheets, Sara. Because of Carin having an affair with our grandfather, Dean, everyone Axel and Erik Colton fathered has that dubious background."

"Thanks," she said, feeling as if a burden had lifted. "Thanks for not hating me for my connection to Axel."

"Hate you? You're kind and smart and you've helped Mom and Rick with new business. I'm glad you came into our lives."

For the first time since last night's fiasco with Harry, Sara felt a genuine smile touch her lips. "I'm glad, too."

"Families are so complicated at times." Lila sighed. "Especially with the Coltons. I hope your mother's side of the family is normal."

A short laugh. Normal? What defined normal anymore? Since Lila opened up to her, she told her the truth.

"Not exactly. My mom was an only child. Her parents died when she was in college. The few aunts and uncles on her side are either long gone or never acknowledged my mother after she had an affair with Axel and I was born."

She thought about the cold attitude of her mother's relatives and how they judged Regina instead of reacting with kindness when Regina asked them to visit for the holidays.

Regina never did reveal how her relatives had reacted, but Sara could see the hurt in her mother's eyes. It made her determined to never make contact with that side of the family. *I guess I'm as protective of my mom as she is of me.*

"They considered me to be a stain in their eyes because I was illegitimate. I never discovered this until much later, when Mom told me the truth about my origins. They never were close to us growing up, would only send a Christmas card, when they remembered."

"It's just you and Regina?" Lila's eyes widened. "I wouldn't know how that feels. But I bet it was nice at times, having your mom's undivided attention."

Now that she thought about it, Lila was right. Sara smiled. "My mother had a way of making every holiday special. I think she did it because I always wanted brothers and sisters, and a father. So she lavished lots on me each holiday."

Lila grinned. "Well, now you have a lot of Colton cousins and relatives. Maybe too many. I have to get back to work. Maybe we can do lunch tomorrow?"

If Carin had been icy, Lila was positively warm, shattering the cold Sara felt. "That would be lovely. I'll text you."

After Lila left, Sara looked at her cell phone, considered calling Harry Cartwright. Her mother had been gone for a long time. If she had left town, she'd have informed Sara.

It simply wasn't like her mother to leave and not call, or at least text. Sara thought of the letter and shivered.

If Regina had murdered Axel, even in a fit of rage, would she take the coward's way out and flee town?

Or face up to what she had done and turn herself over to the police?

Sara honestly didn't know. She had no real inkling of the kind of relationship Regina had shared with Axel until this year. But losing a child… She could understand the grief and rage her mother felt when Wyatt died due to Axel's carelessness.

She needed to find Regina. Now. Only one person she knew had the ability to track her like a bloodhound.

With great reluctance, Sara picked up her phone and called Harry Cartwright, hoping he could help.

He answered on the first ring. "Hey."

His deep, rugged voice soothed her the way no warm drink could on a cold night. "Hi. You left in a hurry last night."

"Sorry. My arm was hurting." He snorted. "And me being a manly man, I couldn't let you know it."

Sara smiled. "Consider this your daily nag call. Did you see the doctor?"

"Yes, I saw the doctor."

His impatient tone sounded like all the men she'd ever encountered who loathed visiting the doctor. So much that she could almost consider him as just another guy.

But he wasn't. He was extraordinary, funny, compassionate, courageous, dedicated…and quite possibly the man who'd break her heart.

"And?"

"And it's a flesh wound." He sighed. "I was ordered to rest for a couple of days."

Sara suspected he was not the type to follow orders that restricted him. "So you're working."

"Yeah, you got me. From home. This is the age of high-speed internet and computers. Not that I'd know. I'm still on dial-up," he joked.

"Lucky you. At least you have a phone. I'm calling you from a tin can and a string."

He chuckled and warmth spread through her. Harry was the kind of guy she'd want with her in a crisis, who could navigate through floodwaters and ease panic with a joke about getting his shoes wet.

If this didn't qualify as a crisis, nothing would.

"After I left your place last night, I talked with your neighbor, that nosy Mrs. Pendleton. She wasn't helpful, but admitted she goes to bed early and you come home late at times, so the night Axel was killed, you could have come home and she wouldn't have known it."

Sara searched her memory. That night she'd left work on time at Yates' Yards and picked up takeout from a local restaurant. So much for having a neighbor who could provide an alibi. Then she brightened. "Wait! I still have the receipt. I got Chinese takeout that night. What time was Axel killed?"

"You save your receipts from Chinese takeout?" Harry sounded amused.

"Habit from when I took clients out for dinner. Let me call you back."

She hung up, scrolled through her phone to find the photo of the receipt, then called Harry. He answered immediately.

"The coroner puts the time of death between 7:00 and 9:00 p.m. What does your receipt say?"

Gazing at the receipt, she sighed. "I guess having a receipt that proves I was in a Chinese restaurant at 6:00 p.m. doesn't clear me."

"Not exactly. Unless you can claim a bad case of heartburn that took you to the ER."

He sounded too lighthearted and upbeat for such a serious conversation. Sara frowned. "Well, am I still high on the suspect list?"

Instead of answering, Harry changed the subject. "Since I'm housebound, I did a little checking on your former employer, that POS Ernie."

This sounded interesting. "You think he had something to do with Axel's death?"

"Hardly. I was more interested in his involvement with getting you to work for him again, and how desperate he is." Harry made a growly sound. "He's slime, Sara. The guy is up to his eyes in debt. He actually took a loan from his 401K and now has to pay it back. The company president has been breathing down his neck for new business. Business, it seems from talking to others in the firm, that you were responsible for obtaining."

"Why did you go to all that trouble to look into Ernie if he's not a suspect in Axel's death? Is he a threat?"

"His behavior makes him a threat to you."

Touched he would be so protective, she smiled. "Thanks. I can handle Ernie. He's a bully and like all bullies, they usually back away from direct confrontation."

"Usually. Be careful. I don't like this guy."

I don't, either. But more and more against my better judgment, I'm beginning to like you.

She cleared her throat. "What did you find out about my mother's letter? Did she write it?"

Somehow she knew what the answer was, though it made her heart sink.

"It was definitely her DNA on the envelope. Your mother wrote that letter and mailed it to you."

Gripping the phone so tight in her hand her knuckles whitened, she licked her lips. "How could you know? How could it be a match? Her DNA shouldn't be in the system."

"It wasn't." Harry sounded calm, and she wanted to scream. "I did a little digging and your father's attorney helped. Your mother willingly submitted a sample years ago to Axel Colton's lawyer when your father underwent a paternity test that proved he fathered your brother."

If he had reached through the phone and struck her, she couldn't feel more shocked. "My father didn't believe the baby was his?" she whispered. "You had no right to invade my mother's privacy."

Harry went silent for a minute. "I have the right, Sara. I have a killer to find and I'll go to any lengths to find him."

"I assume that since you have the proof my mom mailed

that letter, which is pretty incriminating, that eases your suspicion of me?" She couldn't help her bitter tone. "Or do you think we're the murdering dynamic duo?"

"Less likely you did it." He drew in a breath, as if wincing. "Sara, Eddie and Dennis Angelo both have connections to your mother."

Oh no. Sara shook her head. "Impossible."

"Dennis worked for the same office as your mother, and as the office manager, she would have paid him, or even hired him. Eddie did odd jobs for Regina."

Sara blinked. "No, he couldn't have… When?"

"Five years ago. We checked his bank and found checks from your mother written to him. She hired him to clear the snow from her driveway. He was running a small snow-plow business. Then she hired him again to haul away a dead tree stump in the spring."

"Mom told me she hired a guy to help her with a couple of projects, but she never mentioned names. I don't remember her saying anything about him."

The sound of shuffling papers. "Both times you were away at college. I can't find a connection to you."

"So that's why you've cleared me, more or less, as a suspect," she said slowly.

"Right. Except for the mug. That may have been placed in Axel's kitchen." Harry's voice deepened. "By whoever wanted to frame you for his murder. Or at least divert suspicion to you. Or it could have been a simple case of someone taking the mug and visiting Axel."

"You said my fingerprints and Axel's were the only ones on it."

"Yours were the only prints we found that we could lift. The others were smeared. So it might have been an innocent case of whoever took the mug put it there and forgot about it. Maybe even Axel himself. He visited the nursery a couple of times before his death."

Relief and fear mingled in her stomach. Relief she'd been cleared. Fear Regina might have killed Axel.

The little cursor on her computer screen seemed to taunt her. *Gone. Guilty. Your mother is guilty.*

Your mother killed Axel Colton, your father.

"I can't believe this," she whispered.

"She may have run away," Harry said gently. "Sara, you have to be prepared for the eventuality your mother killed your father."

The words came out in a rush. "I still can't reach my mother. Not through her cell phone, or emails. Her office has been closed the past two weeks for renovations and they're moving. Mom thought this was a good time for well-deserved vacation. She promised to call me with the new office number."

"The fact that no one can reach your mother is not good for her, Sara."

"Then go find her." She stared at her computer screen. Footsteps sounded outside her door. She was supposed to be working, and she didn't want Vita to find out Regina had been moved to the top of the suspect list.

Sara bit her lip against the grief welling inside her. "I'll have to find her a good lawyer."

"Can you think of any places, favorite vacation spots, a cabin loaned to you by a friend, where Regina would go?"

"No." She started to protest that her mother wasn't the type to run from trouble and then remembered how Regina told her how she'd fled Axel while pregnant with Sara, and changed her last name.

Fleeing definitely fit Regina's personality. Especially if it meant keeping her only living child safe.

"I can't think of anywhere she'd go. Most of all, I know if

she did go someplace, Harry, she would call me. If her cell phone was broken, she'd buy another. This isn't like her."

"People do unusual things under stress."

"Not my mother," she snapped. "She would never cut off contact with me."

"Even to protect you?"

The question made her pause. *Oh, Mom, what did you do?*

"I don't know. It doesn't matter. I want her found safe, and alive. That's what matters most."

"I will. Sara, be careful. Eddie Angelo broke into your apartment building, but he may have been targeting you if your mother used him as an accessory and failed to pay him off. Criminals know the easiest way to blackmail victims is through a family member."

"I'll take extra precautions. Go find my mom."

"I will find her. Take extra precautions, but remember, don't leave town. It won't look good for you with the district attorney if your mother is guilty and you aided and abetted her." He paused. "I'd be forced to arrest you, Sara, and I really, really do not want to be put in that position."

A lump clogged her throat.

He hung up.

Sara felt as if she rode a high-speed roller coaster. She should be happy about being cleared as a suspect, but more and more, it looked bad for Regina.

Where could her mother have gone?

Chapter 10

Harry hated light duty. He itched to be on the street again, but the doctor ordered him to rest for two days after he was wounded.

The following day, his phone buzzed. Harry rolled over, groaned as he rolled onto his sore arm and grabbed his phone. He groaned again.

Sean. Texting at 4:30 a.m.

You okay? How are you feeling?

Harry texted back. I was feeling great until you woke me up. Go get some sleep.

Can't. Twins are up. Did you tell Sara about her mother's letter?

Might as well make coffee and get up. He was too awake now to fall back asleep. Harry padded into the kitchen, put on coffee and sat at his kitchen table, texting Sean about the letter and Sara's reaction and how Sara was no longer a suspect.

He also told Sean he'd started to worry about Sara's safety.

Sean texted back. The Angelo brothers are bad news but now out of picture. Sara should be fine if Regina hired Eddie. She wouldn't hurt her own daughter.

Bristling, Harry texted back. Not taking chances. The Angelo brothers may have accomplices. Sara could still be in danger.

The coffee machine dinged and he poured a mug, added several sugars. When he returned to the kitchen table, his phone blared out two words.

Huh. Interesting.

What? Harry texted back.

You and Sara.

Drawing in a breath, he texted back, Go help your wife and babies then grab some sleep. TTYL.

The last thing he needed was his former partner speculating about a possible romance between him and Sara. That was on the back burner, and that burner wasn't even lit.

I'm only trying to protect her as I would any citizen.

But his conscience warned otherwise.

He drank the coffee, made breakfast and did some work on his laptop. By ten o'clock he shut the laptop and contemplated his day. He felt fine, if not a little sore.

Until Sean called him with bad news. Someone had stabbed Eddie Angelo in what looked like a jailhouse fight.

The DA had been ready to cut a deal with Angelo in exchange for what he knew.

Now their prime source of information was lying on a morgue slab. Harry thumbed off his phone, itching to do something.

Instead of following orders, he decided to circumvent them. It wasn't technically going into work if he met someone for a meal.

After showering and dressing, Harry drove to Naperville to meet with Jimmy Curry, his friend and the lead investigator on the Santa Claus homicide. Brass warned him not to come into the station, fine, he was just having breakfast with an old friend.

An old friend who could fill him in on details about any progress Naperville made on the Colton case.

The breakfast crowd had dissipated by the time he pulled into the parking lot of Belle's Eatery. Too early for the lunch crowd. Harry jingled his car keys in hand as he walked into the restaurant and slid into a green booth by the window. He ordered coffee with two sugars, and pocketed his car keys. If Jimmy, who prided himself on arriving on time, was late, it meant he nailed something.

Harry scrolled through his cell phone while he waited. He glanced at emails and then through his photos, stopping at a photo of Marie and John.

Breath caught in his throat. Damn. He'd forgotten he had this. Left it on his phone when he transferred all his data to the one phone he'd bought a year ago.

A colorful Christmas tree behind them, Marie's wide smile and sparkling eyes met the camera as she held a squirmy, giggling John. He remembered that day…hell, how could he forget? The first Christmas where John really got into opening gifts, tearing at the boxes, playing with the bright, shiny paper. His laughter and Marie's as they tried to keep their baby from eating that same shiny paper. The three of them alone. Her parents had taken a cruise to Europe and he'd felt such relief they had privacy, instead of his father-in-law descending into the usual lecturing about how Harry's salary couldn't provide Marie with everything she needed, how Harry should take the offer to be head of security at her old man's firm…

They'd had a wonderful day. Took John to try skating in downtown, and Harry and Marie had gripped his hands, delighting in his squeals as they lifted him up while they skated. Later as John finally slept, he and Marie had made love downstairs before the fireplace as snow softly fell outside and Christmas carols played over their sound system…

He touched the phone's screen, his throat tight, his appetite vanishing. How quickly life could change in an eye blink. One minute you're worried about the kid's college fund and how you can afford that dream vacation to Disney in the summer. The next, you're spending your vacation money on two coffins and a burial plot…

"Hey, Harry! Good to see you!"

Blinking, he shoved his phone back into his pocket. Jimmy slid into the booth opposite him. Harry pretended absorption in his coffee to hide his face. While Jimmy shrugged out of his coat, Harry grabbed a paper napkin and wiped his wet eyes.

When he looked up, he deliberately winced and crumpled the napkin, stuffing it into his jeans pocket.

"Hurts still, huh?" Jimmy sounded sympathetic.

"Like a bitch. But I hate taking any pain pills." Blame his loss of composure on the gunshot wound. Not on his past.

While they placed their orders, Harry's thoughts drifted to Sara. He felt a tug of deep connection with her, something he hadn't experienced since the day he lost Marie. That spark, that chemistry, was undeniable.

But impractical.

Who was he kidding? Even if she was cleared as a suspect, Harry couldn't begin a relationship with her. The wounds in his heart were too raw, taking too long to heal. He'd dated plenty of women over the past two years to try to forget about Marie. Each relationship ended with him gently breaking it off.

Some had tried to get him to talk about his family. Those women were the ones who lasted longer because they genuinely cared, but in the end, it didn't matter. Who wanted to date a guy who was deeply in love with a memory?

"Got some news for you. Not what you want to hear, but good news all the same." Jimmy stirred sugar into the steaming coffee the waitress poured. "Remember the Santa thief?"

"Yeah." Seemed like a lifetime ago.

"We made an arrest."

Harry's head jerked up. "Yeah?"

"Like you said. Not a simple burglary." Jimmy showed him a cell phone photo. "Maureen Markam, aka Maureen Duell. Vic was her ex-husband. He dressed as Santa, burglarizing homes, but that night he'd planned to visit her and surprise the kid with toys after he did a few homes. She admitted everything. Went to see him before he was released, begged him to stay away from the kid. Turns out Mr. Duell used to beat the crap out of her. He got released, targeted the homes she patrolled. She saw him at the Ladd house while on duty, he threatened to tell the cops she was in on the burglaries and their kid would be sent to social services. He hit her and she shot him, point-blank."

Harry's disgust rose. Men who assaulted women were pond scum.

"Looks like the DA will cut her a sweet deal. She did get the guy responsible for the break-ins."

Harry nodded his thanks as the waitress brought their meals. He toyed with his oatmeal, not hungry anymore. "Glad that's closed. Any news on Colton? Anything?"

"Nothing." Jimmy frowned. "Colton was a lazy bum who lived off his trust fund, made a few enemies but this doesn't make sense. Whoever did it was mighty pissed off, but who hits a guy over the head with an antique marble candlestick? That seems so…"

"Angry?"

Jimmy sat back. "Yeah. It was convenient. So we know it was a crime of passion, no prints or DNA on the weapon, except for the vic's. But it wasn't even in easy reach."

Harry's mind sorted through the details of the crime scene and suddenly it dawned. After taking out his phone, he scrolled through the photos of the crime scene he'd stored for referral.

The candlestick. The markings on the bottom.

"Damn. Why didn't I see this before?" he muttered.

"What?"

"This candlestick…" He showed his phone to Jimmy. "Antique, marble, with real gold. Expensive. What did the other one appraise at?"

"Around $6,000 each. But a lot of stuff in Colton's home is expensive. He was rich."

"Yeah, but most of the things in his home, they were not antiques. His decor was modern." Harry snorted. "I know about this stuff from my ex-mother-in-law. She prides herself on her traditional French Provincial home. I couldn't tell Asian from mid-century modern, but heaven forbid you dare gift Arlene with an Art Deco photo frame for her antique desk. She actually lectured me for half an hour after I gave her that frame before Marie and I got married. I liked it, thought it would look great on her writing desk."

Jimmy shook his head. "Beats me. I don't know how you put up with your in-laws, Harry."

I did it for Marie. Because I loved her and when you love a woman that much, you'd do almost anything for her.

"Those candlesticks at Axel Colton's…they're ornate, almost as if they don't belong. Colton's living room was all high-end contemporary. Lots of glass, look at this living room."

He showed Jimmy the photo he'd taken of the pristine cream sofa and the mirrored coffee table with matching end tables. "The candlesticks don't fit in. They don't match."

Jimmy shrugged. "Maybe Colton liked them and was trying to figure out a place for them. We never could trace their origin. Family said they always saw them around."

"His immediate family. Colton was from the wrong side of the sheets, remember? Maybe one of the Coltons on the right side of the sheets wanted them back, family heirloom and all that, and thought it a fitting demise for Colton… beaming him with a candlestick he refused to hand over." He stared at the candlestick photo and it jogged a memory.

"I keep all the photos from past crime scenes, and the vic's houses, on my phone," he muttered. "There. Look at this house. Italian decor. Fits right in with the candlesticks."

"What house is that?"

"Alfred Colton's. One of the twins murdered by the serial killer earlier this year."

Jimmy's eyes widened. "Damn. So what's the connection?"

"None right now. But what if Axel, being an illegitimate brother, stole something of his father's that was an antique that had been in the Colton family for years?"

"And this would make the murder not about Axel, but about the candlesticks. Personal property. But why not simply take the candlesticks after killing Colton?"

"Because if this is the motive and the suspect used the candlestick to kill Colton, whoever did this knew they could be traced back to them." Harry tapped his phone. "I remember the Alfred and Ernest Colton case. Sean's wife, January, would know. She's Alfred's daughter."

He texted Sean, knowing his ex-partner would probably yell at him for being out instead of home resting. So what? He told Sean he needed to talk to January at their home. Set up the time.

Harry set his phone down and dug into his now-cold oatmeal. "Jimmy, I need you and your guys to go over every inch of Axel Colton's home one more time. See if anything else looks like it doesn't belong. If Colton took the candlesticks, chances are he might have taken other things."

"It's still the same with you, huh, Harry? All work and no play. Always the job."

Jimmy's voice was quiet, but Harry sensed a deeper meaning. "So? I'm working a hot case. Same with you, buddy."

"Not anymore. Pauline and I are getting married."

Harry set down his spoon carefully, his stomach tight. "Whoa, that was quick."

"Eight months? Naw, I'm getting older. I'm thirty-four, same as you. I want to settle down, have a family. Have someone to grow old with."

"I used to have that." He shrugged. "Not anymore."

"You can have it again. You're not dead, Harry."

Part of me feels that way at times.

"Congratulations. She's a nice girl."

"I wasn't gonna tell you, didn't want you to feel like I was rubbing it in your face."

"I'm happy for you, I really am." He was happy for Jimmy, who'd been a bachelor his entire life. Jimmy had sworn he'd never get married because he never wanted to make someone a widow, and uncertainty always filled a cop's life.

"Then stop feeling sorry for yourself and stop living in the past."

His guts churned. Harry felt his temper start to rise. "Who says I am? And who are you to tell me how to live my life?"

"A friend. A friend who knew Marie long before you did, buddy. She wouldn't want this for you. Harry, you have to let it go and start living again." Jimmy's voice caught. "She was a sweetheart and there'll never be anyone like her again. But Marie wouldn't want you to live like this."

"Don't go there, Jimmy. Not into my personal life. Not if you want to stay friends."

"Someone has to go there. Harry, it wasn't your fault. It wasn't anyone's fault except the con who killed her and he's never seeing freedom again."

Harry leaned back against the booth and snorted. "You mean, live the high life like this? I've moved on, Jimmy. Back in Homicide where I belong. Sean and I are friends again and work together again. I'm focused on the job. To protect and serve."

"The job. Always the job." Jimmy sighed and dug into his eggs.

He ate a few forkfuls quickly, the way cops always did when they needed to eat fast because you never knew when a call would blare over the radio. Never knew when you'd have to rush off to investigate a fresh lead or provide backup during a gun battle.

Never knew when you'd get a dreaded call to come to the hospital to say goodbye to a fellow officer or in Harry's case, say goodbye to your wife and little boy...

Suddenly no longer hungry, Harry pushed his bowl aside. He drained his coffee and threw some bills on the table. "I have to run. Keep in touch, let me know what you find in Colton's house. Text me a photo of any suspicious items so I can show January."

Jimmy nodded. "Take care of yourself, Harry."

The words seemed to have a double meaning, which Harry ignored. But as he slid behind the wheel of his sedan, he hesitated in turning on the engine. Thoughts of Sara kept entering his mind.

Maybe Jimmy was right. He focused too much on the job, never made time for a personal life. Sean had moved on, married and now had a family. Jimmy was moving on as well.

I'm stuck in the past.

It was time to push forward.

Then he remembered the internal screaming in his mind when the doctors grimly informed him Marie and John were dead. The pain so deep and sharp he couldn't breathe, couldn't even cry. When he did cry, he clung to the grief as if it were a living thing because they were connected to the grief. He feared the moment he stopped grieving, his memories of his wife and child would fade into twilight. Only work had saved him from dissolving into a puddle of depression. Work had nudged him each day to get the hell out of bed, shower, keep putting one foot in front of the other. The world hadn't stopped spinning and criminals still broke the law. He found a solitary comfort in that routine, even if it proved cheerless at times.

When all else failed, he had the job.

Gritting his teeth, Harry switched on the ignition. Time to move on? Not today.

He had a murder to solve.

Chapter 11

Sara wasn't certain meeting another Colton cousin was a terrific idea, but she couldn't resist the temptation. Especially when the invitation came from January Stafford, the daughter of Alfred Colton, who'd been murdered by a serial killer.

January had been so sweet when she'd phoned Sara and expressed interest in meeting her. Sadly, they had something in common more than being Coltons—both their fathers had died at the hands of killers. At least January had closure, unlike Sara.

Her new husband, the father of their twins, was Detective Sean Stafford, who happened to be Harry's ex-partner.

Sara smelled something fishy when January mentioned something about Colton heirlooms and how perhaps Sara could be a help in recalling anything her mother said about Axel's lifestyle.

She drove straight from work to the Stafford home, releasing a sigh of relief. Harry's car wasn't here. Dusk had started to drape the sky with vivid colors of lavender and rose, streaking the clouds that scuttled past. A hint of snow lingered in the air.

The house had a wide front porch with twin Christmas trees flanking the double doors. Gold light from a brass overhead fixture highlighted the homey touches on the porch—a basket of pine cones, white rocking chairs and a table sporting a Santa Claus on skis. Garland adorned the porch railing, along with strings of Christmas lights.

Impressed they had time to decorate with the whirlwind of having twins, Sara rang the doorbell, knowing it was one of the high-tech security ones and they could answer from their smartphones. But instead of a voice speaking from the doorbell's microphone, a good-looking man with a rag over one shoulder opened the door.

Sara stuck out her hand. "You must be Sean. I recognize you from the other night in the alley when Harry was shot."

He shook her palm. "Come on in. January just finished feeding the twins."

"And you got burping duty."

Sean frowned, looked down at the towel where Sara pointed. He beamed. "Yeah, Leo's a little piggy."

He led her into a spacious formal living room with elegant furniture, a brick fireplace and a large portrait of Sean and a pretty blonde woman hanging over the mantel. Garland threaded with lights adorned the mantel. A fir tree sat in one corner, fully decorated with lights, red and green ornaments and tinsel. Several colorful packages with Christmas wrapping sat beneath the tree. The tree and decorations softened the formal look of the room.

"Have a seat. I'll be right back."

"Nice house."

"Thanks. It's all so…shiny still." He glanced around the

to do something other than breastfeed or change diapers or grab quick meals."

She listened to January chatter about her twins as Sara helped set out the teacups, sugar and cream on a serving platter. January frowned and began measuring out coffee for the coffeemaker on the counter.

"Oh darn. I forgot. Sean's cutting back on caffeine, he gets so little sleep these days, and Harry drinks only coffee, not tea."

"Harry's on his way here?" She felt that little flutter in her chest that had nothing to do with apprehension, only excitement. Then she remembered that last text she'd sent and stifled a groan.

Bad timing. Terrible.

When the drinks were ready, Sara brought the service out to the living room and set it on the coffee table as Sean padded down the stairs carrying a baby monitor. January followed with a platter of chocolate chip cookies.

"I didn't know Harry was coming here. Maybe I should leave…" Sara sat on one of the chairs and wondered if it wasn't too late to make her escape.

Setting the monitor down on a nearby table, Sean peered out the window. "He's parking his car right now."

She pasted on a polite smile as her heart did little skip-hops. Harry didn't bother with the doorbell. He came right inside, pounded Sean on the back with a guy slap and then walked into the living room as if he belonged there. He wore jeans and a navy sweater and carried a small satchel.

He kissed January on the forehead, took a seat and only then did he realize Sara's presence.

Harry stared.

"What are you doing here?" His voice came out as a deep growl. "Or are you determined to annoy me in person and not just through texting."

Sara stirred sugar into her tea. "I was invited, same as you were."

"I thought Sara would like to meet a Colton cousin." Sean handed Harry a mug of steaming coffee and sat on the sofa next to his wife. "Besides, you crossed Sara off your suspect list. I thought the four of us could brainstorm. Sara might have valuable information her mother passed on about Axel's habits and if he were brazen enough to steal family heirlooms from Alfred or Ernest. Maybe Axel said something in passing to Sara's mom that Sara can remember."

Dead silence.

"And since you and Sara seem to be so…involved in the case, we thought it would be good to have both of you over at the same time," Sean added, sounding less convinced.

Right. You couldn't come up with a better explanation? She began to realize just why January and Sean had invited her over.

She looked questioningly at Harry, who kept his expression placid, but his eyes spelled fury as his jaw tensed beneath his well-trimmed beard. Oh yes, this was a setup if there ever was one. Harry didn't want her here and could have kicked his friend for inviting her.

Softly, Sara began humming, "Matchmaker, matchmaker, make me a match…"

Sean and January looked at each other. "Oh dear," January murmured. "Are we that obvious?"

For a moment, no one said a word. Then to her surprise Harry threw back his head and laughed.

"As obvious as coal on snow, January honey, but you're forgiven." He glared at Sean. "Your husband, on the other hand…"

Sean threw up his hands. "I thought it was a good idea.

Besides, you needed to meet January, Sara. And you do have a unique connection to Axel and why Harry's here."

"Right. Sara has many unique things about her." Harry sipped his coffee. "In case you're wondering, Sara, my arm is much better thanks to a delightful painkiller I took earlier. Sorry to disappoint you."

Sean and January threw her questioning looks. She felt a flush of guilt. "That was rude of me. I lost my temper, Harry, and I apologize."

He raised a dark brow. "Apology accepted if you'll accept mine for being a jerk. Pain puts me into a bad mood."

January brightened. "Now that we're all friends, Harry, what did you need to discuss? You sounded so mysterious over the phone."

"Business in a few. First, tell me how you're doing. You look radiant. Twins good?" Harry asked.

For a few minutes January talked about the babies while they listened. Harry leaned forward, expressing real interest, not mere politeness. His attentive attitude was refreshing. Sara had not met many men genuinely interested in a new mother talking about her babies.

When January finished, Sean chimed in. "She's a real pro at this. Her mom has been fantastic in helping out, but we're thinking, hoping, she'll go home soon. We appreciate her help, but we would like to be alone with the twins to get ourselves into a routine."

"I can appreciate that." Harry rubbed his chin. "I remember after John was born and Marie's mother seemed like she wanted to move in with us permanently. I thought she would never leave us alone to be a real family. Not that we had a lot of time to enjoy being one before…before I lost them both."

Silence descended in the air. Sean and January both looked uncomfortable. They said nothing, and Sara's stomach tightened. She smiled to cover the sudden tension in the air.

"Babies are quite demanding, from what I know. They set their own schedule. My best friend from high school had a baby two years ago and it was amusing how she and her husband were insistent their lives would not change. That didn't last long."

Sean and January seemed to breathe a sigh of relief. Harry reached into his pocket as if fingering the medal he kept there, then he dug into his satchel and brought out some photos.

"Okay, let's get down to business and the real reason I'm here, January. I need your help to identify some items found in Axel Colton's home," Harry told her.

January looked over the photos and frowned. "Yes, I know these. The candlesticks were my grandfather's. Dean bought them in Italy on a business trip and later, he gave them to Mom and Dad. They weren't special, just he thought they would like them since Mom was into Italian decor."

January stared at the photo. "I can't believe Axel had them. How would he get them?"

"Sara, did your mother ever say anything about Axel giving her anything that had been in his family?"

She shook her head, guilt stabbing her at January's woebegone look. Even though she had no connection to Axel other than by blood, it was a horrible thing to learn the father you'd dreamed about idolizing was a thief.

"My mom never wanted anything of Axel's. She only wanted to be as far away from him as possible after my brother, Wyatt, drowned. She even changed her name to protect herself, and me. I didn't know until earlier this year that Axel was my father," Sara told them.

"Maybe Dean asked Alfred for these items back and

gave them to Axel because he felt guilty for neglecting him?" Sean asked.

"As far as I know, my grandfather never did that." January examined the photos of the items as Harry explained what they were.

The two candlesticks. A silver serving platter that had also been in the family for more than two generations.

"Then there's this...something not as expensive."

From a plastic bag marked Evidence, Harry withdrew a wooden box. He opened it to display a pretty Christmas scene of a white-topped house, a gazebo, snow-topped trees and tiny people dressed in winter clothing.

"Jimmy found this music box tucked away in a dresser drawer. It doesn't seem as valuable as the silver platter or the candlesticks, but seemed out of place, so he put it in as evidence."

Sara craned her neck and gasped. "I have one just like that. It's a Thomas Kinkade music box."

All three turned to look at her. Sara felt heat creep up her neck to her cheeks. "I like to collect music boxes. I have since I was a child."

Harry turned it over in his hand. "A trait you may have inherited from Axel. January, do you recall seeing this in your father's house?"

January reached for the box. She examined the interior. "Not really, but Dad liked to surprise Mom with things like this...he enjoyed engraving special messages to her. Honey, can get you get the magnifying glass from the junk drawer?"

When Sean returned with it, January studied the box with the glass. "Yes, here it is. It's so small you can barely read it. There, on the inside of the box. To my darling Farrah, love eternally Alfred."

Sara fisted her hands in her lap. This definitely proved

her father was a thief. Why would anyone give away such a personal, precious memento?

"So this means Axel broke into my parent's house and stole these things?" January looked confused. "I don't understand. Wouldn't Dad have reported them missing?"

"Was Axel ever inside your house? Did Alfred ever have him over on a social occasion?"

January tapped her head. "Sorry, let me think… I have baby brain."

Sean encased her hands in his. "Take your time, honey."

"Let me call Mom. She's out shopping."

A few minutes later, January hung up. "Mystery solved. Dean came by shortly before he died and asked Dad if he could have the candlesticks back, and the silver platter. He said he needed them, but didn't say why. Mom and Dad told him they didn't mind, they were his to begin with. I guess Dean gave them to Axel, maybe he felt bad Axel had no family heirlooms?"

For a moment, silence descended into the room, broken only by the soft crackling over the baby monitor.

"It makes sense," Sean murmured. "So there goes your theory, Harry."

"Well, that clears up the mystery about how Axel got them. But not about the music box." Harry put the box back into the evidence bag.

"Mom did say she had no idea the box was missing. She thought maybe the domestic worker had broken it and thrown it out and was afraid to tell her. That particular domestic worker had done something like that before and Mom caught her."

Harry leaned forward, and judging from the glint in his eye, his mind was clicking over a possibility. "Who was the domestic worker? Does she still work for your mother?"

"Mary Martin. She wasn't very good. Mom had to reprimand her a couple of times and finally let her go after she caught her stealing from the liquor cabinet."

"I'll check her out." Harry glanced at Sara. "I don't want to take up any more of your time…"

A soft wail sounded over the baby monitor. January brightened.

"But you're here so you need to meet the twins. Wait and we'll bring them down," she told them.

Sara's heart sank at the tight expression on Harry's face. *Don't, January. Please don't. He's not ready for this…it's too soon. Give him time…*

He glanced out the window as if desperate to escape, and then shrugged. "Ah hell," he muttered.

Sean and January came downstairs, each carrying a sleepy twin, one wrapped in a blue blanket, the other in a pink blanket. The pride and joy on their faces as they gazed at their children touched Sara's heart.

January beamed at her. "Would you like to hold Laura?"

Although she had little experience with babies, she held out her arms. January instructed her to keep Laura's head upright. The baby slept peacefully, her little fingers close to one cheek. She smelled heavenly and for a wild moment Sara felt a tug of wistfulness.

Growing up as an only child, without any family, she'd missed out on moments like this with family members. Only when her friends started marrying and having babies did she experience them. Even then, relatives took precedence over friends.

Maybe someday she'd have children of her own. It would be lovely to have a family.

Sean handed Harry the twin in the blue blanket. "Here. Alfred Leo Stafford, meet the best cop in Chicago, your uncle Harry."

Harry held baby Leo, staring at the newborn as if he

were the most unique and precious thing in the world. Tension knotted his entire body. Sara realized it wasn't a person's natural tension at fearing to hurt the little one, but something else.

Something much more personal.

"I forgot how tiny they are," he mused. "So small... John was this small... I counted all his fingers and toes. I was afraid to hold him when he was first born."

He shrugged and kissed Leo's forehead. "Welcome to the crazy world, Leo. You picked good parents."

Beaming, Sean took baby Leo from Harry's arms. "You're great with babies, Harry."

"I was," he murmured so softly Sara knew they didn't hear him.

But she did and her heart ached for him. How did you ever recover from losing your child?

When Sean returned downstairs, she was more than ready to leave. She liked the Staffords, but they had moved into a different stage of life, while she was still single and Harry...

Harry had experienced a dual loss no husband, or father, ever should suffer. Her heart went out to him. Beneath his beard, his jaw tightened, but he offered a smile as he clapped Sean on the back.

"Congratulations again, man. Best of luck to you."

"Sorry the visit wasn't a success," Sean told him, and then he shook Sara's hand.

They said their goodbyes and headed outside. A scent of pine and crispness layered the cool breeze ruffling the fringes of her scarf. Inhaling the fresh air, she felt glad to be free from the tension inside. Sean and January were proud new parents, joyous because of their babies, and oblivious to Harry's quiet pain.

She was not unaware.

Instead of heading directly for his car, Harry lingered by her vehicle. Sara didn't open the door, but turned to face him. Someone had to acknowledge what he endured. Even if he didn't want to admit how much it hurt.

"That was tough for you," she murmured.

Harry jammed his hands into the pockets of his jeans and leaned against his car. "I guess."

Shutting down. Any light had vanished from his blue-green gaze. He looked cold and distant.

The hard-nosed attitude might work for interrogations, but she sensed something deep struck a nerve with him.

"He's your good friend, but it's got to be hell seeing him so happy with new babies."

Harry blinked. "Ah, hmmm."

"Especially when you hold one of them, and you remember holding your own child."

His brow furrowed. "Don't go there, Sara."

"I don't want to cause you more pain, Harry. I only want you to know I see you…" She pointed to her eyes. "Here."

Taking a gamble, she stepped forward and touched his chest. "And here."

Harry looked away. "I'm fine. I'm a cop, Sara. We learn to deal with death."

"Death of strangers, yes. Death even of your friends at times. But a wife and child…that's something you never get over. You only get through it."

At first she feared she'd overstepped her bounds, for he scowled and started to pull away. Harry took two paces, stopped. He brought out the St. Jude medal and looked at it, returned it to his pocket as if putting away fragile glass. He rubbed the back of his neck and suddenly he seemed to emotionally crumble.

"I miss them," he whispered. "Damn, I really miss them, and seeing the babies, holding Leo…it brought it all rushing back. It was always supposed to be me who never walked through our front door again. Me. Not them. I even bought a funeral plot because I'm a cop in Chicago and I warned Marie there might come a time when she'd lose me. I wanted her to be taken care of and get through something like that without having to worry about arrangements or expenses. I never imagined…using it for my wife and kid."

She could never understand what he felt or the depth of his grief. Sara approached him, took his icy hands into hers. "She must have been a wonderful woman. Tell me about her and your child."

Harry stared at their linked hands. "Marie was quiet and shy, but had a fierce streak when it came to protecting those she loved. The proudest I ever was of her was the day she told her parents we were getting married. Her old man blew a gasket, said I wasn't good enough and I was marrying Marie for the family money. Marie told him she'd live with me in a run-down trailer because she loved me and no one would stand in her way."

Moisture glistened in his eyes, making them brilliant. "John, he ran us ragged at times. So curious and alive… everything fascinated him. His personality started to shine through. He was only two, but you could see he was smart and loved puzzling things out and putting them back together. Marie was a terrific mom, loved John with all her heart and when they pulled her out of the car wreck, she'd been twisted around, as if trying to shield him in the back seat from the impact."

Now her own eyes dampened. Sara didn't dare let go of him. If she did, she had the funny feeling he'd vanish back into himself, sinking as if immersed by a body of water so deep he couldn't find his way to the surface.

"I'm so sorry," she whispered.

Harry's jaw tightened. "I wish it had been me instead of

them, oh God, why wasn't it me who died that day? Maybe I shouldn't have gone on living."

She shook her head. "No, don't you go there. I don't know why ugly things happen, or why our loved ones die and there's nothing we can do to save them, but, Harry, I know life is worth living. And each day you're above-ground, breathing and placing one foot in front of the other, it's a victory. We don't know the answers. All we can control is getting through times like that as best as we can."

Sara cupped his face in her hands. "You're not alone. You're never alone. I never met her, but your wife sounds like a wonderful, loving woman. Marie wouldn't want you to join her and John. She'd want you to go on living and be happy."

Acting on instinct, she kissed his cheek. He lifted his head, stared at her and suddenly kissed her on the mouth. Harry cupped the back of her head and devoured her lips, kissing her as if his next breath depended on hers. She opened her mouth to him, welcoming the surge of passion and heat.

Needing it as much as he did, she wrapped her arms around him, giving in to the feelings she'd suppressed ever since the moment she'd awakened from a dead faint and saw him administering aid to her. He kissed her as if he never wanted to release her.

When he finally did, Harry leaned his forehead against hers. "Damn, I didn't mean to do that."

"I'm glad you did."

A slight knocking drew their attention to the house. Sean and January stood at the large picture window. Both beamed. Sean did a thumbs-up sign.

Harry swore softly as Sara flushed, then she laughed.

"I guess they consider the visit a success after all," she mused.

"I'll say." Harry kissed her mouth again, gentler this time. "Thank you, Sara. I'll be okay now. I just had a moment. Someone warned me, I forget who, that grief is like a river that trickles down to a low creek as the months and years pass, but there would be times something triggers a memory, or a thought and it comes bursting out like a broken dam again, as painful as the day you lost them. Today was one of those days."

She touched his cheek. "I understand. The day I found out my father was dead, I guess all that grief rushed forward and overwhelmed me. But he was a stranger. Your loss is greater."

Harry took her hand, turned it over and studied it. "You have such lovely hands, Sara. Mine are big paws."

That made no sense. She frowned as he kissed the inside of her wrist.

"Don't ever make comparisons, Sara. Comparing your loss to mine is like comparing your hands to mine. You suffered a huge loss. I have memories to comfort me."

The familiar tightness rose in her throat. Sara tried to stem the flow of tears, but they leaked out of her eyes and began trickling down her cheeks. The harder she tried to stop crying, the worse it got.

"Aw damn, I didn't mean to make you do that." Harry took the edge of her scarf and gently wiped away her tears.

"I'll be fine. I'm just overwhelmed, oh no, are they still watching?" Sara couldn't bear to look.

Harry did. "No, fortunately. We must look like a couple of crying fools in their driveway."

She smiled and wiped her eyes. "Falling apart in the cold."

He studied her a minute. "You okay?"

Nodding, she drew in a deep breath and opened her car

door. "Thanks, Harry. I haven't really permitted myself to do that in front of anyone. I needed it."

He kissed her cheek, his mouth warm and slightly wet. "You'd best get home, get warm."

Solid advice, and yet he lingered. Sara ached for him. She knew what it was like to head into an empty apartment, the quiet so dense it made the air heavy, when all you wanted was company. Because being alone with your own haunting thoughts made the loneliness even worse.

On impulse she made a decision. "Do you want to go with me and grab a bite of dinner? Or just sit and talk? Nothing expensive, but good, homemade food. It's not exactly in an upscale area, though."

For a moment he said nothing and she thought she'd misread the torment in his gaze. Then he nodded. "Thanks. Yeah, that would be great. I'm not eager to go home yet."

"I'll drive and then drive you back here to get your car."

"Or you can follow me and we'll leave from the restaurant. It's closer to my house." Sara thought the idea of returning here might be too much. All he needed was to pull into the driveway later and see Sean and January silhouetted by the living room lamp, cooing to their bundles of joy.

"Sounds fine." Harry glanced at the house. "Too many memories right now. Let's go."

Never had a woman read him so thoroughly as Sara had this evening. Even Marie, as much as she loved him, sometimes got upset when he'd distanced himself because of the job. She had wanted to be part of his life, every part of it, even the ugliness of crime. Sometimes Marie had missed cues from him after a particularly grueling day when he'd desperately wanted her company, but didn't want to discuss his job. She'd end up hurt, and he'd end up comforting her and failing to be comforted himself.

Not now with Sara. Astute and empathetic, she'd realized how difficult being around Sean and January had felt for him.

The restaurant Sara selected was a diner in a questionable part of town. But it was well-lit, cheerful and had plenty of security cameras. Instead of getting out of her car and heading inside, Sara popped her trunk. She removed a small bag of dog food.

"I have to do something first. Want to come with?"

Curious, he nodded, and then walked with her to the building's rear. Sitting against the building in a spot shielded from the wind was a man sitting on the ground with a large, shaggy dog. Both the man and dog had seen better days and were obviously homeless. Harry's guard instantly went up and then relaxed when he saw the man jump to his feet with a big smile.

"Miss Sara! I was hoping you'd come by. I'm almost out."

"Hi, Rob." She petted the dog and then handed Rob the bag. "Here you go."

"Thanks, Miss Sara. Here. Just like we agreed." Rob handed her two crumpled bills.

She took the money and stuffed it into her coat pocket. "Rob, it's cold out here. Why aren't you inside?"

The man scratched his graying beard. "I'll bunk down later."

"Did you eat yet?" she persisted.

A shrug. "Naw. They told me it was okay to eat in the kitchen, but I can't leave Rex alone out here."

"This is my friend, Harry. Harry, Rob."

"Pleasure to meet you." Harry squatted down and petted the dog. "Hey there, buddy."

The man cast a dubious look at Harry's badge, glinting in the parking lot light. "His name is Rex. Are you here to arrest me?"

Harry stood, and shook his head. "Nope. Miss Sara promised me a hot meal of good food. That's why I'm here. Food good here?"

"The best," Rob said gravely.

"Great. I'm starving." Harry took Sara's arm and nodded at Rob. "Thanks."

The diner inside was informal and cheerful. A silver Christmas tree sat near the counter and garland threaded with white lights decorated the tops of the booths. A few patrons ate at the counter, and more crowded the booths.

Harry looked around. "Need to wash my hands."

"Me, too," Sara told him. "The restrooms are back this way."

After they emerged from the restrooms, the hostess led them to a quiet booth in back. Harry helped Sara remove her coat, and then took his off, hanging both on the hooks by the booth. He took the seat opposite her, watching the door as always.

She studied him with her amazing green eyes. Such a beautiful woman, inside and out.

"Thanks for helping me with Rob and Rex. It's my way of making sure his dog gets fed and Rob has a little pride. He hates taking charity, but when it comes to Rex, he'll do it."

"The restaurant owners don't mind? That's good of them."

Her face fell a little. "Vinnie and Lorraine have been wonderful to Rob and Rex. Rob came here over the summer, asking for a job. He washes dishes for them at night. During the day he works at the garage across the street as a mechanic, which is what he used to do in the Army. He's terrific at repairing engines. That's how I met him. He fixed my transmission."

A homeless vet. Harry was sadly familiar with their plight. "Does he sleep here on the restaurant grounds? Some homeless people prefer being outside."

"No. He wants a place, but with the cost of housing, especially with a dog, he can't afford an apartment. The repair shop owner lets him sleep in the garage and store his things there, but he doesn't want the heat run at night. Now that it's getting cold, I'm worried he could freeze."

Harry watched Sara as she talked. So animated and fierce in her conviction of helping others. It was insightful seeing this side of her.

Their waiter came over and took their drink orders, leaving them to peruse the menu.

"I love their mushroom risotto. It's how I found the place on the way home from work one day. They had a special."

He considered. "A diner that serves risotto? Impressive."

Sara grinned, her green eyes sparkling. "Isn't it? Vinnie is from Italy. Lorraine is Greek, so you'll find lots of cultural favorites on the menu. They consider you family if you eat here more than once."

"You sound like me. You eat out a lot or you nuke something at home." Harry scanned the menu.

"I like finding different restaurants with good food that doesn't cost a month's paycheck." Sara shrugged. "Even when I was making better money, it became a fun hobby. You can find little, tucked-away places where the cooking is excellent, served with a dash of culture and friendliness."

"Same here. I like gourmet dining once in a while, but would rather eat someplace less pretentious." He pointed to his jeans. "In case you can't tell, I'm not a pretentious kinda guy."

Sara smiled and looked pleased. "Me, too. I never had

the need to Instagram my food to show the world what up-scale restaurant was worthy of my money. Guys I've dated in the past who tried to impress me left me cold when they bragged about how much they knew about dining out or wine pairings. It's not my style."

Harry loved that Sara wasn't afraid to voice her needs. She knew what she wanted and liked and how to assert herself.

A guy would always know where he stood with her.

With a start he realized Marie was far different. With his wife, he always wondered if she went along with him simply to please him, much as she had pleased her parents.

When the waiter came, they both ordered the mush-room risotto.

"What's your favorite winter sport?" he asked when the waiter left.

"I like to ski when I can save up money for trips. I do have a friend who has a time-share in Aspen. Comes in handy."

They talked about winter sports for a few minutes. Lost in thought, Harry recalled a time when he tried to get Marie to ski.

"She never got off the bunny slope. Marie preferred sit-ting by the fire with hot cocoa. But she tried to learn, to please me, I guess. We had some good times on vacation, but the snowball fights and snowshoeing, especially after John was born, made them even more special because those were things we could do as a family."

"She sounds like a wonderful wife and mom," Sara said softly.

Harry toyed with his water glass. "I don't talk about their deaths much, but I need to talk tonight. I'm happy for Janu-ary and especially Sean. For a long time, Sean blamed him-self for their deaths. As if I wasn't blaming myself enough."

Sara reached across the table and gripped his hand. "How did they die?"

Oddly, the question didn't bother him as it once had. In the past when someone asked, he didn't give details. It was too intense and personal.

"She and John were killed in a car accident. The brake lines to my personal vehicle were cut. The man who did it was John Andrews, an ex-con suspected in a murder case Sean and I were investigating for vehicular homicide."

Harry slid his hand out from Sara's to drink water, amazed his hand was steady. Once, he never would have been able to talk about their deaths without shaking.

Tears filled Sara's eyes. "I'm so sorry. You had to deal not only with losing them, but the anguish of knowing it was at the hands of a dangerous criminal."

He had to keep talking, get it out. Sara was different. She seemed to understand he wasn't being maudlin or agonizing over every detail of the accident. Hell, he'd done that more than two years ago. He simply needed to get it out, let her know he carried a lot of baggage with him. Because he truly liked her, and if that kiss was an indication of the way things were going, he knew where they would end up.

Harry felt like he'd been walking in a snowstorm for a long time and suddenly spotted a warm, welcoming inn with a crackling fire and warmth.

"Marie was a wonderful wife and mother, but she never told me she had seen Andrews watching the house. It was only later that her best friend said Marie confided in her that a strange guy was always parked near the house. Marie didn't want to burden me. I didn't know anything was wrong. I was cocky and arrogant and thought nothing could penetrate my home life. If she had told me, I would have driven her and John to her parents', told her to stay there. But she acted as if nothing was wrong."

Harry rubbed his chin. "I should have known she was afraid. I should have known Andrews would have done something like this."

"Are you a mind reader?"

Startled, he frowned. "No."

"Of course not. So how could you have known? You had no indications Andrews was watching your home. You had no idea he'd go to such lengths to hurt you and your family. You had no way of knowing Marie was afraid. It's not your fault. It's not her fault. The only person to blame is Andrews."

Sara's green gaze held his. "I'm not telling you how you should feel, Harry. But blaming yourself is pointless. In your profession, danger comes with the job, even if you don't ever fire your gun."

For a moment, he considered. "I guess you're right."

"I know I'm right."

He looked up as she flushed. "Tell me how you really feel."

"Well, if you insist."

They both smiled at each other, the tension breaking. Harry drank more water.

"I tried to break her out of her shell. I tried to get her to go out and do things she always said she wanted to try, like painting. Actually, that's how I started—it was to encourage her. But she was too shy to join the classes when I had to drop out because of work commitments."

He sighed. "Sometimes I wondered if she married me because she was afraid of life and having a cop as a husband was having someone to lean on."

Life after they died had gone on, though he'd felt imprisoned in grief he didn't know how to release. Being a cop meant keeping emotion in check in order to do the job and solve the crime. Life taught him to be zealous when solving crime. It didn't teach him how to heal his shattered heart.

The art helped. Painting allowed him to express all the rage and sorrow, and if not mend his broken heart, at least start to piece it together again. He started to paint to encourage his wife to learn and grow and continued after her death as a means of washing away the tears he could not shed.

To his relief, their meals arrived. He didn't mind talking about his past with Sara, but he wanted to know more about her. As they dug into their risotto, which Harry praised as some of the best he'd ever had, he asked Sara about growing up in St. Louis. He wasn't surprised to find out Regina had encouraged her to volunteer for charities and had instilled a sense of civic duty into her daughter.

"We're given responsibility to give back to society. I think more parents should teach that to their children. Then again, my mom was extraordinary. Always volunteering, despite her schedule, but always had time for me." Sara's gaze grew troubled. "I wish I knew where she was. She couldn't have killed Axel, I mean, it just isn't like her."

"I'll find her." When Harry made a promise, he kept it. "One way or another, I'll find her, Sara."

She nodded and toyed with her fork. "I know you will. As long as she's safe."

He changed the subject to talk about the city and what they liked best about Chicago. The more lighthearted conversation coaxed her out of her funk.

Harry ordered a hot dog, sans bun, to go, and insisted on paying the check. When they got outside, he clasped her hand and steered her to the back of the building.

Rob and Rex were still there, huddled against the cold. Harry opened the carton and handed the hot dog to Rex. The dog gulped down the treat.

Harry put a hand on the man's shoulder. "Go inside, Rob. There's a hot meal waiting for you."

Rob shook his head. "Not without Rex. I can't bring him into the restaurant and I won't leave him. What if someone steals him?"

"Go inside," Harry said gently. "I'll stay out here and watch him while you eat."

"Promise? Rex is all the family I have. Me and him, we're all we have."

"I promise." Harry sat on the ground and petted the dog.

When Rob headed inside, Harry glanced up. "You don't have to stay, Sara. You can go home."

Sara sat on the ground beside him. "I think Rex needs two bodyguards."

While some women he'd dated might have fed the dog as Sara had, they would have been horrified at the idea of sitting on the cold ground in elegant silk trousers to watch the dog while his owner enjoyed dinner inside. Not Sara. His admiration for her rose.

Harry removed his cell phone and dialed a number. While it rang, she scratched the dog's ears. Never mind that the dog might have fleas. Sara didn't care.

He was beginning to realize exactly how special and compassionate Sara Sandoval was.

Two phone calls later, everything was arranged. Harry thumbed off his cell, his fingers slightly frozen. But inside he felt warm all over.

Gaze rapt with admiration, Sara studied him as if he'd given away his last dollar instead of finding a place for Rob and Rex.

When Rob came outside, Harry jingled his keys in his hand. "Come on, Rob. I've found a warm place for you and Rex to stay. Buddy of mine has a small, furnished studio for very low rent. Utilities included, though not cable, just electric, heat and water. It's not in walking distance, but on the bus route so you can get to work."

It was sort of a white lie, for he'd promised his friend he'd pay the security and first month's rent in exchange for Rob having a lower rent for the annual lease term.

He didn't do it to look like the white knight in Sara's eyes.

But he had to admit, it felt damn good to see her happy he'd helped.

Harry Cartwright seemed like a kaleidoscope of colorful layers. At first she'd wanted to dismiss him as a cop who might be a thorn in her side. Now she was getting to know the real man behind the badge, and the compassionate soul within.

Finding a home for Rob and Rex had cost him. Rob never could have saved enough for the security or first month's rent.

They packed all Rob's belongings in Sara's trunk. Harry drove Rob and Rex himself to the studio apartment. It didn't take long to move in Rob's few things. Sara made sure to turn up the heat as Rex ran around, sniffing the small, but comfortable space.

Turning to Harry, Rob stuck out a hand, his mouth trembling. "Nobody cares about me and Rex except my bosses and Miss Sara here. Rex would have starved if not for Miss Sara. Thanks, Harry. You're not a bad sort yourself."

Harry made sure to escort Sara out to her car and lingered as she got behind the wheel. She rolled down her window and pressed her gloved hand upon his.

"Thank you, Harry. Not many people would care about the fate of a homeless man and his dog."

He nodded, as if such a magnanimous gesture was an everyday occurrence for him. Maybe it was.

"When you get home, make sure to lock up behind you, Sara. Someone is out there who may be targeting you. I'm determined to find out who killed your father. It may be your mother and you'd best prepare yourself for that."

Sara put her keys into the ignition. "I'm prepared. But first we have to find her."

He tapped her nose. "No, sweetie. I have to find her. I'm going tomorrow, first thing in the morning when the doc clears me. I'll find her, I promise."

Relief washed through her. It felt like someone had taken a heavy load off her back. All this time she'd fretted and worried alone. Now she had Harry at her side to help. Harry didn't seem the type to make such promises easily.

He's also going to find Regina to question her and perhaps arrest her.

The flicker of doubt winked on and off like a neon sign. Sara took a deep breath. Later, she would deal with those consequences, like she had with other matters ever since she made the decision to move to Chicago and introduce herself to Axel Colton.

Harry dropped a brief but sweet kiss on her mouth, leaving her lips warm and tingling. When she returned home, Sara went straight to her apartment and locked the door, making sure to check the locks.

That kiss swept her breath away. She still felt the pressure of his mouth against hers, the blood humming in her veins, desire zinging all the way down to her toes.

Frustrated, she roamed around her apartment, too restless to settle down.

Harry had shared a special part of himself, showed what kind of man he really was and had awakened passion he'd stirred inside her that sparked into an inferno. One kiss. Sara hugged herself, thinking about how he'd be in bed. Desire sparked again. She wanted him.

He wasn't right for her. He was a cop with a job to do.

But he was the only one she did want.

Her phone chimed. She glanced at the text and smiled. Harry, checking on her.

Lock up?

Sara smiled. Yes, I locked up.

Good night, Sara.

Then, as if an afterthought, I miss you.

Miss you too, she texted back.

Sara set down her phone and picked up a book to read about landscape ideas in winter. Finally she went to bed. But for a long time she lay awake, thinking about Harry and how they desired each other.

And how he might end up finding her mother tomorrow, and arresting her.

Chapter 12

The next morning after the doctor cleared him to return fully to work, Harry wasted no time.

An urgency drove him onward, more than yesterday. He'd run Mary Martin's name in a thorough background check. Alfred and Farrah Colton's domestic worker was married, had two children and was clean, no priors, but digging deeper, he discovered a disturbing connection.

Mary was the sister of Dennis and Eddie Angelo.

The threads on this case were twisting together in a pattern that made sense. But he knew someone had to be the driving force behind all of this. Trouble was, that person remained elusive.

Harry set out to find Regina Sandoval, but decided to take a detour first. He needed to follow the thread on Dennis Angelo. Wasn't as if he delayed the inevitable.

No, not because he couldn't forget kissing Sara. Last night after he got home, he'd fallen asleep, dreaming about her. He'd been wandering in a dense fog, the scent of rain and tears on his cheeks, and she emerged from the mist like a beacon lighting the way. Sara had taken him into her arms and melted against him like she had last night.

For the first time in months, he'd awakened feeling hopeful and energized about something other than the job.

It was the kiss. The best mistake he'd ever made.

But man, if he ended up arresting her mother, the relationship was over before it ever began. Maybe he needed to end it. Cut it off before it progressed. He hated admitting he cared about her, more than he thought he would ever care about a woman again.

If he wasn't careful, Sara Sandoval could hurt him more than any bullet graze could.

Harry drove on the exact same route as Dennis Angelo had on his last trip after the ex-con had planted the murder weapon in Nash's trunk. Most people drove I-55, the quickest way to St. Louis. Dennis Angelo had not.

Angelo had driven a less traveled road, I-57, stopping at a no-tell motel north of Kankakee. The manager had already told Harry and other investigating officers the motel's security cameras were broken. However, he'd seen Angelo's old, rattling Buick. He had noted it because the muffler was broken and the car thundered into the motel parking lot.

Not very inconspicuous.

A few miles down the road, Angelo had crashed his car, dying almost instantly.

Something warned Harry the manager neglected to be totally honest and forthcoming with the police.

The Love Inn looked seedy and sagging as he pulled into the parking lot. A pink neon sign blared out Rooms By The Hour. He'd been here at night after Angelo was killed. Daylight didn't improve its appearance.

A musty smell of cigarette smoke and stale body odor

hit him as he walked into the office. Yellow tinted the white walls and ceiling, signs of a heavy smoker. Using his knuckles, Harry dinged the grimy front desk bell a few times.

Out of a back room came the same rumpled man he'd interviewed right after Angelo was killed. His eyes bleary and squinting, he waddled to the counter. A greasy brown spot stained his blue T-shirt beneath his frayed sport jacket. Harry immediately detected the odor of old cigar smoke, stale beer and the unmistakable smell of pot.

"Room for a night or an hour?" the manager asked, scratching his belly.

Harry flashed his badge. "Chicago PD. I'm back to ask you about a motel patron. Dennis Angelo."

"Oh. That guy." The man scratched his nose. Harry stepped back in case the guy had something contagious, like scabies.

"Yeah, that guy. You said…" Harry flipped through his notebook. "Angelo was here, alone, the night he was killed. You spotted his car, but he did not check in."

"Yeah, I was taking a smoke break."

Judging from the walls and smells in the office, the guy took too many smoke breaks.

"You're absolutely sure Angelo was alone? Here, in a motel most people rent rooms by the hour?" Harry made his way around the counter. Got close. Forget the contagion. He could shower later. Answers were more important.

The man blinked and backed off. "Maybe someone else was with him."

"Who? What kind of car?"

"I didn't see the car. But I did see Angelo with a woman."

Harry swore under his breath. "And you didn't tell me this earlier because…"

The man shrugged. "We see a lot of men here with women. My boss would fire me. I'm paid to collect money, not spy on customers. We pride ourselves on discretion. It's our reputation."

Harry got into the man's face and fisted his hands in the manager's worn coat lapels, scabies or no scabies. "Listen, you lying shyster, I want the truth. I don't give a damn about your customers or your rep. Tell me what I need to know or I'll go over this place inch by inch until I find something to haul you in for."

The manager swallowed. "Okay, okay, I'll tell you what I know!"

Harry released him. "Good man. Who was the woman with Dennis Angelo?"

Paling, the man swallowed hard. "I don't know! It was dark. I just saw a woman. I think it was a woman. I didn't really pay attention because like I said, there's lots of women who come here with men."

"Did they arrive in separate cars?"

"I guess. I only remember them because Angelo had paid for a room for an hour and kept pacing in the parking lot, like he was waiting for his date."

Some date.

Harry began writing notes. "What kind of dress?"

"I think, I think it was a dress. Dark. No wait, pants."

He groaned, tempted to shake the man to rattle his brain cells.

Minutes later, he had little to go on. The woman was about Angelo's height, maybe a little shorter. Or taller. Wore a hat and a shapeless coat. Or maybe it wasn't even a woman. The manager couldn't tell Harry if Angelo left before the woman did, or vice versa, because he'd suddenly been busy checking in other customers. An hour later, Angelo was gone, the key to the room left on the front desk.

It could have been Regina. Regina was tall, like Angelo.

Or maybe Angelo had stopped here for a quick bout of sex, like most of the motel's less upstanding patrons.

Soon Harry was back in his car headed to St. Louis. When he arrived at the suburban neighborhood where Regina Sandoval lived, it was nearly two o'clock.

Regina's house looked vacant. Newspapers piled up on the driveway. No car. Nice house, two-story middle income. Quiet neighborhood where kids' bikes piled up in the driveway and you didn't have to worry about anyone stealing them. He gave the house a long, appreciative look. He could envision Sara growing up here, backpack slung across one slender shoulder, her long legs coltish as she walked to school. That little frown line of concentration, maybe, as she thought about an upcoming test. Doing a background check, he'd discovered she'd been an honor student, a trait following her into college. No priors with Regina or Sara. Not even a parking ticket.

No one answered when he knocked. He went around the back, peered through the back door. Everything was too quiet. His gut warned him this wasn't going to be good. But before he went breaking inside, he needed to ask around.

Legwork served a purpose, but gave no answers. By the time he finished talking to neighbors, he learned Regina was an outstanding mother and a good neighbor, and Sara was her darling. Only the Miller family hadn't gotten along well with the Sandovals, according to the neighborhood gossips. But the Millers were known snobs who shunned others. The family had moved six years ago after the husband lost his job due to a drinking problem.

Regina seldom drank, always pitched in at PTA and school events, and whenever someone in the neighborhood needed a helping hand, she was there.

He walked down the sidewalk, feeling he'd either received the snow job of his life or Regina had been respected and liked by everyone. Except the Millers.

No one could tell him where Regina was, though. She'd said something to Carla Harrison, Regina's friend, about taking a vacation since her office was closing for renovations.

Time to check with the Harrisons.

Harry knocked on the Harrisons' door. A sullen teenager answered. "What?"

He flashed his badge. "Chicago PD. Your mom or dad home?"

"Should they be?"

Normally he had lots of patience dealing with unruly, sarcastic teens. Not today. "Where are they?"

"Dunno." The girl started to push the door shut. Harry shoved his foot inside, preventing her.

"I asked you a question. Where are your parents?"

He caught the scent of pot. Ah. No wonder the kid was trying to shove him out the door.

"I'm not here to check up on you," he said, softening his tone. "I'm investigating the disappearance of Regina Sandoval."

No answer.

"No one knows where she went. Her daughter says she's missing."

A blank stare.

He sighed. "Look, I won't tell your parents what you're doing. Just tell me where your mom is."

Relief flitted across the teen's face.

"Regina Sandoval. Your neighbor," he said helpfully.

"Oh her." The girl made a dismissive gesture. "My mom's visiting her. The Good Samaritan thing, you know? She's in the hospital. St. Good Hope."

No wonder the woman hadn't answered her daughter's concerned phone calls. "What happened?"

"Some kind of freak accident. Coma, I dunno. Mom just found out today and went there."

Harry plugged the hospital name into his cell. "There's no hospital in St. Louis by that name."

"Duh. 'Course not. It's in Springfield, where Regina was staying."

Harry gave her a level look and the kid had the good sense to look away. He plugged in the name and city, got an address and directions. "Why aren't you at school?"

"Half day today."

"When is your father getting home?"

"He texted to say he's about a half an hour away. Why?"

"Because you shouldn't be alone. And don't smoke. You'll ruin your lungs."

The sullen expression returned. "No, I won't. Everyone says that. And you promised you wouldn't tell my parents."

"I did promise. I won't tell them. However…" Harry grinned. "I may stop by the station, have a chat with their narcotics division. I used to work Narcotics."

Blood drained from the teen's face. She scurried inside and slammed the door shut, locking it.

Oh yeah, a little fear did wonders for the younger law-breaking set.

The hospital wasn't too far, but traffic already started to build up. Harry thought of all the moms and dads heading home to their children and maybe a good meal around the dinner table. Small talk, maybe someone had earned an A in math or their daughter had scored a winning goal in soccer.

His throat tightened. Once he'd thought he might have the same happy suburban life. He'd thought about it, considered quitting the force so Marie wouldn't wait up, worrying, wondering if he would make it home. Always the worrying when you were a cop's wife.

He was going to tell her he would consider her father's job offer as head of security.

Going to...but that night she and John were killed. For weeks, his world had spun on its axis in a crazy tilt, like a ride he desperately wanted to abandon, but was strapped in for the duration.

He finally reached the hospital, a sterile three-story building that looked like every other hospital he'd visited. Harry pulled into a parking space reserved for police and shut off his engine. For a moment, he sat in the car, staring at the hospital.

Damn, he hated hospitals. Nothing good there. Even after Marie gave birth...that had been a happy memory, but now it only reminded him of the vast hole in his heart. The emptiness he still felt when he examined his personal life.

Dating hadn't helped.

Meeting Sara Sandoval had.

He rubbed his chin and then climbed out, heading inside to find out what the hell happened to her mother.

After paying a courtesy visit to the chief operating officer and explaining the purpose of his visit, he entered Room 405. A woman, her head wrapped in bandages, lay on a hospital bed near the window. Another woman, plump and middle-aged, sat reading a book in a chair by her bed. The woman glanced up.

Harry showed his badge. "Harry Cartwright, Chicago PD. I'm here to see Regina Sandoval."

The woman shut her book and set it on the hospital table next to the bed. "Thank goodness. I was frantic with worry when the Springfield police called me and told me she was here. I'm Carla Harrison, Regina's friend and neighbor."

Though the woman in the hospital bed was pale, he saw

the resemblance to Sara in her high cheekbones and heart-shaped face. "What happened?"

"She hit her head falling down some stairs at a house she was visiting. The cleaning lady found her and paramedics brought her here. The police think it was a robbery gone wrong, or a home invasion. Her purse, cell phone and wallet were stolen. If not for the cleaning lady finding her…" Carla brushed at her eyes.

"Why was she in Springfield?" Made no sense. If Regina was guilty, she'd be halfway across the country.

"Her firm is opening a satellite office here. Regina had taken a vacation and on the way home, stopped at the house."

Harry gave Carla Harrison a long look. "How did the police find her and contact you?"

"I contacted them. Regina was due home two days ago for the neighborhood meeting on the Christmas parade. She's the honorary chairwoman. She hasn't missed a parade in twenty years. I knew something was wrong, but she didn't answer her phone. So I started making calls and gave the St. Louis police a photo to circulate. The Springfield police finally reached the homeowner where she was found. He's going to be the manager in charge of the satellite office. He had no idea who she was, but called the company president. The president said Regina had a key to the house and was overseeing the furniture being moved inside. It was typical of her to go into the house to stock it with drinks and some food before the family moved in, to help them feel welcome. She is thoughtful and organized that way."

Carla wiped at her eyes again. "Look at her. Who could tell who she is by using a photo to identify her, with her face all bruised and her head banged up? The only good thing is Regina has a distinctive birthmark on her right arm, like the map of Italy. I used to tease her that was the reason why she loved making Italian food because I didn't think it was in her blood."

At Harry's stare, she added, "Regina is Hispanic. But that doesn't matter… Are you investigating who robbed her?"

Harry touched the medal in his pocket, thinking of how the murder of Axel Colton was turning into what seemed like an impossible case to unravel. He needed to focus on each thread and unravel it and not get distracted.

"Do you have the address of the home?" he asked.

"The police have all that information. Don't you work together?"

"I'm here on another matter, ma'am."

"Such as?" Carla sounded hostile. He couldn't blame her.

Harry decided on a partial truth. "Her daughter, Sara, has been desperately trying to reach Regina."

Blood drained from Carla's face. "Oh dear, I didn't even think about that. Poor Sara! She must be frantic. She and Regina are quite close. I'll call her now. Oh no! I don't have her phone number, I think she changed it when she moved."

"Leave that to me." He removed his cell phone, texted Sara that her mother had been found and was safe, and he'd call her later.

"Mrs. Harrison, please have a seat. I need to ask you some questions."

Knowing that even though Regina was unconscious, she might be able to hear, he decided to question Carla in front of her. Maybe it would coax her into waking up. He couldn't get all softhearted now just because he could imagine Sara here, crying over her mother, wondering if she would ever wake up, crazy with worry and guilt over not reaching her earlier…

Harry took out his notebook and pen and remained

standing at the opposite side of Regina's bed so he could see her in his peripheral vision. He grilled Carla about Regina, and any association she had with Eddie and Dennis Angelo. Carla told him Eddie had done odd jobs around the neighborhood after Regina recommended him, but no one ever heard of his brother. Or their sister, Mary Martin.

"Eddie was down on his luck, a nice, polite man, and Regina helped him out by hiring him to do some odd jobs around the yard. But he ghosted her after she needed him to help move some inventory at the warehouse and she had to formally fire him. I had the feeling Eddie wasn't cut out for a regular job." Carla kept glancing at her cell phone.

"How did Regina find Eddie? Was he knocking on neighbors' doors, asking for work?" Harry scribbled notes.

Carla's thin blond brows narrowed as she thought. "No, it was almost odd…he found her at her office at first. He was hoping for day labor after he moved from Chicago to St. Louis. He said he came with recommendations from some rich person in Chicago."

Harry stopped writing. This was peculiar. "Who was this person?"

The woman shook her head. "I can't remember. Regina mentioned it in passing and laughed, but she was a little startled. I remember that. I had the feeling she was bothered this acquaintance knew where she lived. As if she had run far away from something bad in her past and didn't want to be found. Do you think it was an ex-husband? Regina's my friend, but she's a private person and I never did find out if she'd been in an abusive relationship. She did act like that when we first met, always looking over her shoulder."

Looking over her shoulder to see if her old lover, Sara's father, would ring the doorbell after finding out about the daughter Axel didn't know existed? Yet another thread he had to follow.

"You have absolutely no idea who recommended Eddie to Regina? Try to remember, Mrs. Harrison. This is important."

"I don't see why. Eddie was just a down-on-his-luck man who couldn't quit drinking."

"He may have been more than that," Harry said grimly. "Was this person's name Axel Colton?"

Carla wrinkled her forehead. "Colton, that sounds familiar. I saw on the news about him, isn't he the one who was murdered?"

"Yes. Was it Axel Colton?"

"I don't think so. But the last name may have begun with a *C*. She was rather vague."

He had only more questions and no real answers. He needed to check out the house where Regina Sandoval had her accident.

This time, he needed to bring Sara along. She knew her mother and just might provide a link to all the broken threads in the case until Regina regained consciousness.

Chapter 13

Sara felt as if someone had put her on a turntable and spun her madly around. Her life had flipped in hours. Sheer relief at discovering her mother had been found. Extreme worry knowing she was unconscious and injured in a hospital.

And now Harry wanted her along with him as he checked out the crime scene where Regina had been injured.

Vita graciously gave her the day off to accompany Harry. Shortly after seven o'clock in the morning, he picked her up in his sedan in front of her apartment and handed her a cup of hot coffee prepared exactly as she liked.

She accepted the coffee with grateful thanks as she settled into the passenger seat. Harry looked different this morning and then she realized why.

"You shaved off your beard!"

"I thought it was a good idea." Harry rubbed his clean cheek. "The beard was sort of an act of rebellion and when I was working in Narcotics, it helped with undercover work."

Sara scrutinized his cheeks. "It makes you look younger."

To her surprise, he flushed. "Yeah, just what I need, the look of a baby-faced cop."

"Not baby-faced. Just younger. I like it."

He smiled. "Feels strange not having it. But I'll get used to it."

As they started for Springfield, Sara mused over her mother being found. "I don't understand why the police didn't inform me sooner about finding my mother. Or why they didn't contact anyone at her office. Wouldn't they have asked the home's owner right away who my mother was and identified her that way?"

Harry nodded. "The house was recently bought by the new hire taking over the satellite office. They contacted the real estate agent, who told them the owner and his family are driving across the country from California. The Springfield police had trouble reaching him. When they finally did, he said your mother's company had a skeleton key because they had all his furniture delivered to the house. When the police called your mother's company to get more information, the president said it was probably Regina found in the house. She oversaw that project. There was a car there that matched the description the president gave the police."

Sara sipped her coffee. "Are you allowed to bring me onto an active crime scene?"

A side glance. "I called Springfield PD and told them. It's not much of an active crime scene now, plus the vic is still alive."

Vic. Her mother. "You mean if she dies the police will change their minds?" She couldn't help the bitterness in her voice.

"They have priorities just as every other PD does. Right now your mother's case is a robbery. They're not even calling it a home invasion because there's no signs of forced entry. Your mother knows whoever did this."

A shudder snaked down her spine. Hard to believe someone would want to hurt her mother that badly, let alone someone Regina knew well enough to admit into the house.

"How did this person find her?" she asked.

"That's what I'd like to know," Harry said grimly. "It would have to appear that whoever did this contacted your mother and she arranged to meet him at the house. But we won't have solid answers until she wakes up."

Harry finally pulled into the driveway of a two-story green house with white shutters. It was in a solid middle-class neighborhood, not unlike the one where she and Regina lived. Regina's car was nowhere in sight.

"My mother's car is gone." Sara's hands tightened on her now-cold cup of coffee.

"Springfield had it towed to their impound lot. We'll get it back soon." Harry unbuckled his seat belt and turned, facing her. "Sara, you should know something. This wasn't a home invasion. Your mother was deliberately targeted. The only things stolen belonged to her. Nothing else was taken, not the new electronic equipment worth thousands, or the home computer, or anything else in the house of value."

Maybe such knowledge would help the police narrow down leads on her mother's attacker, but it only made Sara more uneasy. Whoever did this to Regina had wanted her dead. It was the only explanation.

The house was still and too quiet when they went inside. The carpeting smelled new and she detected a hint of pine. Tears welled in her eyes as she spotted the Christmas tree in the corner with tinsel, lights and decorations.

"Mom must have done that. She would want the family to feel happy and welcome here. It's one reason she's so good at her job—she oversees so many details and knows moving is tough on a family."

Harry pointed to the kitchen beyond the living room.

"Your mother was working in the kitchen and she was found lying on the basement stairs. Stairs are right off the kitchen."

The kitchen was modern with polished granite countertops, stainless steel appliances and a farmhouse sink. Several bar stools were arranged along the island.

"Do you see anything that would belong to your mother? Anything?"

Sara shook her head. "If she was here helping out, Mom wouldn't have many personal items inside. She respected someone else's space."

The kitchen was tidy, but for a stack of papers on the island that immediately caught Harry's interest. He clasped Sara's hand. "Don't touch them. I need to process this."

Harry pulled gloves from his pocket, snapped them on and picked up a pink flyer from a neat stack. "Grand opening of Larkspar Insurance. Come see us for all your home, auto and personal property needs!" the flyer advertised.

"Pink," he mused.

"One of the owners of Larkspur Insurance is a woman. That's her signature color—in fact, Mom said this satellite office is targeting busy businesswomen who don't have time to shop for insurance. They planned to decorate the office with pink accents."

But Harry's attention was elsewhere. He began opening bottom cabinets.

"What are you looking for?" she asked, bemused.

"Trash." He pulled out a bin under the sink. "Not here. Empty. Come on."

He led the way outside to the attached garage and handed her a pair of surgical gloves. "You allergic to latex?"

When she shook her head he instructed her to don the gloves.

"Put the gloves on. Start looking through the trash cans, see if there are envelopes. If you see any or anything else odd, tell me," he instructed.

But only newspaper and bubble wrap littered the trash bin she saw. Then she heard Harry call it. "Got it, you bastard."

Glancing up she saw him hold up a pink envelope in one gloved hand. He turned it over. Sara's breath caught. "That's like the pink envelope my mother used to mail my letter!"

Harry held the envelope up to the light. "Whoever did this is clever, but sloppy. Or in a rush. They forgot to check all the trash."

"But you said my mom's DNA was on the envelope seal and she must have written it."

"It was her DNA, but I'd bet a month's salary she did not write that letter." Harry dropped the pink envelope into a bag marked Evidence. "You know your mother and her habits. You said she liked to write letters and always mailed notes to clients that were handwritten. Think, Sara. Did she seal them and then address and stamp them?"

Sara nodded. "Usually she used a software program to print out mailing labels."

It dawned on her. "You think someone else mailed that letter to implicate my mother? How did they open a sealed envelope?"

"Freeze a sealed envelope for about an hour or two and the glue will unstick. All you have to do is pry open the envelope, slip in whatever you wish and reseal using a sponge to avoid fingerprints. The glue gets tacky again after it thaws out."

Harry shook his head and quietly swore. "The DNA the lab lifted was just enough to incriminate her, but slightly compromised. They did lift a fingerprint that matched Regina's as well. Whoever is behind this is determined to make it look like your mother killed Axel."

"And that person is the real killer." She shuddered, fear skidding down her spine on crawling legs.

She was horrified someone tried to frame her mother for the crime. Her mother, who lay in a hospital bed.

"Maybe. I doubt Regina killed Axel. Not with what happened." He peeled off the gloves and stuffed them into his pocket. "Let's go inside."

Harry showed her how to peel back the gloves. Sara placed them in her purse so as not to leave anything behind, same as Harry had done.

"Why would anyone want to hurt my mother? She'd never harm anyone. She has no enemies and she's a good person." Her voice caught and she struggled to prevent her emotions from taking over.

"I don't know, but trust me, Sara. I will find out. I promise this." Harry's quiet, reassuring voice settled her raw nerves a little.

"I have to call and see how she's doing. Maybe…oh I hope so…she woke up."

The cell phone shook in her hand as she dialed the hospital for a status update on Regina. Her hopes crumbled as the nurse relayed the news.

Sara thumbed off the cell. "No changes. The nurse said it takes time with a head injury. She had woken up a couple of times previously…"

She had to hold it together for her mother's sake. Believe that Regina would pull through and everything would be okay. But it was really tough when you were alone.

Harry put a comforting hand on her shoulder. She felt grateful for the touch. It centered her, made everything less hectic and terrifying. He reminded her she wasn't entirely alone.

"Let's go outside for some fresh air," he told her.

They walked onto a wood deck overseeing an expansive yard. Playground equipment sat off to the side. Sara hugged herself.

"Look at that. Typical of my mother. I bet she told the movers to make sure the equipment was set up, even though it's winter and the kids wouldn't use it for a while. But that was a detail Regina specialized in overseeing. She was like that at home as well, always making sure I was comfortable."

Cold penetrated her bones, a deep cold that had nothing to do with the weather. She stared at the yard, trying not to see her mother lying in a hospital bed, never fully waking up.

"I love her so much. She's my only family. I don't know what I'll do if she dies," she whispered.

Suddenly she was in Harry's arms as he engulfed her in a warm, comforting hug. He rested his cheek against her head. "Never think like that, Sara. She's alive and as long as she's alive, there's always hope. Always cling to that hope."

The softness in his voice, edged with a slight pain, told her Harry spoke from experience. Harry, who had suffered a tremendous loss, but still had the capacity for compassion and understanding. Some people might have turned hard from grief and lost their sense of humanity.

Harry had not. He was a good cop who sought to do the right thing, and seemed to honor that goal. He always seemed to be working and focusing solely on solving cases. But moments like this gave her glimpses into the real Harry Cartwright, a man who cared about more than the job. Even if he didn't like showing it.

They stood motionless on the deck, the icy wind billowing the edges of her scarf still penetrating her thin coat, but the chill inside her lessened. It felt wonderful to be held with such tenderness.

He stepped back and she lost the wonderful warmth of his arms. Harry brushed aside a strand of her hair, his fingers warm against her chilled cheeks. "You're not alone, Sara. You do have other family now. Vita thinks of you like a third child. You have a lot of family members now."

She smiled, glad he reminded her of the possibilities. "Yes. Vita's family are wonderful."

"I'm sure the other Coltons would welcome you as much as Vita has." Harry kept stroking her cheek and his touch sent delightful shivers down her spine. Delicious warmth filled her.

"A few might. Maybe not Uncle Erik or my grandmother."

Harry raised his eyebrows. "Carin is something else. Not the milk-and-cookies type."

"My grandmother…" She gave a humorless laugh. "No, more like the Rodeo Drive sort. I bet she never has a hair out of place."

"But she does seem like she has a hair up her butt."

Sara laughed as he grinned, and she mock punched his arm. "Harry!"

"Got you to laugh," he said softly. "Knocked that sad look off your face."

She stepped closer to him, leaning against him. "Yes, you did. Thanks."

"Sorry, shouldn't have said that about Carin. It was inappropriate, even though she's been a pain to the department, saying we're working too slow to solve Axel's murder. She's grieving in her own way. She lost a son."

His voice grew quieter. "I know what that's like. It's something you never get over."

So true. Sara felt a brief stab of guilt. She may have lost a father she didn't know, but her grandmother lost a child. It was the wrong order of life. Most parents expected to die before their children did.

"It's cold out here. I used to like winter before I heard Axel died. Now winter reminds me we're all mortal," she mused.

Harry took her bare hands into his and rubbed them.

"My grandmother was getting a tree for Axel's grave when I saw her at Yates' Yards. Carin doesn't know who I really am, and I'd like to keep it that way. She seems like a cold person and I don't think she'd welcome me with open arms." Sara snuggled into his coat as he wrapped his arms around her once more. "Not like Vita and her family have done."

"Maybe you should give her a chance." Harry tilted her chin up with one finger so she gazed into his face. "Everyone deserves a second chance."

Sara had the suspicion he was talking about himself, not Carin. She wrapped her arms around his neck and parted her lips.

He needed no other invitation as he brushed his mouth against hers. His lips were slightly cold and firm, but as they sank deeper into the kiss, sparks leapt between them. Sara was no longer chilled. She was heating from the inside out, the amazing warmth searing her as she pressed closer, needing and wanting more.

Groaning, he took her deeper into the kiss. Sara felt as if she stood on the edge of a cliff, ready to skydive. The parachute strapped to her back assured her she would not fall, but the thrill of the experience overrode any natural fears. She'd been kissed by experts—men who considered themselves great lovers and knew how to please a woman in bed.

But this was different. This wasn't a kiss of seduction

and pleasure. This was a kiss of comfort and reassurance, a kiss in the middle of a crazily spinning world that calmed the vertigo. She knew it would be great in bed with Harry not because he was a good-looking man she was wildly attracted to.

She knew when they finally ended up in bed it would be amazing because he had a good heart and he would make love with the same dedication and intensity he showed with everything in life. Harry wasn't a one-night stand. Not with her. Not with this blazing passion and intensity that was far deeper and richer than she'd felt with any other man.

He would give everything, body and soul, when he tangled with her between the sheets.

They broke apart and he gave a small smile. "Cold still?"

"No. I'm warm." A little laugh. "Nice and warm."

Harry made her feel as if everything would turn out all right. *But will he stay? Will he break your heart because you're starting to fall in love with him? All those other men meant nothing to you. Not like he does.*

Hard as it was to ignore the voice whispering doubts inside her, for now she would. Sara needed Harry.

His hands grazed her jacket and he frowned. "Sara Sandoval, you need to get a thicker jacket if you're going to survive winter in Chicago. This isn't St. Louis anymore."

She smiled. "I suppose I should."

When she first arrived in the windy city, Sara had no intentions of really staying. Settling here seemed unlikely, especially if Axel had wanted nothing to do with her. But lately she thought she could learn to live here on a more permanent basis.

It has nothing to do with Harry, right? Oh no, nothing at all...

Right. She gave a little laugh. "I suppose we should go inside. Much warmer in there."

Harry turned serious. "I need your help. I'm going to search every inch of this house to see if your mother's attacker left anything else behind, and you can identify any personal objects as your mother's."

An hour later, they had covered every inch of the house except the basement. Sara couldn't bring herself to explore the area where her mother had fallen. The only questionable item Sara found was a business card advertising Larkspur, with Regina's name on it. She'd spotted it on the bedroom dresser.

Harry's nose wrinkled. "Smell that? Heavy, spicy…like perfume."

Sara inhaled. "Not really, but Mom liked to freshen the air with scent, especially if she knew the family's preferences. It's not unusual."

"Strange choice for an air freshener. I think I've smelled this before…more like men's aftershave."

She marveled he could detect such a faint fragrance. "You have a good nose, Harry. Does it come with the job of being a detective?"

His mouth quirked upward. "More like it comes with the territory of being an epicure. Although with my beer, I'm much more pedestrian."

The fact he'd caught it was a grim reminder they were in a crime scene. Sara gazed around the kitchen and wished they could leave. Right now. She couldn't help but feel the ghost of violence remained here.

His gaze sharpened. "Stay here. I want to check out the basement."

Lingering in the kitchen, she studied the flyers on the counter. Then she remembered something she'd seen in the trash that she'd dismissed.

Harry trudged up the stairs. "Nothing. No smell of cologne."

"These flyers." She pointed to the stack. "When I was going through the trash in the garage, I saw a cardboard box from a printing company. Could it mean anything? Mom wouldn't have tossed the box for the flyers once she finished mailing them. She always orders extras and would have stored them in the box."

"Which means someone else, maybe her attacker, threw it away and there could be fingerprints. I'll call Springfield, ask them to dust the box and everything else in the trash for prints."

She pulled out her cell phone. "One more thing I remembered. If she was in someone else's house, Mom would never open the door to anyone, even someone she knew, without warning. She made a rule they had to call her first on her cell phone. She didn't care if it was the company president."

"Whoever attacked her called her first." Harry pulled out a notebook and scribbled something. "I can pull the phone records for Regina's cell and find out. Good job, Sara."

Not that she'd done anything spectacular.

"You ready to leave here?" he asked. "I have to go to the Springfield PD to let them know what we found, but after, I thought we could stop at the hospital."

Her breath hitched and her heart beat faster. "To see Mom?"

As he nodded, she threw her arms around his neck and hugged him tight. "Yes, please, thank you!"

Harry patted her back. "As long as I'm with you, it's okay. But I don't want you making any trips back there without me."

His gaze turned hard. "Whoever did this is upping their game and they may target you next. I want you to promise me you'll go to work, go straight home and if you need to go out, call someone to go with you."

Her joy faded a little. "You're really worried someone might come after me?"

"They've already attacked your mother, for what reason, I don't know. Regina is still under suspicion, Sara." He framed her face with his warm hands. "I want to make sure you're safe."

So protective and concerned. Sara understood his reasons. It didn't make it easier. She was accustomed to freedom and living her life as she pleased. But she knew he was right.

"I promise."

He kissed her palms, one by one. "Good. Let's go see your mother. Then after, we'll stop by a hardware store. I need to copy your front door key."

Sara's heart fluttered. "Why, Detective Cartwright, do you plan to take liberties with me?"

Harry's mouth twitched briefly. "Not right now. Later, perhaps. Will you be at work all day tomorrow?"

"Yes, why?"

"I plan to try to break into your apartment. I'm not convinced that building is secure. After I'm finished, I'll stop by your place after I have dinner at my sister's, and we'll get the locks changed if they don't meet my satisfaction."

Sara felt another flutter, mixed in with rising indignation. Pushy much? "That's extreme, Harry."

"These are extreme circumstances, Sara. You're under my protection now and I do everything I can to make sure those under my protection are safe." His jaw tightened. "I'm not going to fail like I did last time."

Anger faded as she realized the implication of his declaration. Last time, meaning when his wife and child died. "Okay, we'll make you a copy of my keys. I'll do it because I get it. I do, Harry. But I'm not someone you can wrap up in a cocoon, shielding me from the world. I won't live like that. I cherish my life and my privacy."

Then because she had begun to care, and wanted to start a real relationship with him, she added, "I like you, Harry. A lot. I want to see if we can be more than friends. So if you plan to swaddle me in cotton wool and put me away in a box like a gemstone, know this. It won't work out so we might as well stop before we take any kind of romantic leap."

She took a breath. "Into anything, including intimacy."

Harry's eyes darkened as if he liked the idea of being intimate with her. He took the key and stared at it a moment. Nodded. "I know. Give me a chance, Sara. If I know you're safe, I can relax a little. Right now things are moving too fast with us, and too slow and complex with this case. I need to control…something…not you, but knowing you're safe will let me sleep at night. I'm not the domineering type who wants to keep you on a leash. If I think the locks are secure, I'll meet you at your place tomorrow night and return the keys."

He gave her a long, lingering look that had her heart doing backflips. Oh yes, the chemistry between them grew more intense. "I need to level with you, Sara. I don't consider us the cop and the former suspect, or even friends. I'm starting to care, Sara, and it's scary for me to do that with another woman. Let me do this one thing to make sure you're okay in your own home. Just trust me, okay?"

Sara bit her lip. "Okay. Will you at least let me know when you plan to enter my apartment and let me know when you leave?"

His mouth twitched. "Of course. I plan to call you and keep you on the phone the whole time."

That made her feel better. It wasn't as if he planned to sneak inside and comb through her belongings. "Good.

Stay away from my bedroom, though. Mornings get hectic and I seldom have a chance to tidy up the way I wish."

"Of course." Then his voice deepened and he got that intent look in his eyes once more. "I don't plan on entering your bedroom until I'm asked, and then I have no plans to leave right away. I'm the kind of guy who likes to take his time in bed, Sara."

There it was, the sexual gauntlet thrown down. She felt another flutter much lower, signaling she was up to the challenge. She smiled slowly, and licked her lips, knowing he tracked the move. "Good. I like things that…last all night long."

For a moment they regarded each other, and then he tucked the key away and turned brisk and professional once more. "Thank you for trusting me on this. Let's go see your mom. Maybe, by some miracle, she'll have awakened."

As they drove away from the house she couldn't imagine who Regina would have allowed inside the house. Whoever it was, it was someone her mother trusted. Someone who might turn out to be the same person who killed Axel.

And wanted Regina dead as well.

To his relief the next day, Sara's locks not only seemed secure, but he had a good feeling about her staying here. Her nosy neighbor, Mrs. Pendleton, had peeked outside her door when he walked toward Sara's apartment and threw all kinds of questions at him. Nosy neighbors were almost as good as security systems.

Unfortunately, he didn't have the same luck with the phone records to Regina Sandoval's cell or the box with the flyers. The box held no viable prints. Frustration filled him as he drove that afternoon to Carin Pederson's house to meet with her son Erik.

Whoever had called Regina Sandoval had done so from

a cheap prepaid phone that had no records. It made her attack even more planned, and whoever had done it had meant to deliberately harm her. Even tracking the pings the phone had made had been fruitless. Regina's attacker had called her a mile or so from the satellite office her company planned to open.

Carin Pederson lived in a stately mansion in an upscale Chicago suburb. Although Erik had a condo in the city, Harry had found out Carin's son spent more time living with his mother. The condo's ownership was in question as well, since Erik had mortgaged it to the point where he had no equity in the property.

Harry had talked with Nash Colton, who admitted his father was tightly wound and even angrier than usual. It gave Harry another reason to question Axel's twin further.

But the man was hard to find. Every time he tried to pin him down for an interview, Erik either wasn't answering his phone or blew him off.

It was only when Harry left him a message that he could either answer questions at home or at the police station in handcuffs, that he was able to nail down a time.

Erik was staying at his mother's house in Overland Park. The mansion looked like a relic from the 1800s, majestic and stately once. Now it appeared dowdy and neglected, with dirt covering the antique windows like cataracts. Harry rang the doorbell. At least it worked.

A domestic worker in a uniform grayer than the front windows answered. She escorted him into a parlor and left. Harry stood by the fireplace, gazing around. He suspected the room was in better shape than most of the house. But after dealing a few times with Carin Pederson, he knew impressions were important to her.

To his surprise, Carin entered the room. In a cream Chanel suit and cream pumps, she looked impeccable and stylish, but the severe expression on her tight face spoiled the effect. No wonder Sara hadn't wanted to reveal her true identity to her grandmother. He wouldn't want that, either.

"I understand you're here to torment my only surviving son. Isn't it enough you police have put us through misery by failing to do your job and find out who killed Axel?"

Diplomacy was never his strong suit, but he needed it now. Harry summoned all his tact and thought of her tremendous loss. She had a right to demand justice.

"I'm truly sorry about your loss. Let me reassure you, we are working around the clock to solve the case and bring your son's killer to justice."

Carin sniffed. "If you worked as hard as you say you are doing, you'd have found the killer by now. I heard you're the lead detective and yet there are reports of you wasting time with Sara Sandoval when you should have locked her up already. She was a suspect, was she not?"

His temper slipped a notch, but Harry managed to keep a polite smile in place. "I wouldn't call it wasting time, ma'am. Miss Sandoval has been cleared as a suspect and she's been instrumental in aiding the investigation, especially since her mother was found attacked and left for dead. We believe whoever attacked her mother is the same person who killed your son. It's why I need to question Erik."

If Carin grew pale at the news he could not tell. The woman wore too much makeup.

"Talk to my son, but I warn you, Detective. I have considerable influence and power in this city with elected officials. If you and your Keystone Cops keep making the kind of amateur mistakes you have made, there will be consequences."

"Of course." He struggled to keep his temper in place. "I must speak with Erik. Or did he slip out from your leash again?"

Now the woman flushed red beneath her cosmetics. "Watch yourself, Detective."

You watch it, lady. Keystone Cops? "Is Erik here? The sooner I can talk with him, the sooner I can leave."

Her thin lips pursed. "Very well. I will send him downstairs."

She waved a hand. "You can let yourself out when you're finished."

Harry watched her walk toward the back of the house. Sara wasn't exaggerating when she claimed her grandmother could be icy. His blood warmed as he thought of Sara. He missed talking with her.

Erik finally trudged down the stairs and entered the parlor, looking like a sullen child instead of a fifty-nine-year-old man. In his gray trousers, neatly starched white shirt and red tie, the man looked as if ready for a business meeting. Yet to his knowledge, Erik Colton had never owned a business in his life. Like his twin, Erik preferred to live off his trust fund.

"Detective. I apologize for ah, our domestic worker's, lack of courtesy. She should have known better. You should have been offered something to drink. Coffee? Tea? Please sit."

Not the domestic worker's fault. "I'll stand. Nothing to drink for now."

He started right away with questions about Erik's whereabouts the night of Regina's attack and if Erik ever talked recently with Regina Sandoval. Erik had an alibi, albeit a weak one. He was home with his mother.

"If we're finished here…" Erik started to rise.

"Not quite. I'll take that cup of coffee now."

Erik yelled for the domestic worker, who scurried into the room.

"Coffee, please. Two sugars, no cream. And a mug if

you have it, not those little china cups that barely hold a mouthful of liquid," Harry told her.

She returned with a steaming mug of coffee. Harry looked at the inscription.

WORLD'S GREATEST TWIN.

Accepting it with thanks, Harry sipped. The domestic worker left.

"Interesting cup. Seems customized mugs run in your family. Did you know one reading WORLD'S GREATEST DAD was found in Axel's kitchen after he died?"

Erik grew red-faced. "What does that have to do with anything?"

"That same coffee cup was found in Axel's kitchen with Sara Sandoval's prints all over it. As if someone were trying to set her up, planting evidence she was in Axel's house the day of the murder."

"Maybe she was. Talk to her, not me."

Erik ran a finger under his collar. Good. He was sweating. Harry planned to coax a little more perspiration from him.

"Tell me about Axel and his relationship with Regina Sandoval. When was the last time your brother saw her?"

"That slut?" Erik scoffed and brushed at his trousers. "We were glad he finally got rid of her. She was a menace, always demanding money and Axel's time. It was her fault Vita divorced my brother."

Blame the victim. Classic psychological trait. Harry locked gazes with him and switched tactics.

"Do you have any association with a man named Eddie Angelo?"

Now Erik looked away. "Never heard of the man."

"No? What about his brother, Dennis Angelo? Their sister, Mary Martin?"

Erik's gaze shifted left and he squirmed a little. "Who are these people and why are you asking me about them?"

"Leave the questions to me. You've never met a Mary Martin? She used to be a domestic worker for Farrah and Alfred Colton. Your half brother Alfred."

Erik sighed. "Why would I know her? Perhaps I've heard her name before, but that would be because my children or another relative mentioned her."

Right. *And you don't even remember to call your own domestic worker by her name.* Servants were below recognition to a person like Erik Colton.

"Did you love your brother?"

Erik blinked several times, glanced away, adjusted the hem of his trousers. "Of course."

Slow on answering. Interesting.

"You were twins. I'm sure he talked with you. Was there anyone Axel worried about, anyone threatening him?"

"There may have been. People were jealous of us and our money."

Like I'm jealous of a television detective. Such a fantasy. "Did you and your brother have a good relationship with your father? Did Dean ever gift you or Axel with family heirlooms?"

Erik looked away again. "He set up our trust funds."

Evasion.

"A trust fund is one thing. But what about personal items that your father may have wanted to give you that belonged to the family? Items that you could pass on to your own children, such as a silver platter that belonged to his mother? More sentimental than valuable."

A short laugh. "I'm not a sentimental man, Detective. Neither was Axel."

"Your father never gave you anything that belonged to him?"

"Never and I don't see where this is going. Are we finished?" Erik snapped.

Raw nerves were a good sign. "Maybe Dean gave personal items to Axel."

Erik sniffed. "My brother and I shared many things, but we were not alike. Axel craved recognition from our father and his heritage. He had started to distance himself from the family."

"Meaning you and your mother?"

A shrug. "Everyone. He talked as if he wanted revenge, although for what, I don't know. It was typical of Axel to create drama where there was none."

Harry consulted his notes, while keeping one eye on Erik. "You're certain you were nowhere near Springfield that day? Never contacted Regina Sandoval about your brother's death or anything else?"

No makeup on Erik's face, so it was easy enough to detect the flush. Rage? Or guilt?

Erik stood. "I think we are done, Detective. If you want to know anything about Regina Sandoval, ask her illegitimate daughter, not me. But I understand you've already been seen around town with her."

Slapping a lid on his temper and the urge to punch Erik Colton in his face, Harry followed him out of the room. As Erik opened the door for him, a gust of wind blew past the man. Harry caught a whiff of the man's aftershave.

He stiffened.

Damn if that wasn't the same, or close to it, cologne he'd smelled at the house where Regina Sandoval had been attacked.

Harry turned, looked him straight in the eye. "Know this, Colton. You and your mother may think we're dragging our heels on this case, but I'm damn good at my job and I always find the bad guys. Always. I've solved every case I've had. With or without help from families as obstinate and unpleasant as yours."

As Colton started to sputter, Harry smiled slowly. "Nice aftershave. I just came from a crime scene where I smelled the exact same scent. Odd, isn't it?"

Colton slammed the door behind him, but not before Harry caught the unmistakable look on his face.

The man was scared. He knew he'd slipped up.

You couldn't convict someone based on a fragrance. But he knew he was getting close, much closer, to finding answers. Even if he hadn't killed his brother, Erik Colton was looking more likely for another crime.

Attacking Regina Sandoval and leaving her for dead.

The weather had turned unexpectedly warm for Chicago in December, and the sudden change had many people enjoying the outdoors. At work, Sara took advantage of the warmth and strolled on the grounds of the nursery during her lunch break.

She'd found it hard to remain cooped up. She hadn't gone for a run in days. Every day when she returned home after work, the walls of her apartment seemed to close in around her, suffocating and squeezing.

Sara had promised Harry to never go out alone. She always kept her promises.

At least tonight she could open her windows and let in fresh air. Then she remembered Harry's stern warning about someone trying to break inside and sighed. He would come over tonight anyway to return her key.

The thought made her lady parts tingle in anticipation. Maybe they would make a night of it. All night long.

She trudged up the stairs and started past Mrs. Pendleton's apartment when the elderly lady opened the door.

"Sara! Wait."

Turning, she saw her elderly neighbor marching toward her with a plate in her gloved hands.

"I finally got my baking done. Here, dear. Let me put it inside for you. It's still hot, so be careful."

After unlocking the front door, Sara let Mrs. Pendleton inside. Her neighbor placed the pie on the counter.

"Enjoy, dear, and thank you again for getting groceries for me." Mrs. Pendleton beamed at her and glanced around the kitchen. "It's so warm in here. Why don't you open a window? Or better yet, go for a nice walk? I would if these old bones could handle the stairs better."

"Good idea. Thank you." Sara escorted her neighbor to the door.

Mrs. Pendleton turned, her rheumy blue gaze unreadable. "I really would get some fresh air, Sara. I know you're new to Chicago's winters. Days like this are meant to be enjoyed outside."

She thanked her again and closed the door behind her neighbor. Sara opened the living room window a couple of inches, securing it with the sturdy lock Harry had given her. She didn't dare try it with the kitchen window because of the fire escape.

After eating her take-out salad, she pushed it aside. Her appetite wasn't terrific. Maybe it was the pie waiting for her. Sara inhaled the delicious scent of freshly baked apples. Pie was her one weakness and Mrs. Pendleton was thoughtful enough to indulge.

Now I'm really going to have to make up for these calories with an extra-long run.

She cut herself a healthy slice, heated it in the microwave and settled back on the sofa to watch her favorite cooking show.

Somehow it held little appeal tonight. Maybe it was the

pie. It tasted okay, not as good as she anticipated. That was life. Sometimes reality didn't live up to your anticipation.

Harry had. He'd held her attention from the moment she'd seen him gazing down at her with concern after she'd fainted from the news of Axel's death. The man had deep layers she had only begun to peel back.

She finished the pie and grabbed her phone, checking the hospital for a status update on Regina. Still no change.

She texted Lila, asking about lunch tomorrow. Lila was busy with her art gallery and a new show starting soon. Sighing, Sara clicked on an app to read a book.

Soon, her eyes started to close. She blinked, tried to focus. No use. Odd. The novel had fascinated her earlier in the week when she'd downloaded it to her phone.

Something smelled odd, too. Was that gas? Had she accidentally left the oven on?

As she tossed aside her phone and stood to race into the kitchen to check, she swayed. The room spun as if she were on a fast-moving carousel.

This was crazy. Another fainting spell? Sara turned and saw her phone on the sofa as if from a long distance away. She stumbled toward it. *Have to call Harry. Something's wrong.* Her vision blurred.

Grabbing the table for support, she knocked over the lamp. Her vision grew gray and she could no longer stand.

As she collapsed to the floor, her last thought was calling Harry for help. But her phone seemed so far away.

So very far…

Chapter 14

The pounding kept up a steady rhythm outside. It had turned warm and the neighbors decided to take up the garage renovations they'd abandoned in the cold weather.

Lifting the curtain with the back of one hand, Harry peered out the dining room window. Seemed like everyone was out enjoying the weather. He dropped the curtain, musing over things.

Once he and Marie had a house like this. He'd sold it after she died and opted for an anonymous apartment in the city, closer to the station. But sometimes it was nice to visit suburbia again.

"Harry, dinner's ready," a voice sang out.

He headed into the dining room, where his brother-in-law and eight-year-old niece were already seated. Offers of help with meal preparation had been politely refused. Linda said he deserved to be pampered for a change.

He sat next to Amelia, who beamed. "Uncle Harry! I learned to skate today all by myself! I didn't even fall!"

She gave him a beseeching look. "Do you remember your promise?"

Laughing, he took a dollar from his wallet and gave it to her. "Here you go. I remember. One dollar when you learn to skate. But remember, falling is part of learning. You only need to make sure to get back up again."

Such a sweetheart. Glad as he was to have family in the city, sometimes he didn't visit enough.

Or make the time. Tonight, Linda and Elliott insisted he join them because they had news to share.

Certainly he had no news to share. Talking about a murder investigation was hardly dinner talk, even if Amelia wasn't present. Very few times did he discuss active cases with his family. Elliott still asked questions, which Harry dodged, but Linda never did.

When you grew up with your father as a cop, you learned what subjects were off-limits at the dinner table.

He dug into Linda's excellent roast as he listened to them talk about Amelia's school, and how they canceled the annual ski trip to Colorado in February. The last caught his attention.

"Why aren't you going?" he asked his sister. "All okay?"

"Better than okay." Elliott beamed. "We didn't want to risk it."

"I'm pregnant." Linda squeezed her husband's hand. "We wanted to tell you in person."

Harry squelched the hollowing feeling in his chest. Another baby. He was thrilled for them, but it was yet another reminder of his personal loss.

This was their joy and he would never spoil it. He stood and gave his sister a quick, affectionate peck on the cheek. "Congrats."

Then he hugged her. Linda and Elliott had been trying for another baby for years.

Elliott glanced at his wife. "We talked it over and we hope it's a boy and if it is, we want to name him John, after my father. We hope that's okay with you."

The excellent roast turned sour in his stomach. "Of course. It's a good name."

Simply because his own son had been named John didn't mean he couldn't tolerate a nephew with the same name. At least that is what he told himself. The pain he felt deep inside would go away eventually, certainly after Linda gave birth.

"Congratulations again."

He asked basic questions about the baby and their plans, listened as they held an animated discussion. Yet for all their joy, and Amelia's excitement about having a little brother or sister to boss around, something inside him twisted with disquiet.

What was wrong with him that his only sister's news had him feeling uneasy? Was he that much of a jerk?

As Elliott and Amelia helped Linda clear the table, insisting he relax and enjoy himself, the feeling grew more intense. Harry frowned and walked to the window again. In the past he'd followed his gut and it served him well. He stared at the neighbors pounding hammers on the garage extension. Such a nice evening out. The kind where people in the city would get out for fresh air...

Sara.

Groaning, he turned from the window. That was it. Not his sadness over his own child's death. It had to do with Sara.

He knew Sara liked to go for long runs and this weather might prove too tempting for her. Even though she'd promised him she would remain inside her apartment. Time to check up on her, letting her know he would be over soon.

Fishing out his cell phone, he called her number. No answer.

Harry tried again, left a voice mail, and then hung up. He tapped the phone against his open palm.

Something was terribly wrong. Sara always answered her phone.

On impulse, he called the dispatch in Evanston to see if anyone reported an emergency in her area. No one had. But an elderly woman with a shaky voice had reported she might have smelled gas in the hallway of her apartment building.

Harry's blood went cold when the dispatcher gave him the address. Sara's apartment building.

"Get uniforms over there, ASAP," he told the dispatcher.

Harry went into the kitchen and kissed Linda's cheek. "I have to run."

Linda turned from the sink. "But we haven't had dessert yet! I made strawberry shortcake, your favorite!"

"I'm sorry. Rain check. I have to check on something— otherwise, I'd stay." Then because he loved his sister and her family and didn't want them worrying, he added, "A friend isn't answering her phone."

"Her?" Elliott's eyes lit up. "Are you dating again?"

"Which friend and why haven't you told us about her?" Linda demanded.

"Uncle Harry, are you shagging with someone?"

All three adults turned and stared at Amelia.

"What did you say?" her father demanded.

Amelia turned beet red. "Uh, uh…"

"Young lady, where did you hear that word?" Linda demanded.

"From that show you watched." Amelia twisted her hands together. "It means getting together, right?"

Harry laughed and swept up his niece in a bear hug. "In a way, sweetheart. She's a friend I'm hoping will turn into more than a friend." He kissed her and grinned at Linda. "And you wanted another one. Good luck. I have to run."

Worry filled him as he put on his flashers and raced to Sara's apartment. Still not answering her phone. Could be she decided to silence it to read or take a snooze. Anything was possible.

But that call from Sara's building…

Outside Sara's building, a patrol unit had just pulled up. Harry used the key she'd given him and yanked open the door as he and the two officers ran inside. Heart racing, Harry took the steps two at a time. She had to be okay, she'd open the door and laugh, making an excuse about taking a bath and not having her phone close by.

Her door was locked. Harry pounded on it. "Sara? Sara!"

"I smell gas," one officer said.

Harry unlocked the door with shaky hands. Bursting inside, he whipped his gaze around, searching, calling her name. Then he came to an abrupt halt as he spotted a body on the living room floor.

Sara. His nose wrinkled as he smelled the distinct odor. Damn it.

"Get all the windows open," he yelled. "And be careful, this place can blow any minute."

Harry lifted Sara into his arms and raced out into the hallway. Gently he laid her on the hallway carpet. Not breathing.

He began CPR and chest compressions. *C'mon Sara, breathe, c'mon sweetheart, breathe…*

Someone in the apartment building down the hallway

opened their door. "Is everything all right?" an elderly woman called out in a quavering voice.

"Gas leak! The whole building could go up! Get out of here!"

Ignoring her gasp, he focused on CPR. Sara's lips seemed so cold against his...when they had been warm and filled with life only hours ago. She had to live. He wasn't going to lose anyone else. Not on his watch.

After a minute she woke up, coughing. Harry's relief was short-lived as he realized the gas was still leaking. The officers were going door to door now, getting the tenants to leave.

He called 9-1-1 on his cell phone.

"I have a female victim, possible poisoning caused by gas leak." He rattled off the address. "Evacuate the building, source of the gas leak not identified. Advise caution."

No time for conversation as Sara kept coughing, and looked dazed. He stood, threw her over his shoulder in a fireman's hold and ran down the stairs. Another patrol vehicle pulled up as he carried her outside into the fresh air.

He set Sara down carefully on the sidewalk. "It's okay, sweetheart, you're going to be all right now. Breathe deep."

Harry looked at one officer and identified himself. "Watch her, I have to go back and secure the scene. Two officers are inside, helping to evacuate the building. There's still a gas leak and this whole place could blow."

The officer crouched by Sara, called for an ambulance on his shoulder mike. "What happened?"

Rage filled him, pure and hot. He fought it. Emotions did no good in a crisis. "Someone tried to kill her."

Two hours later, the building had been totally evacuated and public works gave the all clear for people to return to their apartments. From the hallway, Harry watched a forensics team at work determining the source of the leak. Much as he longed to be at the hospital with Sara, his work was here.

The ER doctor had confirmed high levels of doxylamine, an over-the-counter sleep aid, had been found in Sara's blood. Sara was resting comfortably and they planned to admit her.

He'd called Vita Yates and asked her to stay with Sara at the hospital, briefly explaining what happened. A patrol officer would also stand guard in case the suspect tried to return to kill Sara.

Anything could happen. Whoever did this was clever and determined.

The valves on Sara's stove had all been turned on. If not for the window Sara had cracked open, she might be dead.

He couldn't think about that. Had to focus on the investigation. Why did someone want to kill Sara? Was it the same person who'd injured Regina Sandoval?

Maybe even the same person who had killed Axel Colton?

He knew the threads were starting to come together to form patterns, but a clear pattern wasn't discernable yet. Harry walked into the kitchen. Though the gas smell had dissipated, he scented something else—a faint but discernable strong smell. Like men's cologne. He frowned. Damn if that wasn't the same smell he'd detected in the house where Regina Sandoval had been attacked.

"Detective Cartwright?"

A crime scene tech marched into the hallway, bearing a plate in her gloved hands. "We found this in the kitchen sink…looks like it could be the remains of dessert the victim ate. We found a pie in the refrigerator with a slice cut out."

Harry's stomach tightened as he sniffed the plate. "Apple, maybe. Inform me after you get the forensics on it."

Then he remembered Sara talking about her neighbor who liked to bake pie. An elderly woman…the same one who'd poked her head out into the hallway when he frantically tried to breathe life into Sara?

He marched down the hallway, knocking on doors until a tenant told him in Apartment 302, Emma Pendleton lived alone. Sara had sometimes shopped for the elderly widow.

No answer at Apartment 302. Harry went outside and checked with the patrol officers.

Everyone had returned inside to their apartments. No one recalled seeing an elderly woman from the third floor. "Where's the building superintendent?" he asked.

To his dismay, he discovered there was no building super. The man had been laid off four months ago. Rumor had it the building's owner was in financial straits. Tenants with maintenance issues had been complaining to the attorney who collected the rent, but nothing had been done. Some had withheld rent until the problems were fixed. They were forming a group and had pooled their money to hire a lawyer to fight for them to pressure the landlord into fixing the building's problems.

He called Sean on his cell phone, instructed him to find out who the building owner was. Harry hung up, glanced around at the patrol officers.

"I need to get into Apartment 302. The woman who lives inside may have information connected to this case."

Upstairs, they pounded and pounded on the door. No answer. Harry didn't want to frighten an elderly woman, but his gut warned this wasn't an ordinary tenant. Not with the remains of an apple pie in the sink and Sara found unconscious after eating it.

He looked at the patrol officer pounding on the door. "Break it."

The officer kicked open the door. Harry entered first,

his sidearm drawn. In his experience, innocent-looking civilians could brandish weapons.

The officers checked every room. "All clear," one called out.

Harry replaced his gun and looked around. The apartment seemed innocuous if not poorly furnished. He snapped on a pair of gloves given to him by a crime scene technician.

"Detective!" an officer called out.

He went into the bedroom. The officer pointed to the closet and a battered, scratched chest of drawers.

"Clothing is missing. Looks like someone packed and left in a hurry. Probably when the building was being evacuated. Good time to slip away without being noticed." The officer shook his head.

Returning to the kitchen, Harry opened drawers and cabinets. He didn't have to look far. Mrs. Pendleton had several apples in the refrigerator and containers of nutmeg and cinnamon discarded in the trash. Both containers were full and still had price tags.

In the trash, he found an empty bottle of sleeping tablets and bagged it, telling an officer to give it to the crime scene technicians down the hall. Harry scowled as he snapped off the gloves and issued instructions to a nearby officer.

"Tell the techs to sweep this apartment. I have to go to the hospital. Put a BOLO out for Emma Pendleton. If I'm not mistaken, she's our prime suspect in trying to kill Sara Sandoval."

Her head pounded like someone had nailed iron spikes into her skull. Pressure squeezed her right arm and a beeping sounded. Sara winced at the bright lights over her head. She could hear something outside, noise, voices droning. Something was in her nose… Sara moved an arm and felt tubing protruding from her nose. She wanted to close her eyes and go back to sleep, but someone kept urging her to stay awake.

"Sara, how are you feeling?"

That voice…it seemed familiar. She tried to focus, and realized Vita Yates leaned over her.

"My head aches." She put a hand to her throat. "Thirsty."

Vita gave her a cup of water. "The doctor said you can have this. Small sips."

Gratefully she drank it and handed it back. Her thoughts cleared slightly as she realized the tubing in her nose was an oxygen cannula. Her right arm felt pressure from the cuff attached to it, taking her blood pressure automatically every few minutes.

"Where am I? What happened?" Her voice sounded shaky and raspy.

Vita placed the cup on a bedside table. "You're in the hospital. Detective Cartwright found you in your apartment passed out. The gas from the stove was on. If he hadn't found you…"

Vita stopped talking and wiped a tear. "Oh, Sara, why would anyone hurt you?"

Harry saved her. Suddenly more than anything, she needed to see him.

"There's a police officer outside your room. He told me to get him when you're awake." Vita squeezed her hand. "I'll be right back. Don't go to sleep again. They want to question you."

Despite Vita's warning, she couldn't help closing her eyes. And then she heard a deep, gruff voice that instantly made her eyes fly open in abject relief.

"Harry," she whispered, her left hand reaching out for him.

Vita wiped her eyes again. "I think I'll search for a decent cup of coffee, and leave you alone."

Harry sat at her side, took her hand into his as Vita left the room. "Sara."

His voice sounded shaky and it made her wonder exactly how bad she was.

"Am I going to die?" she whispered.

A slight laugh and a head shake. "Not if I have anything to do with it. No, you're going to be fine, but they want to keep you overnight to make sure you're okay."

She fingered the cannula. "This…it feels odd."

"Leave it." A gentle squeeze of her fingers. "Honey, I need to ask you what happened and then you can rest. What do you remember before passing out? What was the dessert you had? Who gave it to you? Mrs. Pendleton?"

Sara tried to gather her scattered thoughts. "Yes…she baked an apple pie for me. I had some salad for dinner and I ate the pie and then started reading a book. I got up…" She frowned, pressing fingers to her temples. "Got dizzy. It was odd, because it felt like I was going to pass out again, like I did when I found out Axel was dead. But this was different. It was…"

"Foggy?" Harry leaned close. "As if you needed to sleep and couldn't stay awake?"

She nodded. "Exactly. I tried to find my phone, but it seemed so far away."

He swore softly. "The doc found sleeping pills in your blood. Lab confirmed the scrapings from the dessert plate contained apple pie with a high amount of sedatives. There's a warrant out now for Emma Pendleton's arrest."

If her head was foggy before, it was clear now. Sara struggled to sit up. Harry helped adjust her.

"Mrs. Pendleton? My nice neighbor lady? Impossible. She wouldn't hurt a fly…"

"No, but she sure as hell planned to hurt you." Harry's jaw clenched and he took a deep breath, his grip on her hand tightening. "She knocked you out with sleeping pills and then turned on the gas in your apartment so you'd suffocate. If you hadn't opened the living room window, you'd be…"

His voice trailed off and looked away. She understood. *You'd be dead.*

Suddenly despite the oxygen pumping into her lungs, the room seemed to compress around her and it was hard to breathe. Her blood chilled. Emma Pendleton tried to kill her.

The nice neighbor who had little money and baked pies. Sara's stomach roiled. The pie, the pie with the funny taste to it…

"It makes no sense," she rasped. "She never had a problem with me. Why?"

"We'll find out why when we get her into custody, and we *will* find her. She fled the scene when the building was evacuated and all the residents were in the streets in case your apartment blew up from the gas being on."

He glanced toward the hallway. "I've asked for an officer to remain outside your room at all times in case she returns. Vita was kind enough to stay with you until I could arrive."

Needing an anchor, Sara gripped his hand. Calm, capable Harry. He'd saved her. Amid the aching pounding in her head flashed a warning hard to comprehend…

Mrs. Pendleton tried to kill me. She hates me that much she wants me dead.

"How long do I have to stay here? When can I go home?" She feared the answer. After knowing she wasn't safe in her own apartment, Sara wasn't certain she wanted to return anytime soon.

Harry ran a finger down her chilled cheek. "They're keeping you overnight as a precaution. I promise, you're safe now. Sara, can you think of any reason why Emma Pendleton would want to hurt you?"

Air seemed to suck out of her lungs. Sara took a deep breath, glad for the fresh oxygen flowing into her body. "No. I mean, we weren't close. I did favors for her because I felt sorry for her. She had little money and offered to bake pies for me when I refused money for buying her groceries. I never took money from her. Maybe she was insulted?"

It was all too bizarre and terrifying to think someone she trusted, and helped, turned out to be that cold and calculating.

His hand felt warm against her face as he cradled her cheek. "Sweetheart, I don't know. What about friends visiting her? Relatives? She has a daughter named Amy DeLucca who lives in South Carolina. Married to a Mario DeLucca, has three children under the age of fifteen. Did Amy or her family ever visit her?"

Police must have already found out about Mrs. Pendleton's relatives and searched her apartment for evidence. Sara tried to focus. "She mentioned her daughter once, and said they were not close. She seemed sad when she talked about Amy, so I never questioned her again. I don't remember any friends visiting her, either, but it wasn't as if I spent much time with her. I bought her groceries when I could. Is this important? I never met any of her friends. Why would she want me dead?"

Sara fell back against the pillows, suddenly exhausted again. Harry cupped her cheek, his blue-green gaze filled with tender concern. "I'll find out. I promise I'll get answers."

Harry's phone dinged a text and he scrolled through it. Rest seemed impossible, but she felt exhausted. Sara gave a longing glance at his cell phone.

"Can someone go to my apartment and bring my cell phone?" she asked.

He withdrew a phone from his jacket pocket. "Here. The crime scene techs had to go over it, but they cleared it for me to bring to you."

Shuddering, she looked at her phone, realizing her apartment, in fact, her life had become a crime scene. Her mother also lay in a hospital bed, only Regina wasn't conscious. It was too much. She fought the tears welling up.

"I need to check on Mom."

With the edge of his thumb, Harry wiped a stray tear trickling down her cheek. He handed her a box of tissues, silently took her cell phone and dialed. Despite her distress, she felt a surge of wonder. He understood. Harry knew she was too upset to call the Springfield hospital and check for herself.

By the time she restored her composure, he'd hung up. "No real change, but the charge nurse said Regina is showing promising signs of waking up. She's had more bouts of consciousness. That's a good sign, honey."

The distant look came over him again. Sara recognized it. He was deep in thought.

"Sara, you've lived in that apartment most of the year. You're from out of town... How did you find that place? Were you searching for a low-cost rental?"

She nodded, her thoughts muzzy again. Sara pressed her fingers against her pounding temple. "I wasn't sure how long I'd stay in Chicago, so I needed a place with either a month-to-month or a six-month lease term. Maybe even a sublet. Rents are so expensive. I was ready to move further away from the city when Lila told me about the apartment. She knew I was searching."

His gaze sharpened. "Lila used to live here?"

"No, she said she'd heard of this place and they offered

month-to-month rentals with a low security deposit. Lowest I found. In fact, the real estate agent I worked with told me the landlord agreed to split the security deposit into five payments I could pay each month with the rent."

"Generous landlord." He frowned. "Maybe too generous."

His phone pinged again. Harry's brow furrowed as he read the text. He stood, kissed her cheek.

"I have to go, Sara. Get some rest. I'll return when I can."

Sara's eyes closed as he left the room. So tired, so very tired. Yet for a few minutes she could not sleep. The image of Emma Pendleton's careworn face kept floating before her.

The woman who wanted her dead had almost succeeded. But why did such a nice elderly neighbor wish to kill her?

Someone tried to kill Sara.

There had to be a nexus between Emma Pendleton and Axel Colton's murder. Regina Sandoval had been assaulted and left for dead and then Sara was targeted. The threads connecting all of these incidents seemed stronger, but he couldn't pinpoint a motive.

At his desk in the police station, Harry sifted through Colton's file. He must have missed something. Regina had not had contact with her ex-lover in years. She hid Sara's existence from him. Had Pendleton known Regina or even Colton? Nothing in Colton's background or in the intel they pulled on Pendleton indicated anything.

Detectives had already been in touch with Amy De-Lucca. The woman insisted she had not heard from her mother in more than a year, not since she and her family had moved from Chicago to South Carolina. They had a fight when Emma refused to enter an assisted-living center close to Amy's home and insisted on staying in Chicago.

Eyes weary from strain, he sat back, drumming his fingers on the desktop. The green banker's lamp on his desk provided a warm glow, but the words in the file provided no answers. Out in the squad room, the major case squad detectives worked overtime, taking leads, trying to track down Emma Pendleton. Pendleton had tried to kill someone close to Harry, and his team didn't take that lightly.

They would work tirelessly until they closed this.

A knock sounded on the open door of his office. Harry glanced up to see Sean, bleary-eyed and wearing rumpled clothing. The guy looked as tired and sleep-deprived as Harry felt. "What are you doing here? You have kids. Go home."

"Not until we find Pendleton." Sean dropped a file on his desk and then plopped into a chair. "The daughter's insisting her mother isn't a killer."

He snorted. "They all insist that, even after the relative confesses."

"It doesn't make sense. Nice old lady tries to kill the woman down the hallway, the one woman who runs errands for her and cares for her." Sean ran a hand over his face and yawned. "Can't make the connection. Even the neighbors were stunned."

"What about the landlord?"

Sean pointed to the file. "It's all there. Not much. Building's owned by a shell company. Ajax Real Estate, LLC. We have a guy researching it now, but there's no clear paper trail. Landlord is listed as an attorney. They're questioning him now, but he just collects the rent and deposits it into the holdings of Ajax Real Estate."

"Did you talk with Lila about why she recommended that apartment to Sara?"

"Briefly. She honestly doesn't remember, just heard it around that they had cheap rents. Maybe one of her clients."

Harry's tired brain pinged a sharp thought. He sat up. "Maybe we're looking in the wrong place. The rents in the building are all inexpensive…building is old, somewhat run-down. I'm going back to the hospital to check on Sara. I want to know how and why she ended up in that place. Check on Emma Pendleton's background. Go back, way back."

"Her marriage record? Already checked. Her husband, Mark, died of a stroke two years ago."

"Before that. I want birth records, school records, medical records. There's a connection here we're missing. If she skinned her knees as a kid, I want to know it. She's our prime suspect right now and until we find and question her, I need to know everything about her. I also want to know if there's a connection between this shell landlord and Pendleton. Tie that damn attorney up until he barks out how much rent Pendleton paid. Or if she was late with the rent."

Sean nodded and left. Harry's phone rang. Sara. He was relieved to hear her voice sounded stronger.

"When can they spring me, Harry? I'm bored and can't rest. They keep checking my pulse to make sure I'm alive."

Harry grinned. "By tomorrow you'll be released."

Someone rapped at his window and he glanced up. "Gotta run. If you're bored, watch the Food Network. Think of some new way I can get indigestion."

A breathy laugh and a whispered "Thank you for saving me."

Too emotional for words, he grunted a response and thumbed off his phone.

His gut kept telling him there was a connection that would tie all the threads neatly together. They just had to find it. In the meantime, Sara remained in danger. But he'd be damned if anyone tried to kill her again.

I'm not losing her, not like I lost Marie and John. Never again. Not on my watch.

Chapter 15

Afer a restless night, Sara was ready to leave the hospital. The doctor had released her late the next morning, under strict orders not to drive for at least a full day. But instead of Vita arriving to drive her home, Harry showed up in her room.

"My personal escort?" Sara smiled up at him as she sat in the wheelchair the medical aide pulled up to the bedside.

"You're staying with me." Harry picked up the bag with her personal items. "Sorry sweetheart, you are not going back to that place. Not until Emma Pendleton is found. I brought your coat and a hat. It's cold out again. So much for our warm spell."

Her heart fluttered with excitement at the idea, though she dreaded knowing she couldn't go home. It felt horrible to think of what happened in the one place she should feel safe.

"Much as I love the idea of spending time with you,

Harry, I need to get to my stuff. All my things are back in my apartment."

"I have everything you need. Toothbrush, you name it. Let's go."

He drove his department-issued sedan, moving carefully through traffic. Sara wanted to throw questions at him, but she was emotionally spent. He glanced at her as he pulled up before his apartment building.

"You okay? You're awfully quiet."

"Tired. Worn-out." She studied her hands. "Did you get any answers yet, Harry?"

"We're working around the clock. Got a lead on Emma Pendleton that Sean's checking out now. Soon as I get you settled upstairs, I have to return to the station."

His apartment was neat and tidy, with modern furnishings, and far larger than hers. The sofa was butter-soft tucked leather, and there was a glass coffee table and a wide-screen television on an entertainment center. He even had a separate dining room with an antique wood table and six chairs. In the corner of the living room, an easel held a half-finished painting of a snow-covered landscape.

"This is quite good," she told him, admiring the painting. "Pretty."

"Look at the left corner."

When she did, she saw a small splotch of red lying on the snowy field. "Is that a body?"

He grinned. "I told you my job interferes with my art. Case I solved not long ago. Good way to get it out of my system."

Harry set down her suitcase in the bedroom. "You can stay in here. Take a nap if you wish to rest." He gazed around. "I changed the sheets and there's fresh towels. If you want to shower, let me know—I don't want you to do it without me."

Images of them naked and wet sucked her breath away. "That sounds amazing. I'd love it. But don't you have to return to work?"

Sara felt her cheeks pink. Then he grinned and touched her face.

"Much as I'd love to shower with you, I meant I need to be here in case you feel dizzy again. Don't want you passing out."

A faint ping of disappointment. "Of course. I could use a hot shower."

He jerked a hand at the bathroom. "Help yourself. I'm going to make us lunch."

After she showered and dressed in the yoga pants and the oversize Chicago PD sweatshirt he'd left for her, Sara joined him in the kitchen. Harry set a plate before her.

"Homemade beef stew. Thought you'd like a hot meal."

She sat at the table, inhaling the scent. "A man who cooks and lets me use all his hot water. What more could I want?"

After lunch, Harry washed up and left for the station. Sara wandered around for a few minutes, but his king-size bed looked too tempting. Sara lay down on the quilt and fell fast asleep.

She woke up to the sound of the front door opening and closing. For a moment she felt disoriented. It was dark outside and she was famished. Then she inhaled and smelled Harry's cologne, distinct and spicy. She was no longer in the hospital, nor at her apartment, but his place.

Harry came into the bedroom, flipped on the light. Sara winced.

"Just woke up, huh? How did you sleep?" he asked.

"It was wonderful." Sara yawned. "Thank you. Just what I needed."

She sat up and hugged her knees. "What's new? Did they find Emma Pendleton? Please tell me they did."

Funny how she never knew she could fear an elderly woman so much. But there was little doubt the woman tried to kill her.

"She's in police custody. They're bringing her in from South Carolina." He tugged off his tie, dropping it on a nearby chair. "You're safe now, Sara."

Sara knew she should feel relieved, but felt only empty. Sad. Her elderly neighbor would spend the rest of her short life behind prison bars. Everything seemed topsy-turvy.

"Hold me," she whispered. "I feel like my world is collapsing."

Immediately she was in his arms, snuggled against him. Here she felt utterly safe. Harry was a rock, her anchor.

For a moment she rested there, and then her stomach gave a loud grumble. Harry laughed and kissed her head. "I think my lady needs food. I'm neglecting my host duties. How about some dinner after I shower and change?"

In the kitchen, she watched him bustle around in jeans and an old CPD police shirt. The delicious smells of stir-fry made her mouth water.

They ate at his dining room table. She sipped her wine as he told her how he'd found a place to live.

"After Marie and John died, I sold the house and moved here. Buddy of mine gave me a break on the rent. It's not far from the station, and there's a terrific gym for working out and an indoor pool, plus the view can't be beat."

Sara sighed and sipped the excellent vintage he'd poured. "My apartment is a box compared to your palace. But it's cheap. I never planned to live there as long as I have. I needed a place that was closer to work, and wouldn't break my budget."

After dinner, she helped him load the dishwasher. Harry wiped his hands on a towel and grabbed a roll of duct tape from a drawer. "I need to show you something."

She followed him into the bedroom, watching as he removed a white terry-cloth bathrobe from the closet. "Sit on the bed."

Curious, she did as he requested.

He took the belt of his terry-cloth robe, set it aside. "Hold out your wrists. I'm going to tie you up."

She tilted her head. "Kinky, aren't we?"

Winking at her, he turned serious. "Later, maybe. For now, I want to show you how to get out of restraints if something ever happens to you. You need to know how to protect yourself, Sara. I don't want anything happening to you."

A little worried, she watched him tear off a piece of duct tape from the roll and hold it up.

"Duct tape is usually what many criminals use because it's easy to buy without suspicion. If you're conscious while someone is binding you, lean forward. Make fists with your hands and bring your arms together so you can break the tape easier. It's not impossible to break duct tape."

He instructed her to raise her arms over her head. "Now bring them down and make sure your elbows go all the way down."

She tried. No luck. But on the fourth try, she did it. Sara beamed. Harry gave an approving nod and gently removed the rest of the tape. Then mischief flashed in his blue-green gaze. "Shall we try tying you up with the belt now?"

She licked her lips, a different hunger rising. "I have something better in mind."

When he joined her on the bed, she wrapped her arms around him and kissed him deeply.

Sara opened her mouth beneath his, drawing him deeper

into the kiss. When they parted for air, both breathing heavily, she watched his gaze darken.

"You sure about this?"

Sara kissed him again. "As long as you have protection, and I don't mean your gun, Harry, I'm absolutely sure."

It was as if she'd opened floodgates. They shed their clothing, tearing it off each other in their eagerness to get naked. Her breath caught. Harry was rock-hard all over, solid muscle over his flat abdomen, his biceps. Her breath caught again as she spied pockmarks in his shoulder and stomach. They were deeper and more puckered than the recent scar on his arm. Sara touched them.

"Bullet." He shrugged as if it were nothing, as if everyone had bullet scars. "Got careless during a pursuit."

Shivering at the thought of him lying on cold pavement, bleeding, maybe dying, she slid her arms over his chest. "Stop being careless."

Muscles jumped beneath her touch as she touched him, then he shuddered as she kissed his neck, tasting the salt of his skin.

Heat smoldered in his gaze. She wasn't innocent, but Sara knew this was different. Sex was sex. This was far deeper, and lasting. She felt it with her whole heart.

Naked, she shivered as he touched her in turn. Sara arched as Harry thumbed her cresting nipples. When he bent his head and took one into his mouth, she clung to him, everything inside her spinning with sheer desire. He swirled his tongue over the taut peak, then suckled her. She was growing hotter now, a fire stoking inside her as the sweet tension braced her body.

They fell onto the bed, as he kept kissing her breasts. She whimpered, her hips rising and falling, driven by instincts of her own.

Gathering her close, Harry kissed her deeply, his hand

drifting over her belly, down farther. She made a startled sound, which he soothed with his kisses, as he slid a finger across her wet cleft.

Sara gripped his wide shoulders as he began playing with her. Slowly he began to pleasure her. It was consuming. Sara strained toward him as he teased and stroked, his hands sure and skillful. The ache between her legs intensified and she pumped her hips upward. Every stroke and whorl sucked air from her lungs until she gasped for breath, ready to burst out of her skin. Tension heightened, spiraling her upward and upward. And then the feeling between her legs exploded. Sara screamed, crying out his name as she dug her nails into his wide shoulders.

Her eyes fluttered as she fell back to the bed, spent and dazed. She watched him open the nightstand drawer, reach for a condom. Spent from orgasm, she saw the puzzled expression on his face.

"Damn. It's been a while. Not sure I remember how to put this on. Help me?"

The teasing look in his eyes made her laugh. Sara helped him roll on the condom, then they kissed once more.

Nudging his hips between her legs, he braced himself on his hands.

"Sara," he murmured, his gaze dark and burning. "You're so damn beautiful. So sexy."

Harry laced his fingers through hers. Slowly he pushed into her. He pulled back, and began to stroke inside her. His muscles contracted as he thrust, powerful shoulders flexing and back arching.

Sara drew him close as they moved together. The delicious friction was wonderful, the closeness of his body to hers, his tangy scent filling her nostrils. She pumped her hips, as he taught her the rhythm, feeling the silky slide of the hair on his legs. He began to move faster, his gaze holding hers.

Emotions crowded her chest as she gripped his hard shoulders. It felt as if he locked her spirit in his.

His thrusts became more urgent. Close, so close...she writhed and reached for it, the tension growing until she felt ready to explode.

Screaming his name, she came again, squeezing him tightly as she arched nearly off the bed. He threw his head back with a hoarse shout. Collapsing atop her, he pillowed his head next to hers.

They fell asleep in each other's arms. Twice more in the night Harry made love to her again. It wasn't sex. Sara knew it with every fiber of her being. It was deeper and richer.

She had never felt anything like this before, and knew no matter what, Harry had nestled deep into her heart and wouldn't leave.

Sara could only hope he felt the same way.

Harry couldn't believe it. Felt as if every cell in his body responded when they made love. Sex was sex, but this was something more. Lasting. Even with his wife, much as he loved her, it hadn't been this electrifying.

And that made him feel vulnerable in a way he hadn't since Marie died. Sara wasn't the one-night-stand type. She was the marrying type. But he couldn't think about that. For now, he wanted to hold her close, and watch her as dawn slowly crept over the sky.

Sara roused, her long black hair silky to his touch as he tunneled his fingers through the strands. He loved looking at her like this, languorous and sultry, a small smile playing on her mouth.

His own smile died as he remembered how he could

have lost her. Harry felt all the night's pleasure evaporate at the memory of that visceral pain. Seeing her so pale and still on the floor, his emotions raging with fear and pain…

Like seeing Marie at the medical examiner's office when the doc had lifted the sheet. For the first time, he became one of those grieving people like the ones he'd had to tell many times in his role as a homicide detective… *I'm so sorry for your loss.*

I can't put myself through that again.

Being numb and indifferent to life had pulled him through one day after another. He learned to present a facade to the world that fooled several. But with Sara, it was different. She'd peeled him back like an onion, and got to what he furiously guarded for more than two years.

His heart.

Sara raised herself up on one elbow. Harry watched her, his heart beating fast once more. She looked so sexy with her long hair curtaining her face, her big eyes studying him with such tenderness.

With a jolt he realized she was not basking in the afterglow, but had something on her mind. He steeled himself.

"Harry, there's something I need to say. Something in my heart." She bent her head and plucked at the sheet. "After losing Axel before I had the chance to get to know him, I resolved to never again waste time."

"Go on," he said, knowing what was on her mind.

"I love you, Harry. I know we haven't known each other long, but I'm pretty sure I love you."

Fire died in her eyes as he sighed. She swallowed hard.

"I guess this is a little premature." She laughed a little as if to cover her embarrassment.

He caught her arm. "No, it's not you." He cursed. "That sounds bad."

Harry sat up, took a deep breath. Damn, he hadn't

wanted to hurt her, and here he was, about to do that very thing.

"I can't say it, Sara. I don't even know if I'm capable anymore of saying it, to anyone." He looked directly at her. "I care for you, Sara, and I know you're feeling vulnerable now after what happened, but you deserve the truth."

"Harry, what are you telling me?"

His body tensed as he forced the words out. "All my love died that day with Marie and John."

She put a hand on his arm. "I understand, Harry. I do. But life goes on and there are better days ahead. You have to have hope that you can love again."

"Maybe." He shook his head. "I don't think so. Not now, and maybe not ever. You deserve the truth, Sara. You're a wonderful, caring woman. If you're expecting me to fall in love with you, it's not going to happen."

Sara clutched the sheet to her breasts. Then he watched as the light dimmed in her brilliant green eyes. He knew, and cursed what he'd said.

But she deserved the truth.

Her voice remained steady. "Have they cleared my apartment as a crime scene?"

When he nodded, she inhaled. "Good. I'm going home."

Sara slid out from between the sheets and reached for her clothing. Harry reached for her. "Sara, don't do this."

Dismay filled him when he realized tears shone in her eyes. Tears he had put there. No one else.

"Don't do what, Harry? Don't go home? Don't stop seeing you?" She laughed, but there was no humor in the sound. "It's best we end this now, before it really begins."

He rubbed a hand over his tensed jaw. "Emma Pendleton may not have worked alone. It may not be safe to return to your place."

What a stupid-ass excuse to get her to stay. Sara was smarter than that. He knew it and she knew it.

She shrugged into her shirt and then buttoned it. "You say you're a great cop, Harry. I'm sure you'll find out what you need from Mrs. Pendleton. Goodbye and thank you for everything."

"Sara, please. I don't feel right about you going back there. Wait, let me get dressed at least and I'll take you…"

"Fine."

Sara left the bedroom and went into the living room. Never had he dressed in such a hurry. He was pulling on his jeans when he heard the front door quietly click shut.

Damn it.

By the time he reached the street she was gone. Frantic, he kept calling her phone. No answer.

Half an hour later, his phone pinged with a curt text. I'm home. Safe. Good luck with the case, Harry.

Harry closed his eyes, not sure who he hated most at that moment. The dirtbag who'd wiped away all his hopes and dreams when he'd killed Marie and John.

Or himself, for letting Sara walk away.

Chapter 16

Work became everything for Harry after Sara walked out on him. He focused on the case. Always the job. The job was there for him, would always be there for him as a salve for wounds that never healed.

Emma Pendleton was due to arrive this morning at the station. She had purchased a one-way bus ticket to Myrtle Beach, South Carolina. Police halted the bus before it reached its destination.

He'd wanted everything on Widow Pendleton and finally got it. Two yearbooks, one high school and one from middle school, sat on his desk, along with piles of papers.

Harry began leafing through the middle school book. On impulse, he called Sara. Still not answering his calls. He left a voice mail.

Suddenly his phone dinged, indicating a text. He glanced at it. Harry, I understand. I do. I do care about you, more than I should, so please don't call me anymore because it hurts too much. I'll find out from Sean and January what happened with the case.

He pocketed his phone, ignoring the tightness in his chest.

It was important to be thorough in an investigation. Much as he itched to interrogate Pendleton, Harry knew sometimes suspects wouldn't talk and had to be cracked. Holding something over them, a piece of evidence that could connect them, helped to make a suspect break down.

When two uniformed officers finally brought Pendleton into an interrogation room, he closed the yearbook. Harry left his office, went to the room and stared at her through the one-way glass.

"Let's do this," he muttered to Sean.

Sean would stay with him, in case Harry lost control. Surely he wanted to throttle the woman for trying to kill Sara.

They sat at the table across from Pendleton. Harry's heart pounded and his rage simmered on low. Sean glanced at him. He nodded.

"What happened, Emma?" Sean's voice was soft and reassuring. "We found traces of sleeping pills in the remnants of the pie you baked for Sara. Why did you do it?"

The woman burst into sobs. Unsympathetic, he watched Sean slide a box of tissues over to Pendleton.

"I didn't want to," she wailed.

"Sara was your friend."

Pendleton nodded and wiped her eyes.

Enough of good cop. Harry leaned forward, locked his gaze to Pendleton's. "You wanted to kill her. Sara, the person who bought you groceries and looked after you. You tried to kill her with the same damn apples she bought you. Admit it."

"No, never, I didn't…"

"You baked the pie. We found a container of sleeping pills in the trash, Emma. Your prints were all over it. The DA is going to send you away for a long time. Forget the assisted-living center in Myrtle Beach. You'll spend the rest of your days in a cold prison cell."

"No, please. I had no choice! She made me do it!"

"Who?" Sean asked. "Who put you up to this?"

The elderly lady shook her head. "She said I didn't have to pay rent if I kept an eye on Sara. I didn't want to do it. But if I didn't, she would kick me out and I'd be on the streets. She even threatened to hurt me at one point."

"Who?" Harry practically shouted the question.

Pendleton shook her head. "She'll kill me if I tell. She has money, the means to do it. I'm just an old, penniless lady."

The rheumy blue eyes darted around the room. "I tried to protect Sara."

"Protect her?" Harry had to fist his hands beneath the table in his rage.

"The plan was for me to mix an entire bottle of sleeping pills into the pie so she could slip into Sara's apartment. I didn't know she would turn on the gas! But she mentioned something about how I should leave right after I gave Sara the pie because something bad might happen in the building. It might blow up. And then she laughed, and it was an awful laugh. Evil."

The woman took a deep breath. "I tried to warn Sara. I told her to open her windows, it was so nice out, maybe take a walk. And then, then I called 9-1-1. I got a taxi to the bus station. I'm sorry! Sara was so good to me! I didn't want to hurt her!"

Harry forced himself to calm down. Yelling would accomplish nothing. "I'm sure you didn't want to harm her. It must have been hard on you, knowing you had to do something you didn't want to do. This person sounds terrible. Was it an acquaintance?"

"We were friends once." Pendleton wrung the used tissue in her hands. "Good friends in high school. Best friends. We did everything together, shopped, dated. She once gave me a pair of her expensive nylons when I had a date and money was tight."

"A good friend who asked for a favor?" Sean asked. "Tell us about this friend."

"I hadn't seen her in a long time, and then she sent a sympathy card after my Mark died. We started exchanging letters and I told her I was down on my luck."

Now they were getting someplace.

"Who is this friend?" Harry demanded.

"I want a lawyer," the woman said in a quavering voice.

Sean exchanged glances with him. Harry rubbed a hand over his face. "All right."

Damn. She had to clam up just as they were getting someplace. Now all they could do was wait.

Sara couldn't believe it when Vita called her with surprising news. Her grandmother Carin wanted to meet with her.

"I hope it's okay that I gave her your number, Sara. She said she knows who you are and wants to get to know you better. She sounded pretty upset, and nice, for a change." Vita sighed. "Maybe losing Axel has made her aware of what's really important."

Telling Vita it was fine, she hung up. Sara couldn't believe it. After all these years, thinking she had no family interested in her, her grandmother had not only acknowledged her existence, but wanted to meet with her.

Carin's voice had sounded quavering with emotion when she called Sara minutes later. "I want to take you to my late son's house, my dear. Your father's house. There are a few things of his you should have."

She'd told her grandmother the doctors prohibited her from driving for another day. Carin told her she would come and drive her to Naperville.

"I want to get to know you better, Sara," Carin had said.

Pacing the living room, she kept glancing out the window. A real grandmother at last! Maybe Carin wasn't the warm and fuzzy type, but they surely could find something in common. The fact Carin acknowledged her and wanted to know her better fired her with excitement and anticipation.

Her phone buzzed. Harry.

I can't do this. Not now.

Sighing, she turned down the volume on her phone, and then pocketed it in her trousers. Carin might be old-fashioned and frown upon cell phone interruptions. Sara wanted to make a good impression.

Smoothing down her cranberry sweater, she ran to the door and flung it open.

Carin Pederson was short, elegant and rail-thin, wearing a Chanel coat, leather gloves and a felt hat. She smiled at Sara. "Sara, what a pleasure to meet you."

Resisting the urge to hug her, Sara smiled back. "Welcome, Carin. Please come inside."

Her grandmother entered, but did not remove her coat. She shivered. "May I have a cup of tea. It's rather chilly in here."

"I'm sorry, I forgot my manners. I was so excited to see you. We can go into the kitchen."

Her grandmother frowned. "I'd rather take tea in the living room, thank you."

It must be an etiquette thing.

"Please, sit on the sofa. The tea will be ready soon."

She bustled around the kitchen, heating up the water on the gas stove, and set sugar and milk in a little creamer on the living room table. Not much sugar, but hopefully Carin wouldn't mind.

Sara set the teacups on the living room table. Her nose wrinkled. Her grandmother, like some elderly women, wore too much perfume. It was rich and spicy, almost like men's cologne.

Carin shivered again. "My, it's cold out."

As Sara started to sit, Carin sighed. "I hate to bother you, but could I have some more sugar, dear?"

Sara returned to the kitchen, calling over her shoulder. "You can take off your coat and gloves. I'll turn the heat up."

When she returned with the sugar packets, her grandmother smiled at her. "Thank you, my dear. When you get old, like me, you get easily chilled."

Her grandmother sipped the tea. "Delicious. Please. I hate to drink alone."

Sara took a sip of tea. It did need sugar. She added a teaspoon and sipped again. It still tasted odd…

Suddenly all her instincts surged like a red flare on a dark road. She'd tasted this aftertaste before…the apple pie.

"Excuse me. Need to use the ladies." Sara barely got the words out.

She sped to the bathroom. Inside, she fumbled for her cell phone, dialed 9-1-1. Everything started spinning. Her legs felt like cooked noodles. She slid to the floor by the bathtub.

"Nine-one-one, what's your emergency?" the dispatcher droned.

The bathroom door banged open. Instead of Carin, her uncle Erik stood at the threshold.

"Hurry." The phone tumbled from her fingers to the

floor. This couldn't be happening. It was a nightmare and she'd soon wake up.

Erik crossed the room, picked it up. Carin entered, shaking her finger.

"For shame, Sara. Such bad manners, leaving me to make a phone call." Carin pointed to the phone. "Erik, dispose of that dreadful thing. I hate those phones. So disruptive."

Too weak to fight him off, she watched, her vision growing blurry as Erik took her cell phone and pitched it into the wastebasket.

"Let's go, Mom. I'll take her," he told Carin.

"Please, don't…" Sara struggled to form the words. "Please."

As Carin turned and left the room, Erik fished the phone from the trash. He met her gaze, put a finger to his lips, then slipped the phone into his pocket. Her eyes closed.

She felt him hoist her upward and drag her out of the bathroom.

Hurry, Harry. Please hurry.

Back in his office, Harry began searching the ancient high school yearbook a detective found. He flipped through it. Class of 1957. Coiffed hair on the girls, short buzz cuts on the guys… He worked his way backward from the W's and found Emma's photo. Nothing popped out. Nothing familiar…

Then suddenly he spotted a familiar name close to Emma's. His blood froze.

"Son of a…" Harry slammed the book shut and returned to the room, rapping on the glass.

Sean came outside.

"Anything?" he asked.

"Not yet. Old lady still insists on a lawyer. We're finding her a court-appointed attorney now."

They had no choice. Had to wait. Harry put an officer in the room with Pendleton and returned to his office. Sean followed. Harry pointed to the yearbook and the photo he'd found.

Sean's eyes widened. He swore under his breath.

He called Sara. Still not answering her phone, or not answering his calls.

Sean jerked a thumb at his office door. Harry looked up and studied the thin, young-looking attorney with a briefcase in hand. Kid couldn't have been more than twenty-five. Wet behind the ears.

"I'm Jonathan Casey, Mrs. Pendleton's court-appointed attorney."

Ignoring the outstretched hand, Harry jerked his head toward the hallway. "Let's go."

He gave the kid two minutes to consult with Pendleton and then went into the room. Sean accompanied him. This time, Sean did not smile. Neither of them did.

But they had to find the nexus to weave the final thread from Pendleton to this case.

"I've advised my client not to answer any questions," Casey squeaked.

Harry focused on Pendleton. "We know who your high school friend is. If you confess everything, we can arrange a deal with the district attorney. We'll do everything we can. You may get off with time served."

Harry gave her his most intent stare, ignoring the sputterings of the kid. He watched as Emma Pendleton's shoulders sagged and she stared at the table. He could almost feel sorry for her.

Almost.

"Tell us, Emma," he said in his softest, most persuasive

voice. "Tell us about the friend who wanted you to do bad things to Sara."

The woman cracked.

"My daughter wanted to move me into a nursing home! So she let me move into the apartment building for free. It was a tiny studio on the first floor, but I had to stay in Chicago. I'm too old to start over and my dear Mark is buried here in the city. Then she asked me to switch apartments to one on the third floor down the hall from Sara. She even paid the movers to take my furniture there. It was a one-bedroom, much bigger than the first-floor apartment, with a real kitchen, not a kitchenette. All I had to do was keep an eye on Sara, and report back to her."

"Carin Pederson." Harry sat back, satisfied. "Sara's grandmother. Why? Because she loved her granddaughter? Or wanted to hurt her?"

Pendleton shook her head. "She said something terrible had happened and it was all Sara and Regina's fault."

Harry's heart skipped a beat. "Terrible as in something terrible Carin did?"

The woman began crying again. "Last time I saw her, Carin said it was an accident. She didn't mean it. If Sara had never come to Chicago, it never would have happened."

All the threads suddenly wove together in a neat, organized tapestry showing the real picture. Pendleton's lawyer patted her shoulder.

"I have more questions," he said tightly.

Casey sniffed. "My client refuses to answer any more questions."

Oh yeah. We'll see about that. He went to Pendleton and leaned close. "Carin tried to kill her own granddaughter."

Emma blinked. "I, I don't know!"

"Tell me! Tell me unless you want to spend the rest of your days locked up in a cold jail cell!"

The woman broke down, holding up a hand as her lawyer protested. "She said she had to do it! Sara had to pay with her life. I tried to warn Sara…"

Harry forced his voice to remain level. "If she tried again, same method, where would she do it? You know this woman, Emma. You were friends. You know what kind of stockings she wears, for God's sake. Where? Her house?"

Emma wiped away a tear. "No. She said she wished she could blow up Axel's house. She hates that house in Naperville…where the accident happened. She wished she could destroy all evidence it ever existed."

His blood ran cold. Harry jerked his head at Sean and they left the room. "Ping Sara's cell phone. We have to find her. She's in danger."

He tried Sara's phone again. No answer. Suddenly his phone dinged an incoming text…from Sara. Yet it wasn't Sara texting him.

Carin has Sara. Axel's house.

Cursing a blue streak, he checked his gun, grabbed his Kevlar vest.

When he returned to the squad room, Sean was cradling the phone to his ear. "Sara's phone pinged off a tower in the vicinity of Naperville."

Axel Colton's house.

"Call Naperville, get backup at Axel Colton's house now. Tell them to approach sirens off. This may turn into a hostage situation."

His vehicle fishtailed as he sped out of the parking lot. Harry prayed he wouldn't be too late.

Sara's grandmother had her. Axel Colton's killer, who now wanted to kill her granddaughter as well.

Chapter 17

He grandmother wanted her dead. Sara blinked as she struggled to wake up. The surface beneath her was hard and cold. She touched it with her fingers. Tile. Her mouth was dry. She licked her lips, tried to fight welling panic.

Slowly her vision cleared. Sara struggled to sit up and realized her hands were tied in front. Something sticky. She tried moving her legs and they were also bound with duct tape.

Fear did little. She had to remain calm if she was going to get out of this.

Remembering what Harry taught her about being tied up, she started to test the tape. Sara tried to focus. Elegant surroundings. Luxurious…a large house. She was in a dining room, could see the kitchen from where she sat.

Smell something foul…gas.

She leaned against the wall as her grandmother entered the room. Carin sat in a chair before her, her careworn face creased into a frown. Sara steeled herself. She had to pit all her wits against this madwoman.

"Carin, why are you doing this? I never hurt you. Whatever it is, we can work it out."

Her grandmother avoided her gaze and stared at the window. "I've always hated this house. So modern, I told Axel. He never listened to my advice. Did you know he insisted on using natural gas for cooking and heating?"

"Carin, please, you don't want to do this…"

"By the time police arrive, the house will be demolished. I failed the last time. I failed with Jackson's kidnapping. I will not fail again."

Shock filled her. "You helped kidnap Jackson? Your own great-grandson?"

Carin sniffed. "He was never in any real danger. I only wanted the thirty million, but Donald, that stupid man I hired to kidnap Jackson, bungled everything. Fortunately he will never talk. I have connections."

The woman smiled and cold dread filled Sara as she realized Carin killed Donald Palicki, her accomplice in kidnapping Jackson.

"Now you're the last mess to clean up. Did you know if natural gas ignites in an explosion, it can do all kinds of damage? It can shatter windows and blow everything apart so that by the time the fire department arrives, little will be left."

"You're my grandmother," she whispered.

Carin finally met her gaze, her face screwed up in fury. "You were a mistake, Axel's mistake, and because of you and your mother, Axel is dead. He refused to listen to me! I told him to get rid of Regina. But he insisted he had wronged her and wanted to make up for everything he had done. I begged him not to. I told him he and his brother would inherit thirty million dollars, I had arranged it. Then he realized I forged the will. It was a fake. He was going to the police about Dean's will. I grew so angry… I picked up the candlestick with both hands and swung…"

Her voice trailed off. "I didn't mean to kill him."

Sara's heart broke. Carin killed her own son. There was no reasoning with her. The woman was insane. She had to stall for time.

"The police thought Dennis Angelo killed Axel."

Carin laughed. "Fools. Dennis was perfect. He was eager to plant the candlestick in Nash's trunk to frame Nash for Axel's death. I had to throw the police off the trail and give them a suspect. But it wasn't enough. I really wanted it all on your darling mother, that bitch. Dennis's brother, Eddie, agreed to work for me after I ran Dennis off the road. He wanted more money. Eddie is younger and more gullible. But he got greedy after he nearly broke into your apartment. He broke into another apartment and got caught. I had to get rid of him as well."

Carin smirked. "It is amazing what prisoners are willing to do for a little money, such as shank a man to death."

Her grandmother had tentacles everywhere, like an evil octopus. "You're insane."

Money can't buy you love, Sara thought wildly. Had Carin ever loved anyone? Even the son she had killed? She'd always harbored hope that her paternal grandmother would be sweet and motherly, like Mrs. Pendleton.

Even that illusion had been stripped away. Was there anyone she could trust?

Harry. He didn't love her, but he wanted to keep her safe.

Erik came into the dining room, saw her, stopped short. His nostrils flared. "Mom, what are you doing?"

"Shut up, Erik. Go start the car. I won't be long."

"Mom, you can't do this! You said you only wanted to scare Sara."

"I said go to the car. Now!"

Erik glanced at her, and turned around, heading for the door.

She was on her own. Had to keep her talking. "But you have money, lots of money. Why couldn't you simply pay him off?"

Carin's face grew red. "Pay him off? I have no money! I needed that inheritance from my sons! Dean owed it to me after all the years I put up with him."

Her grandmother stood, a roll of duct tape in her hand. She thought fast. "Wait! Before you do this, can I at least sit in a chair? This floor is hard and cold."

Carin laughed. "It won't be for long, but I suppose." She yanked Sara up, pushed her into the dining room chair she'd vacated. She tore off a piece of duct tape and slapped it over Sara's mouth. "Enough of this chatter. Accept your fate. You'll die in a blast and this house will be destroyed, as it should be."

Her heart in her throat, Sara watched Carin walk into the adjacent kitchen, twist knobs. Remembering what Harry taught her, Sara stood. Carin went into the basement, perhaps to tinker with the gas heater. Not much time. She raised her hands above her head, brought them down hard.

Nothing, except her arms hurt. She tried again, and again. But she felt too weak from the drugs Carin put into her tea.

The tape wasn't tight around her ankles. Enough room to shuffle slowly into the kitchen. Sara tried once more and succeeded in loosening the tape around her wrists. Not torn.

Frantic, she shuffled to the knives in the stand, and managed to pull one free with her teeth. Sara stuck it between the stove and the granite counter and began sawing at the tape.

Free!

Footsteps sounded on the stairs. The gas smelled terrible, gathering in the air. Sara sawed the tape at her ankles, cutting herself, ignoring the sharp sting. She pulled free.

The element of surprise was with her. Stabbing Carin was too risky. Her gaze wildly whipped around the kitchen. There. Hanging above the island were several pots and pans. Sara grabbed a brass frying pan.

The click clack of heels sounded on the kitchen tile. Close, closer...

Now!

Sara sprang up, screaming and rushing at Carin. Her grandmother made a choking sound, her arms pinwheeling as she tried to balance herself. Carin screeched and swung at Sara.

Sara swung back, the frying pan hitting Carin squarely on the head. Her grandmother moaned and collapsed.

She ran to the stove and began turning off burners when a hand grabbed her ankle. Enraged, she kicked free and then stepped on Carin's wrist. Bones snapped and her grandmother screamed and then moaned, clutching her arm.

The front door burst open and Harry rushed into the kitchen, gun drawn, along with what seemed like dozens of armed police.

"Don't shoot," Sara yelled. "The gas is on and this whole place could explode!"

"We had the gas company shut off the line after receiving a tip." Harry gestured to Carin, who was moaning that her wrist was broken. "Restrain her and take her to the hospital."

Shaking, Sara leaned against the counter, her breath coming in short gasps. All the adrenaline faded, leaving her drained and icy. Harry crossed the room, holstering his handgun.

His eyebrows rose as he picked up her weapon of choice. "You beaned her with a frying pan?"

"She went from the frying pan into the fire," Sara said weakly, her knees suddenly turning to jelly.

He placed it on the island. "Didn't I tell you to try out cast iron for serious cooking?"

Her mouth wobbled as Harry shrugged out of his jacket and placed it gently around her shoulders. "You okay, Sara?"

The nod turned into a head shake. "I'm fine," she managed to say and then burst into tears.

Harry pulled her against him tight. He whispered into her hair, his hands rubbing her back. "Damn, I was so scared we'd be too late. I'm an ass, Sara. I'm so sorry for hurting you. I can't believe I almost lost you."

All she could do was cling to him, feeling relief it was all over.

Chapter 18

Harry took her statement at the emergency room. He insisted on a doctor seeing her, which didn't take long. The cut on her ankle was superficial and she hadn't inhaled enough gas to affect her.

He escorted her to his sedan afterward, and then slid behind the wheel. Harry stared straight ahead.

"What happens to Carin now?" Sara huddled inside his jacket. It smelled like him, spicy and delicious.

"She'll be tried for murder, but the DA will probably work out something to send her to a psychiatric institution after she's released from the hospital. She's totally insane. Killing Axel sent her off the deep end." Harry glanced at her. "Erik helped her, but at the last minute had a bout of conscience. He used your phone to call 9-1-1 and told them about Carin's plan to blow up his brother's house. He's been arrested, but the DA will cut him a deal in return for his testimony against Carin."

Harry shook his head. "We can tie her to Jackson's kidnapping as well. We matched Carin's prints on the tranquilizer dart used to stun Myles Colton when he tried to pay the ransom."

It seemed too unbelievable still. Sara's stomach still roiled from everything.

Harry reached over, stroked her cheek with the back of his hand. "It's all over now, sweetheart. You're safe. She can't hurt you now."

Numb, she nodded. "So much for having a good relationship with my grandmother."

His intense gaze searched hers. "How about focusing on a relationship already established? Your mother is awake and wants to see you."

Sara's heart beat faster. "She's okay? I need to see her."

"I'm taking you there now. I need to officially interview her, and I thought you would want to come along." Harry flipped on the lights on his sedan and the siren.

Sara blinked. "Is that permitted?"

He winked at her. "Official police business. Buckle up. I'll get us to Springfield as fast as I can."

Harry was glad he was sitting and driving. His insides still shook at the idea of how close Sara had come to buying it. It had taken an attempted murder for him to wake the hell up and realize how much he truly cared about her.

How he'd fallen in love with a woman courageous enough to declare her love for him first.

He filled Sara in on the case as he drove to Springfield. Dean Colton had never realized the lives of his two sets of twin sons would end up entangled the way they did. Nor would the patriarch ever imagine his ex-lover, Carin, would forge a fake will to direct thirty million dollars to her illegitimate twin sons, Axel and Erik.

Erik had resented his father's lack of involvement in his life and began asking Dean for favors. Mary Martin had been one of Erik's lovers, so he asked Dean to find her a job in Colton Connections. Instead, Dean had recommended Mary Miller to Alfred's wife, Farrah, after Farrah mentioned she needed a full-time live-in domestic worker.

Seeing he had an inside person at Alfred's house, Erik asked Mary to steal things from Alfred's house. He and Carin took glee in knowing they duped Alfred, Dean's legitimate son.

"The candlesticks and the silver platter were given to Erik and Axel by Dean, who felt guilty after Carin nagged him about wanting to give her twins personal items to remember their father by. Dean gave them a couple of heirlooms belonging to his side of the family. Erik wanted more. Axel did not. He did agree to store the candlesticks in his house, which unfortunately led to his demise. Axel had changed."

He glanced over, saw Sara stare out the window. "I suppose my uncle Erik had a change of heart when he saw his mother trying to kill me," she said.

"Not as much as Axel's change of heart." He turned on Bluetooth to stream blues music. Sara liked B.B. King. It would help to soothe her when he told her what she needed to hear next.

He made small talk about music for several minutes. When she requested a bathroom break, he pulled off I-55 at a rest stop, standing outside the women's room.

Emerging from the restroom, she frowned upon seeing him. "I don't need a bodyguard, Harry."

Here we go. Bare it all, Harry.

"Sara, you need to know something about me." Harry jammed his hands into his coat pockets. "I can be a callous SOB, even when I care. When I care about someone, I get overprotective. It doesn't mean I don't trust you. It means I don't trust myself. I know things ended badly with me, but I'd like to start over."

Sara smiled and kissed his cheek. "Can I trust you to get me a cup of coffee?"

Soon they were back in the car, but he made no attempt to pull out of the parking space. He turned on the music again.

"Sara, you need to know something and it may upset you."

She took a deep breath. "All right. Tell me."

"Six years ago your father hired a private detective to find Regina. Apparently your brother's death haunted him and he wanted to find her and apologize."

Harry's jaw clenched. "Erik told us his twin confided in him that Axel had gone to the funeral of a friend's little boy and all he could think about was the son he lost. Axel wasn't sure how to make contact with Regina again. When the detective found your mother, Axel discovered he had a daughter as well."

Blood drained from her face. "My father knew I existed?"

He gathered her trembling hands into his. "Knew you existed and not only that, wanted to keep tabs on you and your mother. He hired Dennis Angelo to get a job at Regina's office. When Dennis got fired, Erik suggested sending Eddie to do odd jobs for your mother at home."

She began to cry. "My father, the one man I always wanted to know, was spying on us. Why couldn't he have reached out instead?"

Harry gathered her into his arms and stroked her hair. "I don't know, sweetheart. Sometimes a man does things he regrets and needs time to work up the courage to make amends. Sometimes that never happens."

He handed her the box of tissues he'd brought, knowing this news would upset her. When she'd put herself to rights again, he got back on the interstate.

Sara folded and unfolded her hands. "Tell me about my mother's attacker. Was it Carin?"

"Yes. Using a fake name, Carin had called Regina's office weeks ago, pretending to be interested in insurance. They gave her Regina's cell number and Carin waited until she was alone, tracked her down to the house. Regina obviously didn't recognize her."

"Mom had recently gotten her license to sell insurance. She probably thought Carin was a potential client."

So much betrayal and so much heartache. Harry could only hope that Sara and her mother could start fresh.

And that he could be a part of Sara's life, if she wanted him.

Chapter 19

All she'd wanted was a real family to call her own, relatives to celebrate holidays and birthdays with, and a support system. Instead, she'd gained a grandmother who tried to kill her and a father who knew about her, but never sought her out.

Sara tried to sort through her feelings as they entered the hospital, but all she felt was foolish. She'd easily fallen into the spider's web her grandmother wove. Even her apartment was controlled by Carin. Sara had no idea Carin owned the building. Neither did Lila, who recommended it. Erik had confessed he placed the flyer in the employee break room, advertising the low-cost rental, at his mother's behest.

Harry didn't press her to talk. His big presence was comforting as her heart pounded harder as they came closer to her mother's hospital room.

The door was open. Regina sat in a chair by the window. Joy filled Sara as she ran over to embrace her.

Thoughtful Harry hung back as if he knew they needed time.

"Mom, you're going to be okay." Sara hugged her, her eyes swollen with tears. "I thought I'd lost you."

Regina hugged her back, and then glanced up. Her beautiful face was still covered with ugly bruises, but she seemed stronger. "Detective Cartwright. Thank you for saving Sara."

He glanced at Sara. "Your daughter saved herself, Mrs. Sandoval. She's a pretty smart woman. Smart enough to outfox a coldhearted killer."

Regina sighed. "I can't believe Carin did all this."

Harry pulled up a chair, beckoned for Sara to sit while he perched on the bed's edge and reached for his notebook. "I have a few questions. First, I need to know exactly how and why Carin got into the house to attack you."

It didn't take long. Regina clarified that she'd let Carin into the house to talk to her about Larkspur Insurance. Carin was an elderly lady and Regina thought nothing of letting a stranger inside until Carin mentioned admiring the house and wanted to see the basement. Carin pushed her down the stairs.

"Then Carin stole one of the envelopes you had used in order to mail that letter to you and place suspicion on you, Regina." Harry closed his notebook. "Carin was constantly nagging the police for updates. She wanted to frame the both of you for Axel's murder."

Sara clasped her mother's hand, unsure where to begin. "Mom, Axel knew where you were. He knew about me…" Her voice broke. "Axel was the one who sent Eddie Angelo to work for you when I was in college."

Harry nodded. "Sara, I don't know if he knew you were his daughter at that time, but he wanted to make sure you and your mother lived well."

He softened his tone as he addressed Regina. "Axel regretted Wyatt's death and driving you away, Regina. He may have been an irresponsible person in the past, but he did love you. But you heard that for yourself when you went to see him in Naperville, didn't you?"

Regina wiped her streaming eyes and then dabbed at them with a tissue Harry thoughtfully held out. "Right before he died, I met Axel at his house. He called me and told me he wanted to meet with me and promised if I didn't feel comfortable, I could cancel. I had canceled a couple of times previously and then realized for your sake, I needed to find out what he wanted. So I drove to his house…and told him all about you. He promised to make up for all the past pain he'd caused. He wanted to do the right thing. No matter what he had to do, he would do right by you to make up for lost time."

Too late. Axel wanted to know her. And he'd finally worked up the courage to meet her when he died.

Harry filled in the rest. Axel had infuriated Carin, especially when Carin discovered Axel was going to hire an attorney to legally dispute the new will Dean had left. He wanted nothing to do with Colton Connections or the thirty million dollars Carin claimed her children were due.

Regina bit her lip and stared out the hospital window. "Axel told me he was meeting with his mother later. He died later that night when Carin hit him over the head with the candlestick after they argued. I don't know how she can live with herself…to kill your own son."

Harry checked his cell phone. "I need to make a few calls. Sara, I'll be outside. Take all the time you need."

She talked with her mother for a while, telling Regina of her plans to remain in Chicago and continue working for Yates' Yards. The job offered challenges she never anticipated. Regina told her the doctor planned to release her in two days.

When she saw her mother getting tired, Sara called for a nurses' aide to help Regina back to bed. She promised to visit the next day and went into the hallway, where Harry waited.

"I want to remain here with Mom." Sara felt a flutter of hope in her chest. "Maybe you can stay with me and we can spend the night here."

He studied her, his hands warm against her face. "We'll find you a hotel and a rental car, sweetheart. I have to return to Chicago."

Sara felt a stab of disappointment. "Of course. You have to return and wrap all this up."

"Yes, and there's something else I have to do. Something I've needed to do for a long time." He kissed her, his mouth warm and firm against hers. "I'll call you when I'm through."

At the police station, the mood had shifted to relief and joy that the case had finally wrapped up. Harry was greeted with plenty of congratulations and spent time in the captain's office, going over details. When he emerged into the squad room, Sean had news to share.

He and January wanted to have a quick but large Christmas wedding to make up for their elopement earlier in the year. Harry promised to be there.

He hoped Sara would be his date. But he wouldn't ask her, not until he finally took care of personal business.

The trip to Naperville felt less bittersweet than it had previous times. Harry pulled into the long driveway of the Russo house and parked. He jingled his keys in one gloved hand and blew out a breath.

It was time. Long past time, but he was ready now.

A white-capped domestic worker answered the door when he rang the bell, and ushered him into the formal living room. She told him to have a seat and left.

How many times had he sat here before with Marie, stiff as wood, trying to make pleasantries with her father? Trying to assure him he'd take good care of his little girl.

When the Russos entered the room, Harry did not stand. Dominic sat on the sofa across from him, glaring, while Arlene sat beside her husband. Arlene, who had lost her only child and only grandson. He focused on her face, the careworn lines carved there by time and grief. Unlike Dominic, Arlene never blamed him for the loss.

It was for Arlene he did this.

"Well, what do you want?" Dominic snapped. "You asked us to be home because you had something to say to my wife and me about Marie and John. Are you ready to admit it was your fault they died?"

Harry looked at both of them. "It was my fault, in a way. If you want to blame someone for their deaths, blame me."

A soft snort of satisfaction from his ex-father-in-law. Harry continued holding their gazes. He had to remain strong, think of how Marie would encourage him. He could almost feel her at his side, whispering it was okay.

"I can't tell you how many times I wish I had died in that car wreck and they were still alive. I didn't, and nothing I can say or do will change the past. I can only change today and hopefully, make a difference in tomorrow. As hard as their deaths were on me personally, I can't imagine losing a daughter and a grandson."

Dominic started to speak, but Arlene put a hand on his arm. "Hush, Dominic. Let Harry talk."

He gathered all his courage. "I want to apologize to both of you for their deaths, if that makes you feel better. And I want you to know, as much as I loved them, still love them, and will always love them, I'm moving ahead with my life. I've met someone special. She'll never take Marie's place, but she's a good woman and I love her."

Dominic said nothing, but tears formed in Arlene's eyes. She wiped them away. "I'm happy for you, Harry. Marie wouldn't want you to pine for the past."

She glanced at her husband. "Nor would she want us to do the same. It's time for forgiveness."

To his surprise, the old man slowly nodded. "If that's what my wife wants, then so be it. I apologize for anything I've said to you, Harry."

A tremendous burden inside him eased at last.

He took the St. Jude medal and folded it into Arlene's trembling hand. "Here. Marie would want you to have this back. It is your family heirloom."

Arlene stared at the medal and nodded. She smiled through her tears. "Thank you, Harry."

"If there's ever anything I can do for you, let me know," he told her.

"Sometime, if you can, if you have time, I'd like to talk with you about Marie and John. The memories." Arlene wiped her eyes. "It helps me."

Harry smiled gently. "I have time now. And in the future. Take all the time you need."

Chapter 20

It had been a beautiful Christmas Eve wedding and dozens of Coltons attended. Vita and Rick generously opened their home as January and Sean formally said their vows, the twins peacefully napping through the ceremony.

At the end, there was a brief but poignant candlelit memorial for Alfred and Ernest Colton.

After January asked for her help, Sara planned everything, turning the gardens at the Yateses' into a Christmas dream, with potted poinsettias lining walkways and Christmas trees decorated with twinkling lights. Some guests chose to stroll the walkways, admiring the effect. Rick and Vita decorated the spare greenhouse with lights and garland, setting tables and chairs there for those who wished a quiet place to talk and get away from the crowd.

All the women wore red or green or gold, with the men in black tie. Sara wore a new red Dior dress, thanks to the contractual advance her former company had given her.

She'd agreed to consult for them in her spare time after the president of Caymen Reynolds personally assured her he'd fired Ernie for sexual harassment and misuse of company funds after a thorough investigation.

Sara couldn't believe how many Coltons had attended. The buffet reception was a blizzard of names and faces. She met Alfred's widow, Farrah, and many other Coltons. So many her head spun. Damon Colton, an agent for the Drug Enforcement Agency, brought his girlfriend, Ruby. Heath Colton, president of Colton Connections, quietly thanked Sara for the memorial service honoring his father and uncle. Heath's fiancée, Kylie, admired the gardens and told Sara what a beautiful job she'd done in decorating. Myles and Lila were there as well with their significant others.

Harry had agreed to be her date. He'd given her space and time, which she appreciated, but today, she needed him at her side. He helped her navigate through the various guests, always watchful and charming. After an hour of socializing and then eating the delicious food she'd selected, he pulled her aside to a quiet area in the living room.

"Sara, we need to talk." He drew in a breath. "About us."

In his silk tuxedo, the same one he'd worn at the lounge at the Four Seasons, Harry looked resplendent and intent. She smoothed down an imaginary wrinkle in her Dior dress, her stomach tight. They hadn't discussed their relationship or a future.

"Now? Can't it wait?"

"I don't want to wait." He kissed her hand. "I'd like to start over again with you, if you want. I want to make this work. Maybe we could actually have an actual, formal date?"

Joy filled her, and anticipation. "You're not afraid of starting a relationship with me?"

His mouth quirked. "I'd say we already have a relationship. Not exactly conventional, but I'd like to try. I'm a cop, Sara. I'll always be one. I'm damn good at my job. I can't promise there won't be times when the job comes first, but you'll always come first in my heart."

A shadow crossed his face. "I'm ready to try being in love again. I love you, Sara. I didn't realize how much until I thought I'd lose you forever to that stone-cold woman."

He glanced away. "I'll always love Marie and John. But I know Marie would want me to move on and learn to love again. If you're willing to try with me."

Emotion filled her. Sara could barely speak. She blinked hard, knowing how difficult it had been for Harry to reach this point. "Yes. I'm more than willing."

His mouth was warm and firm against hers. She kissed him hard, wishing they weren't surrounded by hundreds of people. Someone whistled and yelled, "Get a room, Harry!"

Her eyes flew open as he released her and mock scowled at Damon Colton. "Go get a room yourself, Colton."

Damon grinned and walked away with Ruby. Harry rested his forehead against Sara's. "So, want to go out with me?"

"I'd love it. But I get to pick the restaurant. No hot dogs."

"Deal. As long as we first get you a new place to live. There's an apartment opening close to mine. A little further of a drive for you, but…"

"It sounds wonderful. I can afford it now. Anything is better than staying at that building."

More people drifted into the living room. Vita headed in their direction, greeted them and then her warm smile dropped.

She lowered her voice. "May we go to the greenhouse? It's private there. I need to talk with you, Sara."

Vita glanced at Harry. "You should hear this as well, Detective."

"Please. It's Harry."

In the greenhouse where Sara once danced beneath the snowfall, Vita drew them over to a corner partly hidden by potted trees adorned with lights and a bistro table and two chairs.

"Sara, please sit."

She sat, Harry standing behind her, his presence reassuring. She wondered if after all this, Vita was going to ask her to leave. Silly idea, but perhaps the memories were too much.

Vita's mouth trembled. "I have something for you. I'm sorry I didn't give it to you sooner, but I felt it wasn't the right time. Now that all has been resolved, I realize it is the right time."

She handed her a white envelope with Sara's name on it. The handwriting was bold and masculine. Sara swallowed.

Vita nodded. "It's from Axel. The attorney handling his estate sent it right after Axel died, along with a note addressed to me with instructions to give it to you should something happen to him. I suppose I held off on giving it to you because I was afraid you'd be hurt."

Holding the letter, almost afraid to open it, she took a deep breath. "Wow. This is intense. He must have trusted you."

Vita's smile held both sadness and cynicism. "Axel feared your mother might destroy it. Or his mother would. Carin did not want him to have any kind of relationship with you. He said in his note to me I was the safest person to hang onto it if he died, until I felt the time was right. He knew I could keep a secret and keep it well."

Another revelation. "You knew I was his daughter?"

A gentle hand on her arm. "Not until after he died."

She kissed her cheek. "I'll give you some privacy."

When Vita left, Sara looked at Harry. She took a deep

breath past a throat clogged with emotion. "I can't…I can't read this. Can you read it for me? You should see it, Harry. There may be something in here that is a clue to what happened between Axel and Carin. Not that it matters now."

Concern filled his face. "You can read it, sweetheart. I'm right here."

Pulling the chair close, Harry sat next to her, his hand gripping hers as she began to read aloud.

"My dear daughter,

"I discovered your existence six years ago, but lacked the courage to tell Regina. Knowing how much Regina did not want me in your life, I decided to wait until you were older. Your mother went to extraordinary measures to hide your presence from me, and I felt I must respect her wishes. I asked my brother Erik to check up on you, and send someone to help your mother if she needed it. He sent one of his former employees, Dennis, to work for your mother's office, but Dennis got fired. So I hired Dennis's brother Eddie to try to get a job doing yard work for your mother. I even provided fake references for Eddie. Eddie reported back that Regina was well and from her talking about your college studies, you seemed happy.

"I came to Yates' Yards one morning to pick up Lila for lunch and saw you in the break room. I wanted to speak to you, I truly did, but failed to work up the courage. Perhaps later I will. You were drinking from a mug that read WORLD'S GREATEST DAD and the irony was bitter for me. I took the cup that you held and wished I could live up to that saying.

"The private detective I hired to find your mother said he could run your DNA from the mug and give me proof positive you were my daughter. I tried to

work up the courage to pursue this avenue, and ended up writing you this letter instead.

"I wanted to be a good dad for you, Sara. I failed with Myles and Lila and utterly failed with poor Wyatt. How I wish I could have started over again with you when you were young! If you are reading this now it is too late for me. But I wanted to let you know I love you.

"I am proud of you, Sara. I wish nothing but the best for you and your mother.

"Love, your father, Axel Colton."

She smoothed down the paper, her heart filled with grief and yet filled also with a sense of needed closure. So much regret. Regret she'd never worked up the courage to confront Axel before he died. Regret for Axel failing to work up the courage to tell her he knew she was his daughter.

And yet in the letter, she knew what she'd always wondered. He loved her. No matter what, he knew she was his daughter, loved her and wanted to make amends.

A heavy weight lifted from her heart. Sara looked at the letter and wiped away tears.

"Bye, Dad," she whispered. "Be at peace."

Then she turned to Harry and sobbed in his arms, partly for all she had lost, but also for all she knew she had gained.

When they returned to the house, Harry knew what Sara needed. Not privacy or isolation, but family.

He fetched her a glass of champagne, told her he'd be back soon. When he returned, several Coltons were with him.

Sara looked confused and then a smile touched her beautiful face. Harry's heart turned over at her joy as the cousins began chatting with her.

He could live with that radiant look on her expression

for the rest of his life. Maybe there would be more than one wedding here at the house.

Carly Colton beamed and hugged him. "I'm so thrilled you and Sara found each other, Harry. You deserve happiness."

He kissed her cheek. "Thanks. I do."

She grinned. "Keep saying that, Harry. I have a feeling you'll be saying it soon at another wedding."

Carly took Sara's hand. "Now, what is this about you decorating and arranging this wedding?"

"There might be more weddings if we can talk Vita and Rick into it." Simone Colton sighed. "This is a beautiful venue."

Sara looked helpless. Harry laughed. "Go on. Go talk weddings and decorating with them. I'll be fine."

Harry watched Sara walk off with her cousins, who looked eager to get to know her better. Once she had no relatives. Now she had dozens, embraced by everyone eager to get to know her. He smiled. Once he never thought he could love again.

Sara Sandoval had changed everything.

Some days life was definitely worth living again. This was one of them.

* * * * *

You'll love previous titles by Bonnie Vanak.
Check out:

Rescue from Darkness
Navy SEAL Protector
Shielded by the Cowboy SEAL

Available from Harlequin Romantic Suspense

#2167 COLTON'S PURSUIT OF JUSTICE
The Coltons of Colorado • by Marie Ferrarella

Caleb Colton has dedicated his life to righting his father's wrongs, but when Nadine Sutherland needs his help proving an oil company took advantage of her father, he wonders if his priorities haven't skewed. Will he be willing to open his heart to Nadine? And will she live long enough to make it matter?

#2168 CONARD COUNTY CONSPIRACY
Conard County: The Next Generation
by Rachel Lee

Widow Grace Hall experiences terrifying incidents at her isolated ranch: murdered sheep, arson, even attempted murder. Her late husband's best friend, Mitch Cantrell, is her greatest hope for protection. But the threat to Grace's life may be even closer than either of them believes...

#2169 UNDERCOVER K-9 COWBOY
Midnight Pass, Texas • by Addison Fox

The instant a rogue FBI agent wants to use Reynolds Station for a stakeout, Arden Reynolds is skeptical of his motives—and his fine physique. She knows attraction is dangerous, but allowing Ryder Durant into her home and her life could prove deadly.

#2170 PRISON BREAK HOSTAGE
Honor Bound • by Anna J. Stewart

When ER doctor Ashley McTavish stops to aid a bus crash, she finds herself taken hostage. Undercover federal agent Slade Palmer's investigation takes a dangerous turn when he vows to keep Ashley alive—even as he finds a new reason to survive himself.

---

*When ER doctor Ashley McTavish stops to aid a bus
crash, she finds herself taken hostage. Undercover
federal agent Slade Palmer's investigation takes a
dangerous turn when he vows to keep Ashley alive—
even as he finds a new reason to survive himself.*

Read on for a sneak preview of
Prison Break Hostage,
the latest in Anna J. Stewart's Honor Bound series!

"Sawyer?" Her voice sounded hoarse. She sat back on
her heels and looked behind her. He was a fair distance
away, moving more slowly than she'd have thought.
Ashley shoved to her feet, her knees wobbling as she
stepped back into the water and shouted for him. "You're
almost there! Come on!" But he was gasping for air, and
for a horrifying moment, he sank out of sight.

Panic seized her. It was pitch-black. Not even the moon
cast light on this side of the shore. No homes nearby, no
lights or guideposts. How would she ever find him?

But she would. He would not leave her like this. She
would not lose him. Not now. She waded into the water,
stumbled, nearly fell face-first, just as he surfaced. He
took a moment to wretch, his hand clutching his side as
he slowly moved toward her, water cascading from the
bag on his hip.